CONQUEST BY SEDUCTION

A NOVEL BY S. W. CHURCH

Published by Jemna Enterprises, LLC.
Colorado, USA

stuartchurch@gmail.com

webpage: stuchurch.com

ISBN 978-0-9970568-2-2

Many thanks to the following talented people.

First Editors:
Jessica Church
Zoraya

Copy and Developmental Editor:
Mia Manns

Cover Artist:
Lazar Kacarevic
planet.caravan@gmail.com

ISBN: 978-0-9970568-0-8

I would like to dedicate this book to
my three wonderful daughters:

Jessica, Emily, and Natalie.

They are the brightest stars in my galaxy.

Special thanks to my friend, mentor, and fellow sci-fi author:
Mark Wayne McGinnis

Enjoy the adventure.

Stuart

CONTENTS

CHAPTER ONE
FIRST CONTACT

"**Y**ou … will kill for me," Simone foretold the impression in her mind.

She opened her emerald green eyes and stood up. Wearing only her black underwear she strolled across the plush carpet to her closet and selected a gossamer evening dress.

Holding the gown against her body she addressed herself in her full-length mirror. "This could be what we've been waiting for, Angel. A man with greater powers than we have." She draped the dress over a chair.

Selecting a rich, brick red shade of lipstick she leaned over the vanity and traced her full lips. She pressed them together and smiled at her reflection. "I wonder what exactly he can do. Perhaps I can help him develop his powers. Then, he can serve me."

She strode back into the main room of her apartment. Her bare toes sank into the thick pile. Picking up her cognac, she peered through the picture window at the dazzling, evening lights of New York City, 38 stories below. She took a long, smooth sip, then set her drink on the lacquered coffee table. "Hmmmm." She tapped her bright red fingernails on the glass and looked up at the twinkling stars. "Will you be able to take us out into the heavens, my new man? That's where I really ought to be."

Changing her focus from the view through the window to her reflection in the dark pane, she stroked her thick, black hair, cocked her hips, and scrutinized her curvaceous figure. She cupped her round breasts and adjusted them into her strapless bra. "We're going to have to move to Colorado, Angel. We'll find him, and introduce him to our charms."

Simone crossed back to her dressing area and pulled the gown over her head. She reached behind herself and closed the zipper, slowly drawing the silky fabric tight against her body, like a snakeskin. She shook her head and tousled her flowing hair against her bare shoulders.

"And as for you, my new man, with you as my vassal we will begin to take back what mankind owes me." She stood up straight and turned side to side, admiring her full figure in the mirror. "Angel, you have been my curse in the past, but now you will be the power that we use to control this man. He doesn't stand a chance."

Three weeks later Mike Kruger wheeled his pickup across Grand Junction, Colorado. His truck sped through the traffic, weaving in and out to pass the slower vehicles. As he approached a yellow traffic light he stomped the gas pedal to the floor, roaring through the intersection as the light turned red.

"Out of my way, you damned hillbillies!" He charged through the Saturday morning traffic.

During undergrad, Mike had majored in aerospace engineering. Fast machines were his passion. He had received so many speeding tickets in his '68 Mustang that he was, at one point, thrown in jail for three weeks. Then one black night he lost control of the powerful car and totaled it. After sixteen days in the hospital, he was sentenced to fifty months in prison for involuntary manslaughter. Everything he had lived for was gone. His plans were shattered, his family destroyed. But since his release from prison, six days ago, he was trying to find meaning in his life again. Intense meditation had helped him to stay sane while incarcerated, and was his main source of rehabilitation as he tried to reenter society. An unexpected side benefit of this therapy had shocked Mike. He had accessed Continuum. This infinite fabric of primordial force and energy was the basis for all elements in the universe. Mike was beginning to understand how this would enable him to reduce any solid matter into pure energy. The new powers that he was developing both amazed and frightened him.

Mike continued speeding through the traffic towards his goal — coffee.

"Good morning, Maggie."

"Hi, Mike." The barista handed him his latte, extra shot. Mike held the door open for an elderly couple, then walked outside to the patio where he found an open bench.

"Ahhh, the fresh air of freedom." Mike squinted at the bright sunlight and breathed the crisp, clear air contentedly.

He sat and admired the immense bluffs that rose to the north. The morning light gave them a phosphorescent, orange glow. "This sure beats prison. But then, so does just about anything." He smirked.

Life on the western slopes of Colorado was pretty damned great.

Mike was feeling that he was in the prime of life. Years of outdoor activity, and a basic diet in the pen, had chiseled his frame into lean muscle. His skin was tanned where the sun shone on it and his shaggy hair was bleached to a light brown. Above his blue eyes was a five-inch scar from when his head had smashed into the windshield of his Mustang, but it suited his rugged good looks.

What a beautiful world we live in, Mike thought as his eyes pored over the details of the ancient view before him. *Three weeks ago this was all just rocks and trees and atmosphere to me. But now I understand that everything is a complex amalgamation of forces and energy. And I am learning how to convert anything back into that energy!* He smiled, partly from contentment, and partly from amazement at his new powers.

"Whoa now," Mike murmured under his breath. An attractive woman, about his age of twenty-six, walked out of the coffee shop and into the dazzling sunlight on the patio. Mike's gaze lingered on her as she walked around, looking for an open seat. The morning light caressed her caramel-colored skin and everything about her looked soft and warm. His azure eyes followed the curve of her neck from her ear down to her collarbone. He felt a healthy hunger grow through his body.

Crap! She was looking right at him, a wry smile on her lips. She seemed to approve of his gaze.

Mike smiled back and shrugged his shoulder. He silently replied, *What can I say? I'm intrigued.*

"May I join you?" she asked as she approached the bench.

"Sure. Please do." Mike scooted over a bit to make more room as she sat down.

The slender woman was dressed in a professional-looking skirt and blouse, yet also looked as if she could hike to the top of the surrounding bluffs. She sat and peered at the drink in her hands as if she were deep in thought. Her thumb stroked the lip of her cup of iced tea, and she brushed the blowing strands of hair from her forehead.

"I've been searching for you, Michael." She abruptly looked up. "I traveled a great distance to find you."

Mike's mind raced as he tried to remember if he had met her before; she seemed familiar, like a friend from a long time ago, but he couldn't place her.

"You don't know me, my name's Tina. We have a lot in common, Michael, and I want us to help each other."

Mike stared at the woman. Her amber hair blew slightly in the morning breeze and her chocolate brown eyes had small flecks of orange in them. They were magic eyes. He felt a curious bond with the woman, as if they had met in a previous life.

"I don't understand, Tina. Why have you been searching for me?"

"You have accessed Continuum, the primordial energy that contains everything in the universe. You are just beginning to learn about your new powers, while I have been developing mine for a very long time," she explained calmly.

Mike was taken by surprise. "How do you know this?"

"My powers also originate from Continuum. I could detect when you first accessed it, three weeks ago." Tina continued, "What can you do with your powers so far?" She placed her straw between her lips and sipped her drink, looking expectantly at Mike.

He hesitated. *I haven't told anyone about this, why would I tell a stranger?* He scrutinized the woman sitting next to him.

Tina gently put her hand on Mike's. "I know that this is sudden, Michael. But there are only three of us on Earth who have access to Continuum, and the third person seems to be pursuing you. I don't know what she wants, but her signature in Continuum seems twisted and dark. I needed to get to you first."

Mike realized that his mouth was hanging open. He shut it.

"I want to help you to use your powers for good works." Tina smiled. Her eyes were filled with peace and trust. "What powers have you developed?"

"Well, I've been examining the composition of my own body when I meditate," Mike began. "And I can break every part of myself down into the most basic element of my physical form: energy." Mike crossed his strong forearms in front of himself. He raised the left arm and lowered the right arm. They passed through each other as if they were made of light. He wiggled his fingers and looked cautiously for Tina's reaction.

Tina watched Mike's demonstration and seemed very satisfied. "That's a good beginning, Michael. You will soon see that you're capable of so much more. Continue to meditate and explore your mind. You have entered a new realm of experience. This is just the tip of the iceberg."

Mike nodded quietly. "What exactly is Continuum?"

"Continuum is the spectrum of energy that composes our universe. At the moment of the Big Bang there was no matter. The primordial energy coalesced into the four forces, then subatomic particles, and finally atoms. Everything around us — those mountains, you, the stars, and the space in between — is ultimately composed of pure energy, and we have tapped in to that power."

"So I'm turning my arms into energy?"

"Basically, yes. Accessing the infinite Sea of Energy will enable you to do some amazing things."

"Like what?"

"See if you can convert other creatures, besides yourself, into energy. Then experiment and try to pass through Continuum." Tina paused and gazed at the stunning scenery surrounding them. She reverently inhaled and savored the fresh air. "Do you understand?"

Mike tried to comprehend what Tina was suggesting. *Convert other creatures into energy? Pass through Continuum?* He looked at the other customers sitting on the deck. "But how will people react to me? I might be shunned, pestered mercilessly, or even persecuted."

"I'm in the same situation that you're in, Michael, and I can help you to expand your powers. Together we could accomplish so much good for this world of ours."

"I'd like that," Mike admitted. He had seen so much of what's bad on this Earth while he was in prison.

Tina looked around the grassy field that surrounded the coffee shop's stone patio. Suddenly she became alert and sat straight up. A rattlesnake, as thick as a rake, was silently winding its way towards the corner of the flagstone deck, where a young family was sitting. The crumbs that they had dropped attracted a field mouse, and this attracted the predator.

A young girl hopped out of her chair and pranced into the tall grass towards some flowers, and the coiling, threatened serpent. The child laughed gaily as she pushed her sandaled feet through the swaying, rustling brush.

"Michael! Do you see what's happening? This is your opportunity! Focus and make that snake vanish."

Mike's mind reeled. "OK, I'll try. I think I can feel how to do it!" He channeled his thoughts towards the twisting serpent and concentrated on the atomic bonds that formed the predator's body. He mentally broke those bonds down until all matter became energy. The snake instantly vanished, blending into Continuum and becoming the first creature that Mike would eliminate with his new powers.

The small child never knew the danger that she had almost stepped on.

Mike returned to his normal state of awareness and

watched the girl picking the yellow blooms. "That was amazing." He shook his head. "You were right, I can convert other animals into energy, and make them vanish." He turned to Tina. "Where did it go?"

"The serpent's body is gone. Its cellular structure has been reduced to atomic forces and was absorbed into Continuum. If it had been a sentient being its individual soul would still be intact, as energy, also in Continuum."

"You mean that after people die, they are still present in this fabric of energy?"

Tina quietly nodded. "Both present and aware."

Mike was fascinated, and excited to see what else he was capable of. "What did you mean a minute ago when you said 'pass through Continuum?'"

"I mean that since you can reduce your body into a field of energy, you can disappear from one location and appear someplace else. Your energy will reform into your body at the new location."

Mike stared at her in disbelief. "It won't kill me?"

"No, turning *another* creature into energy will kill it, as you just did with the rattler. Its body will be reduced to its fundamental elements and be annihilated. However, you will be able to temporarily convert *your* body into energy and pass through Continuum, emerging someplace else, unharmed."

Mike nodded, trying to understand.

"Remember, Michael, you are like a child with a loaded gun. Don't do anything impulsive. Go one step at a time and explore your new abilities; most of all, respect them. Try to think of the good works that you are capable of and enjoy this new experience."

"I agree, but it's difficult to know what to do when you discover that you're a superhero." Mike grinned with enthusiasm.

"Michael, you are not a superhero. You are a fallible

human being that has been touched with the capabilities of a demigod. You must be cautious when you wield your powers. Think very carefully before you act." Tina smiled and touched his knee. "I want us to help each other. We can make a wonderful difference in this world if we work together. Just don't be tempted to abuse your power. It's so easy to be seduced by greed and desire. If you truly wish to help the world, you must resist these enticements."

Tina looked distantly towards the deep blue sky. "You will be tested very soon, Michael."

Mike admired the towering bluffs and the billowing clouds rising above them. He felt the awesome, and infinite, power of nature, a force that he was learning to control.

"What would you like to do, more than anything?" Tina turned to him.

Mike looked back to his hands, thinking about what Tina had said. "If my daughter is out there, in Continuum, I would like to contact her," he replied quietly.

"Hmmm, that's a pretty fantastic wish, but we can talk about it. In the meantime, there is so much that we could do to make the world a better place." She sipped on her straw and it sputtered as she finished her drink. "I need to leave now. I'd like to see you again."

"So would I. Can we meet for dinner sometime?" Mike stood up and looked at the fascinating woman. He moved in for a hug or kiss but Tina held back.

"First things first, if you don't mind," she said calmly.

"You're right," Mike consented, visibly frustrated.

"And yes, dinner would be nice."

The new friends exchanged contact information and drove off in different directions.

What else can I do with these powers? Mike wondered.

As he dodged back through the traffic, Mike noticed a new music store that had recently opened. He swerved into a parking space and peered into the windows. It was full of posters, jewelry, Asian statuettes, guitars hanging from the ceiling, and stacks of LPs and CDs. The place was already popular.

The colorful sign outside said 'Coven Music.' As he pushed the door open it rattled some oddly tuned bells. There was a whiff of incense, and an old Grateful Dead song playing, '… spent the night in Utah in a cave up in the hills.' He bobbed his head to the music and looked around.

"May I help you find something?"

Mike peered behind the counter at the woman who greeted him.

"Aaah, yes, thanks." He tried not to stammer. "I'm always on the lookout for some guitar band stuff." He was also looking for some smooth jazz, but was too embarrassed to say so at the moment.

The tall, graceful woman walked around the counter. "Let's try over here." Mike noticed that she wore a Rolling Stones, *Goats Head Soup* T-shirt. He also noticed that it was amply filled.

"Anything in particular?" She smelled exotic as she brushed by Mike, her heels clicking the wooden floor.

I suddenly have a taste for the Stones, Mike felt like saying, but refrained. He had never seen jeans fit so perfectly. "I really like the Doobies, Steely Dan, the Allman Brothers, that era."

"And not the Rolling Stones?" The woman turned teasingly.

"Oh, sure." Mike tried to keep his eyes above collar level. "Actually, I have the same birthday as Keith Richards." He immediately felt stupid.

"Really?" She paused and appraised Mike. "You're a Sagittarius?"

Who the hell knows that Keith Richards was born in De-

cember? Mike wondered to himself. He could practically hear his mind commanding all of his red blood cells to stop whatever they were doing and head south.

"Yes … my name's Mike."

"I'm Simone, pleased to meet you." Her voice was bewitching.

"It's my pleasure. Is this your business?"

"Yes, I managed a shop in New York City until I convinced the owner to try a branch over here. So I'm a partner in this store."

"Well, it already seems popular, and it looks like you have some interesting stuff." Mike relaxed a bit. Initially he had been overcome by her stunning looks; however, talking to her had made him curious to get to know this person. Nevertheless, his basic urges were being ignited by this black-haired Latin beauty. *She's out of my league*, Mike decided.

"Thank you." Simone paused. Mike noticed her glass green eyes and watched her red lips form the words, "I'd like to get to know some people here in the Valley, would you like to meet for a drink?"

Ten minutes later Mike was tapping his thumbs on the steering wheel as his new Stones CD filled the cab with pounding rhythms.

"She's got some interesting stuff, all right." Mike smirked and laughed to himself as he cruised home. "Damn, what a figure! She moves like a belly dancer."

His fifty months in the pen without female companionship had left an aching void in his life. Going out for a drink wasn't something he'd planned on, but he felt irresistibly drawn to this mysterious and beautiful woman.

This must be my lucky day.

CHAPTER TWO
DUOSOL

"Eight warships! Eight! How can this be?" Tsar Tyrandus gripped the stone ledge as he looked out of his council chamber window. His claws left eight deep scratches in the rock.

"Yes, my Lord, our spies were astonished to discover that the Kaelites have constructed six additional fighter planes," his chief counselor replied.

Tyrandus didn't turn around, but continued to scan the expanse of massive, thick buildings spread out below him. "Until last night our intelligence reported that the Kaelites had developed *two* new warplanes. Our entire defense is based on this information. Now this morning I am informed that there are *eight* new ships." He shook his massive head as he surveyed the kingdom of Pacabria. Blackened areas showed evidence of recent bombings by the rival species on their home planet, DuoSol. "When will this terror ever end, Kota?"

"Perhaps all is not lost, my Lord. Commander Zath is expecting you to review our fleet this afternoon. He might have more recent intelligence. Shall we travel to the airfield?"

Tyrandus turned and faced his chief minister. Like all adult Pacabrians, the Tsar stood seven feet tall and weighed over three hundred pounds.

"Yes, Kota, the air guard will be expecting us." He followed his aide to their transport and headed to the military base of Pacabria. The Tsar looked grimly at the passing dwellings, the citizens of Pacabria, and the beautiful countryside while Kota drove their vehicle to the airbase.

"Everything depends on our ability to repel this new threat." Tyrandus felt the burden of responsibility for the safety of his subjects. "We have fought so hard to secure our peaceful nation. Let us hope that we can persevere."

The two-sun system and three moons gave planet DuoSol erratic seasons and extremely high tidal swings. All of the fauna and flora were adapted to the challenging climate, as well as to the frequent bombardment by meteors. DuoSol was a young planet, located in an immature pocket of the Milky Way galaxy. As such, the interstellar space was still filled with rogue debris from the previous generation of stars' explosions. Small meteors entered DuoSol's atmosphere with regularity, and the roofs of the Pacabrians' structures were thick and strong.

"We must protect our civilization from this new threat, Kota." The Tsar spoke with determination.

"Yes, sir. Have confidence, Commander Zath will design a new strategy to repel this danger." He pulled into the garage at Air Force headquarters.

"Let us hope so; our survival depends on it." Tyrandus impatiently waited for a uniformed guard to approach his vehicle and open the door for him. The military personnel surrounding his transport were as intimidating as any creatures in the universe.

The Pacabrians had evolved to meet DuoSol's harsh environment with brute force. Their bodies were covered with hard scales the size of silver dollars that formed a thick armor over their massive frames. Similar to humans, they had developed bodies that were symmetrical about a vertical axis, with two arms and two legs. Each limb ended in a paw that split into two digits, which split again, giving the Pacabrians four 'fingers' or 'toes' on each paw. Their head sat on a thick neck. Instead of two eyes providing binocular vision, the Pacabrians had one continuous band of light-sensitive tissue extending from ear to ear, giving the impression that they were wearing large ski goggles. This eye band had a surface like a fly's eye, faceted, and varying from silverish to black, depending on the ambient light. With this arrangement the Pacabrians had a continuous, three-dimensional view of what was in front of them.

"Lord Tyrandus." Commander Zath approached and solemnly bowed his head in greeting.

"Why have our spies failed us so miserably?" the Tsar growled at his top military chief.

"The secrecy surrounding the construction of the six additional ships is astounding." Commander Zath was both concerned and impressed. "Our spies have learned that shortly after the first two ships were under construction, the Kaelites discovered improvements and began constructing a second generation of warship in an unknown location."

"Are you telling me that these six additional ships are even more dangerous than the first two?" Tyrandus bellowed.

Zath stood stoic against the barrage of verbiage coming from the Tsar. "Yes, my Lord. However, only the first two ships are ready for battle. The other six are still a few days away from completion. I believe that we can use this scheduling situation to our advantage and destroy all eight of their fighter fleet."

Tyrandus, Kota, and Zath walked through the military headquarters building towards the airfield, where their warships were being readied.

"Explain your plan."Tyrandus exited the large edifice.

"We will bomb the facility that is housing the two operational fighters. That will eliminate the threat of imminent attack until we can discover the location of the other six fighters. Unless …"

"Unless what?" The Tsar needed to raise his voice above the noise of the idling jet engines.

"Unless they attack us first. In which case we will meet them in the sky and destroy these two new ships in battle."

"They have always attacked us first."Tsar Tyrandus surveyed the smoke-filled airfield. The permeating smell of kerosene irritated his eye band. The giant fighter planes were set in three rows of eight. Five of the massive aircraft were running their engines; the noise was deafening as the fossil-fueled turbines roared and blew hurricane-force winds across the tarmac.

"Welcome, your highness." A uniformed Pacabrian bowed at the waist, shouting above the noise. "We are completing our final maintenance and preparation of the aircraft. The pilots are receiving instructions as we speak. We will be on 'white hot' status within hours."

"Very good, Lieutenant." Tyrandus scanned the battle-scarred fighters. Missiles were being attached to the angular wings and fuel trucks filled the planes with flammable propellant. The stench of fuel and smoke was strong enough that Tyrandus could taste the metallic odor.

The Tsar continued thoughtfully, "We have not even seen these new warplanes that the Kaelites have developed, but our reports indicate that they are a completely different level of sophistication, extremely fast and maneuverable. All of our ships must be in top working order and prepared for anything."

"Yes, my Lord. If we must engage them in the air, our strategy will be to use our superior numbers to surround and destroy these two ships."

"That will have to work," Tyrandus replied with reserved confidence. "It must work." He turned and left Commander Zath and Kota.

Three hundred eighty miles away, in Kael, Lord Territhade updated Queen Cassilius on the status of their two new warships, and the preparations for their attack on Pacabria.

"The two Strongforce Attack Warships (or SAWs) are in the hangar being loaded with ammunition, my Queen. The six Generation II ships still need some minor adjustments before they will be operational. However, the two SAWs will be ready for battle in one darkness."

"Thank you, Lord Territhade. We will not wait for the Generation II warships, even though they are the superior fighters. Our counterintelligence reports that the Pacabrians intend to launch a preemptive attack and destroy our new fighters before we can get them airborne."

The queen became more serious. "We will attack the Pacabrian air fleet when the first two SAWs are armed and the crew is prepared. I cannot risk waiting for the Pacabrians to initiate an assault." Cassilius folded her small hands. "At last, we finally have the technology to eliminate these dim-witted brutes. DuoSol will be the domain of the Kaelites, and no one else."

She turned and strode to the balcony of her ornate control room. The masonry and woodwork showed exceptional craftsmanship.

"Our civilization has always been superior to that of the Pacabrians." She admired her kingdom through the open window. "It is time to force them into extinction."

In direct contrast to the Pacabrians, the Kaelites

used ingenuity, rather than brute strength, to adapt to DuoSol's extreme environment and meteor showers. The beautiful nation-city of Kael lay tucked against the towering cliffs of the Shillus mountain range. This offered some protection from the meteors and provided a defensive position against the ground troops of the Pacabrian nation.

Queen Cassilius took a deep breath and placed both hands on the railing, clicking her fingertips against the stone. Her mind was consumed by two impending events: their attack against Pacabria, and the imminent death of her son, Prince Syndor, who was losing his fight against a mysterious illness.

Similar to all Kaelites, Queen Cassilius was covered with delicate scales, giving her flesh a shine like mother of pearl. Two large eyes surveyed her kingdom. These eyes were faceted, not unlike the Pacabrians' eye band, and shone like fine, silver mesh. Although they stood only four feet high, these smaller creatures had continuously inflicted terror against the Pacabrians since before recorded history.

"I will relay your instructions to Commander Mora, my Queen. The two SAWs will be ready to attack upon your command." Territhade bowed and left.

Queen Cassilius inhaled a deep breath of confidence and satisfaction. She headed to her personal vehicle, which would transport her to the hangar where the two new warships were being prepared for their virgin battle. Her airy robes flowed behind her in colorful waves. Attendants followed and traveled to the military development center with their leader. Because of its immense size, this facility, like most of the military outposts, was not nestled against the cliffs, but sat on the valley floor.

"Take me to the assembly facility," Cassilius directed her driver.

As the queen's vehicle approached the hangar they passed what appeared to be a junkyard. The damaged and burned hulls of their previous fleet of fighter planes sat in ruin, rusting and decaying. But a new era was upon them. The two SAWs were a completely higher level of warplane, and the six Generation II planes were a level above that.

"Greetings, my Queen." Commander Mora bowed slightly and escorted her into the complex. He was large for a Pacabrian, standing four foot six. Like all adult males, he had two curling horns twisting from the top of his head.

The twin ships were spotlessly new. Both had two sets of trapezoidal wings, one above the other, and four tail fins. The dual wings gave the SAWs more surface area, which made them highly maneuverable, as well as providing more hard points to attach missiles and guns. Retractable cannon could be extended forward and aft, as well as left and right.

"They are fantastic," the queen praised Mora. "We will attack at first sunrise. No building is to be left standing, and every Pacabrian man, woman and child will be killed."

The commander bowed, excused himself, and hurried to make final preparations.

The new warplanes only carried enough fossil fuel for emergency landings. In the event that the main engines failed, eight smaller jets would lower the crippled fighter to the ground. Unlike these smaller emergency rockets, the primary turbines were fantastically powerful, but were not fueled by a petroleum derivative.

They were propelled by Continuum.

CHAPTER THREE
THE THIRD PERSON

Back in his apartment, Mike had some time to kill and he was interested to see if he could merge with Continuum and transfer through space to another location, as Tina had suggested.

"Yeah, but what about my clothes?" Mike wondered aloud to the empty room. "I understand that the molecules and atoms of my body are organized according to my genetic blueprint. But my jeans and boots don't 'know' what they're supposed to be. What if we get all mixed up?"

He decided to try one thing at a time.

Mike stripped and stood naked in his main room, where he usually meditated. His tanned arms, legs, and face were a contrast to his fair-skinned torso.

"I don't want to risk turning myself into a jumbled mess." He imagined a freakish blob that was once his body, melted together with his hiking boots.

He carefully focused down and concentrated on his form, Continuum, and wanting to be in the bedroom. He drifted deeper into the recesses of his mind and became unaware of his body, like the moment before he fell asleep. He was just a location of consciousness, simply an entity, a soul without a physical counterpart.

Then he was in the bedroom.

There was no flash of light, no puff of smoke, just a transfer of his energy. He didn't feel anything in between the living room and bedroom. Mike checked his body; nothing was missing.

"OK, now this is amazing." Mike was stunned, and elated. He spent the next few minutes bumping between the bedroom, kitchen, guest room, and then dared to appear in his truck outside, nude.

I wonder where I can go. How far does this energy extend? To France? Out into space? He leaned on the steering wheel and stared through the windshield.

He sensed that he had traveled, but not really *through* space. It was more like he had dissolved himself into Continuum at one place, and it had bumped out an equal amount of energy someplace else, where he had reformed. There was no actual traveling between the two locations, which made it instantaneous.

It became time to clean up and dress for his date with Simone. He pulled a Western cut shirt on over his athletic physique and brushed his uncooperative hair as best as he could.

As he sped over to the brewery he wondered about the coming evening. This woman was such a turn-on, but after all, it was just their first date. Mike gave himself a pep talk. "Get to know her first, have fun, and then let things fall into place." It had been over eight years since he had a date, and he felt out of practice.

He parked a few blocks away and enjoyed walking through the cool air as he approached the pub. Simone was not there so Mike relaxed in the foyer, nodding to the loud music, and looking around for an open booth. He felt nervous, but it was a good nervous.

Simone took long, confident steps as she approached the pub. She peered sideways at her reflection in the store windows. *Turn it on, Angel. It's showtime.*

Mike's eyes were drawn to the front of the room as Simone walked past the large windows and entered the establishment. She took Mike's breath away.

"How are you?" Mike smiled.

"I'm glad to be off work and joining you."

"You look wonderful," Mike complimented.

Simone was no longer dressed for her job as the owner of a hippie music store. She wore a skirt and black tights with black boots. The heels were significant, but not spikes. Over her purple top she wore a short-cut jacket. She was certainly dressy, but not overly so.

They found a booth and sat across from each other. Mike ordered a home brew and Simone requested a brandy. They eased into their conversation.

"How do you like the Valley so far?" Mike tasted his beer and leaned forward so that he could be heard above the music.

"It's nice. I'll miss the excitement of the big city, but I'm ready for new adventures." She sipped her drink and peered over the glass at Mike. Her eyes were mesmerizing.

Mike's scrotum tingled. He momentarily lost his train of thought.

"Do you have family here?" she continued.

"No, just friends in this area. I was divorced three years ago and my ex lives near Boulder, with her boyfriend. Aaan …" Mike's voice trailed off. He didn't want to talk about his daughter, prison, or the accident, yet.

Simone noted Mike's reluctance to share something. She was looking for any weakness, anything that she could exploit in order to manipulate him. Focusing through Continuum she was able to get an impression of his thoughts. He was remembering a child, his daughter, and a tragedy.

Mike's mind wandered as he sipped his beer. He assessed Simone. Her hair was as black as a raven. Her makeup and earrings were striking, but not too flashy. She had several rings on her fingers, including a wedding band. Mike's throat gripped up.

"Ah, how about you? Any family in the area?" In his mind he pictured a large, angry man holding a shotgun. *Like a husband, perhaps?*

"My father's family lives in Panama, near the sea. My mother's family is from Spain. They both live in Texas now." She held out her left hand and wiggled the wedding ring. "This is just to keep the hounds at bay." She slowly circled her fingertip around the rim of her drink. The fingernails sparkled as the neon lights in the room were reflected in them.

"Good plan," said Mike, acknowledging the validity of wearing a phony wedding ring. His eyes followed Simone's finger as it carefully traced a curve around the moist glass. There were hints of lip gloss along the edge. His gaze drifted back to the woman in front of him. Although smartly dressed, he noticed that the buttons of her blouse were straining to contain her swelling bust. *Mmmmmmm*, he thought. *Get to know the person first*, he scolded himself.

"So what else do you do for fun?" She smiled suggestively, observing his wandering eyes.

I enjoy driving like hell, bumping through space, and rubbing lotion on big boobs, Mike blurted in his mind, but out loud he replied, "I like muscle cars, and planes. The faster the better. I also enjoy rafting, climbing, and dirt bikes."

"It sounds like you are a bit of a thrill-seeker." Simone looked deeply at Mike and seemed interested, very interested. Her eyes lingered on his strong hands and arms. She noted his discolored knuckles and the scar angling above his eyes. "Were you ever in combat?"

"No." Mike seemed surprised, and then divulged, "But I do have a friend who is retired from the Air Force and takes me up in a fighter once in a while. He's teaching me how to fly an F-4 Phantom II."

They continued getting to know each other, but as they started their second round of drinks the conversation became less guarded.

"How often do you get down to Texas to see your family?" Mike inquired.

"I don't."

Mike realized that he had touched a nerve.

"My father and I had some serious problems." Her voice was strained. "I left when I was fifteen."

Mike searched for something to say, but just looked at her moist, green eyes. They were serious, sad, even bitter.

The pause became uncomfortable.

Simone broke the silence. "I've always been pretty," was all she said.

Mike lowered his eyes and felt his fists clenching.

The implication was sickening.

He looked at his hands and realized that he was also one of the men who had only seen her as a sexy woman. *Get to know the person first.* He tried to redirect his thoughts.

"It's OK," she said. "First impressions are natural." Then her voice tightened. "I will never, ever, be overpowered like that again."

Yikes! Mike could feel the intensity of Simone's emotions. Her eyes were piercing, almost sinister. "That's understandable," was all he could manage to say.

"Michael?"

"Yes?"

"Would you tell me three words that you think describe me? Just right off the top of your head."

Mike tried to comply and not think about it too much. "Beautiful, interesting, enchanting."

"Hmmmmm." Simone was silent for a bit. "Actually, Michael ... I am an enchantress."

CHAPTER FOUR
A TIME TO KILL

Mike smiled mischievously at Simone across the table in the pub. "You certainly are." But then he noticed that she was serious. "What do you mean, you're an enchantress?"

"I mean that I am able to do some things that other people can't."

Mike raised his eyebrows and straightened up. "Like what?"

"Look around us, Michael. All these people, the tables and walls, and the infinite space outside, it's all a Sea of Energy. Over the past few years I have been able to use it to identify who else has connected with it. I am also able to get impressions of what people are thinking."

"That's Continuum." Mike was stunned. He recalled that Tina had mentioned a third person who had access. "You mean that you can read thoughts?"

"Not exactly … it works like this: In our minds we have several levels of awareness. For most of us there is a running dialogue, almost like a narrator, talking in our heads. It says, 'Gee, I think I'm hungry,' or, 'Wow, that guy is hot.' But beneath that chatter are the real thoughts that your brain is having. These thoughts are much faster than the rambling that we pay attention to. It is an instant reaction and interaction with our environment."

Mike was very familiar with this. The first thing that he did when he meditated was to quiet the turbulence going on in his mind. Then his brain opened up to a simple awareness, without all of the interference.

"I can't read minds. That chatter is not part of Continuum, as you call it. Our true thoughts are a deeper form, and this blends with the surrounding energy. So I can get *impressions* of what most people are thinking if I put my mind to it. By the way, you think about my boobs a lot."

"It doesn't take a special talent to figure that out." Mike grinned.

"Think of it this way," she continued. "It's sort of like a calculator, or a smart phone. Many people only use what they need, the basic functions of that device. Our brains are similar. Everyone is connected to Continuum, but most people are unable to get past the level of the running dialogue. Occasionally we have what we refer to as intuition, or impressions, or when we 'just have a hunch.' This is a glimpse of Continuum. Since it flows through everyone's mind, I can use it to get an idea of what people are thinking. Some people have a stronger connection to Continuum than others. You have a very strong connection."

Mike nodded, but was curious. *I wonder why I can't see into people's thoughts. And why can't I tell who else has access to Continuum?* Then he realized that she was probably reading that thought. "Well, I guess that you already know that I can access Continuum myself."

"Yes."

Mike wondered where to begin. "I've developed different abilities than you. My access is more physical than mental."

Simone smiled knowingly; her green eyes sparkled like Christmas tree lights and seemed to absorb Mike.

"For me, this fabric of energy, Continuum, is composed of the most fundamental element in the universe, energy. The stuff that everything else is built from. I have learned to use my mind to temporarily break down objects into that original state of energy. So it allows me to do some incredible things. Hearing you explain the connection of our minds to Continuum helps me to understand it better."

"Good luck with that. Understanding it, I mean. Continuum is beyond our realm of understanding, it is not logical, linear, nor does it have anything to do with time-space coordinates. Our Earthly brains cannot comprehend it, only experience it."

Mike tried to absorb that idea. He pondered the vastness and primordial essence of Continuum. "That sounds like God."

"Hmmm, maybe. Anyway, what abilities have you developed?" Simone leaned forward.

Mike crossed his index fingers. He lowered one and raised the other. Just like his forearms earlier that day, his fingers passed through each other. "So … I can also break down my entire body and bump into Continuum and appear someplace else."

Simone noted every word. "Someplace else? Like where?"

"Well, so far, just around my apartment, and out into my truck," he explained.

"But you should be able to bump anywhere through Continuum, right? Across the country, to the moon, into outer space?" She pressed for more possibilities.

"I guess so, that seems logical."

"Can you travel through time?" Simone's eyes were filled with fascination.

"No, I haven't thought about it. That seems impossible."

"Well," Simone reasoned, "there is no need for time in an infinite realm, so perhaps you can enter Continuum and bump out at a different time coordinate."

Mike couldn't decide if that would be fantastic, of terrifying.

"What else?" Simone continued her probing.

"I can make other beings merge with Continuum and cease to exist. This morning a rattlesnake was about to strike a little girl at the coffee shop, and I made it vanish, instantly."

"That could be very useful." Simone gazed at Mike.

"Useful for what?"

"You could eliminate a lot of bad people with that ability."

Mike recalled the hundreds of prisoners that he had been surrounded by over the past four years. "I suppose."

Simone sipped her drink. "I wonder why we have developed different powers when we are connecting with the same energy?"

"I was just wondering that myself." Mike theorized, "We must share some common predisposition for accessing Continuum, but we have also inherited different genetic coding from our families. I suppose that we each acquired a propensity for different capabilities."

"I wonder what would happen if our powers were combined?" Simone suggested. Her eyes scrutinized Mike as she shifted in her seat. "The world of men can be so hateful, and domineering. I would like for us to do something about that."

Mike sipped his beer. *That's sort of like what Tina said this morning.*

Simone scanned the crowded room and seemed to locate what she was looking for. Discreetly, so that Mike could not see, she caught the eye of a hulking man at a nearby table, and winked at him.

"I need to visit the ladies' room, will you excuse me for a minute?"

"I could use a pit stop too."

They both got up and wound their way through the crowded, noisy restaurant toward the restrooms.

Mike found that two urinals were broken in his, and there was a line to use the two remaining ones. This took some time, but he completed his business and stepped back to where he expected to see Simone waiting for him. She was not there. *Maybe she's already back at the booth?* Mike wondered and returned to the main room.

He could see her black mane of hair above the back of their booth, but sitting next to her was a large man.

Mike was gripped with anxiety. Confrontations in prison were usually fierce and violent. His fists had become fast and hard, but he was not reckless about engaging in a fight. As he approached the booth he noticed three other dudes at a nearby table, apparently this big guy's pals. They were all watching to see what would happen. He could hear Simone saying, "Really, get away from me. I'm here with my boyfriend."

Mike walked up next to his seat. Simone's eyes changed from annoyance and anger to anticipation when she saw him. She smiled slyly. The guy rolled his head around to look at Mike.

"What's up?" Mike asked.

"Jusht shittin' here wiff my new lady friend." The interloper slurred his words. "Wa's it to you?"

"Actually, that's *my* lady friend, and we would both like for you to return to your table." Mike could feel his heartbeat throbbing in his temples.

"I'd like fer you to get the hell outta here sho I ken 'joy sum brown sugar."

Simone's eyes flashed at the reference to her skin tone.

Mike assessed the ursine man. His giant shoulders sloped along beefy arms, ending in fists that were as solid as sledgehammers.

"Miiiiiike." Simone's eyes beckoned him to do something.

Anger swelled up in Mike, nothing like he had ever felt before. *What am I afraid of? I'm all-powerful. With these new abilities, nothing can take me!* He clenched his jaw and glared, challengingly, at the intruder.

The big man flexed his meaty hands and looked at Mike with glazed eyes. "Mebee you'd like to schtep owside and shettle this men to men?"

Mike pulled a twenty dollar bill from his pocket, and put it on the table. He set his half-finished beer on it and looked directly at Simone. She understood. They were leaving.

"Let's go," Mike said flatly to the bully.

He headed for a side door, walking past the three guys. This was obviously a regular form of entertainment for them. The bully placed one hand on the table and the other on the back of the booth to help himself stand up, and he followed Mike through the room. No one else in the crowded pub seemed to notice what was going on.

Simone waited to see what the three guys would do. They clumsily gathered their beers and stood up. She could detect that they were going outside to watch the beating, so she scooted out of the booth and headed for the front door.

As Mike approached the side door he prepared his mind for quick action. He pushed the fire escape bar and entered the cool night air. The side of the building was deserted as he stepped onto the dark, gravel parking lot. He turned to face his adversary.

The big man filled the door as he passed through it. "After I mash yer teef down yer throat, I'm gonna screw that sweet chica of yurs 'til she bleeds." He closed the gap between Mike and himself.

The door clattered shut, cutting off the light and noise from inside the bar.

For a moment Mike considered trying to take him in a fair fight. But the brute's jaw looked as solid as an anvil.

You asked for it, Dude. Mike focused his mind and broke the massive man's body into elemental energy. He vanished, all three hundred pounds of him.

"Holy shit," Mike murmured. "I did it."

Mike stood alone in the dark, looking at the heap of clothes and boots on the ground where the bully had disappeared. Panic stirred in his belly. "I killed him. And those clothes are evidence that he didn't just run off."

I've got to figure this out, now! These things aren't genetically programed, but they still have bonds that hold them together. He concentrated on the atomic forces of the pile of personal belongings on the dirt in front of him. But they wouldn't vanish. *Maybe I should just pick them up and take them with me?*

The door rattled as the three buddies struck the fire escape bar and entered the side lot. Light and music flooded back into the night from the building, but no one was there. Mike had bumped a block away, and was watching Simone walk out of the front door.

"Oh, Michael! That was great!" she whispered excitedly as she caught up to him. "You are amazing. Imagine what we are going to do together."

Mike went from being amazed to being stunned. *I just killed a guy!* Looking down, he noticed that he had managed to bump through Continuum with his clothes on. *How did I do that?*

He peered at the shadows of the three men looking at the pile of clothes and searching for their pal in the parking lot. *I just got* out *of prison, and now I've already committed murder. What the hell am I doing?*

Mike was still surging with emotion as Simone took his arm in hers. It was chilly, but not cold. She tucked his elbow against her left breast and pulled him close.

"Will you walk me to my truck?" she asked.

Mike felt Simone's hips rock against his as they scurried towards her vehicle. His mind changed its focus from the murder to the enticing woman trotting along next to him.

What a superstructure, he observed to himself. His heart started beating harder, partly from the fast pace, and partly from being so close to the sultry woman.

"I parked over there." She gestured with her head.

Mike could barely see her vehicle in the dark but he knew that they were only about twenty yards from where his truck was parked. As they arrived at her red Explorer Mike drew a breath to say goodbye, but it was cut short as Simone pressed her lips against his. He pressed back and they enjoyed a long kiss.

"That was awesome," Mike whispered. His mind reeled as pent-up desire flooded through him.

"Just awesome?" Simone coiled her arms around his torso and neck, then constricted her grip. Her breasts mashed like water balloons against his chest. Mike wrapped his arms around her and pulled her closer. Their mouths collided again. He felt his mind leaving any civil conventions behind and reverting to primal desires that had been dormant for too long. He pressed her against the side of the truck, slid his hands under her jacket and kneaded her chest.

"Oh yeees," Simone groaned, delighted to see that Mike was overwhelmed with desire. He was vulnerable, and this would be how she would control him.

Mike pulled his head back to admire the view of her breasts bulging out of her neckline.

"Mmmmmmmmm," purred Simone. Their faces were touching again.

She grabbed fistfuls of hair and pulled his mouth back to hers. Mike lowered his grip and encircled her pelvis with one arm while his right hand sought out her perfect ass. Over three billion years of evolution were compelling him towards one goal: drive your seed into this body. He reached below her skirt and followed her tights up. But they weren't tights, they were leggings. He went to caress the bare skin between her leggings and panties … but there were no panties, just smooth flesh.

Simone smiled as Mike discovered that there was nothing between him and the source of his passion. He pressed his hand, from behind, into the musky cleavage between her legs. Simone moaned again. She cocked her head and opened her mouth wide, attacking Mike's lips like a lioness biting into her prey. Their teeth raked together.

Man, this woman is primed!

Mike didn't stop massaging her moist folds until she arched her head up and emitted a moan from deep within her chest. She writhed with pleasure while Mike held her firmly against him, burying his mouth under her jawbone. He smiled and gently bit her shoulder.

It was then he noticed that his erection had pushed its way above his belt buckle. It had been more than four years since he was with a woman and his passion surged like a locomotive. He grasped Simone's skirt with both fists and pulled upwards. But she countered with both of her hands and kept covered.

No fair! It's my turn! Mike frantically exclaimed to himself.

"Not here, not now." Simone was breathless.

"Aaaaaaa." Mike's frustration was agonizing. He took a few breaths to calm himself. His shoulders slumped, as he relented and gently embraced Simone. They kissed again.

"Not here, not now." He groaned, "You're right."

He closed his eyes, cradled Simone's head in his hands, and moved closer for another kiss. She teased him with her tongue as she deftly unbuckled his belt and released his hard-on into the open air. She grabbed his bare ass and slithered to her knees.

Thirty minutes after their tryst in the parking lot, Simone was alone in her apartment, standing in front of her large living room window, as she liked to do.

No one can resist you, Angel.

The lights of Grand Junction glittered like stars before her. She sipped her cognac.

"I've got you by the balls, my pet." She smiled with satisfaction. "You can serve *all* of my needs." She raised her tulip glass and toasted her reflection.

CHAPTER FIVE
TESTING THE POWERS

Mike flopped down in a stuffed chair in his own apartment and twisted open a beer. "Damn!" he laughed to himself, "there's nothing like a romp in a parking lot." He took a swallow and became more subdued. "Wow, I just killed a guy. Sure, he was a prick, but did he deserve to *die*?"

He realized that his butt cheeks burned, and shifted in his seat. "Yowch! What the hell?" He went to his bedroom and dropped his clothes on the floor. Upon closer examination he discovered four scratch marks on each cheek. "Damn that wench! She *clawed* me!" He went to wash his wounds in the bathroom but began to wonder, *If I can reduce my body to its elemental energy and have it reform, can I heal myself?*

He concentrated, focused, and entered the channel in his mind that connected with Continuum. His flesh reverted to its original state of pure energy, and then reformed. His injuries were instantly repaired. Mike looked at his reflection in the mirror and patted his round buttocks. "Good as new." He nodded with satisfaction. Something else caught his eye and he lifted his hair, exposing his forehead. The long scar from the accident was gone. "I'll be damned."

Mike's mind wandered back to the beginning of the day with Tina. She was so pretty, and somehow he just felt good being with her, like he could trust her with anything. He wanted to see her again.

When he picked up his phone to call her he already had a text from Simone, and a voicemail from Major Cody Brennevin, United States Air Force, retired.

Simone wrote: "Michael, I have a thrilling idea for us to use our powers. I forgot to mention it earlier. We can begin making the world a better place. Tomorrow?"

"Tomorrow?!" Mike wondered out loud. *This lady moves fast!*

He checked the voicemail from Cody. "What's up, Mad Mike? I'm feeling the need for speed and the desire to go higher! I think I can get a plane on Tuesday. Are you up for some thrills? Or do you need to shave your legs or something?"

"Yes!" Mike laughed. Excitement surged through his body. Flying with Crazy Cody was one of the biggest thrills he had ever known. Major Cody Brennevin was one of only six pilots to achieve five aerial Mig kills and earn 'ace' status during the Vietnam War. Still revered by many younger pilots, the major could wrangle flight time in an F-4 Phantom II fighter jet. Cody had smuggled Mike aboard several times and taught him the basics of flying the sophisticated war machine. Mike never missed the opportunity to buckle into the copilot's seat and tear through the air above Utah with Brennevin reliving his days of flying missions over the jungles of Asia.

He called the major and got his voicemail. "I'll be there Tuesday, you rheumatoid slab of grizzled scar tissue! Take your heart medicine 'cause I'll be slamming you with some serious G-forces!" Mike smiled at the thought of seeing his good friend. They both loved an adrenaline rush, and they both had a bit of a death wish.

He texted Simone: "What's up?"

Immediately his phone rang.

"Hi, Michael. Are you interested?"

"Interested in what?"

"It's complicated. Can I explain it when I see you? Come by my place at six tomorrow morning. Wear hiking boots, and bring your sunglasses. We'll be back the following morning."

Mike set his phone down and looked around his apartment in wonderment. He forgot about calling Tina.

Sunday morning at six o'clock he knocked on Simone's apartment door. She greeted him with an excited kiss. She was also dressed for the outdoors in hiking boots and khaki shorts.

"So, where are we going, what's the plan?" Mike queried.

"We're going to Pakistan."

"Is there a Pakistan in Colorado?"

Simone gave him a 'seriously?' look. "No, my dear, we are going to the country of Pakistan. It's time to take control of mankind. We're going to wipe out some Motishan extremists."

Mike realized that his mouth had dropped open and quickly closed it. "What's a Motishan extremist?"

"Are you kidding? Have you been living in a cave?"

"No, prison."

"Well, the Motishan are a violent faction of an otherwise peaceful religion in the Middle East. They refer to themselves as IPIP."

"That sounds crazy, how about we take a Corvette for a test ride instead?"

"Lame … what could be more exciting than entering a theatre of war?"

Mike stared at her in disbelief. "How about 'living'?"

"Here, look at these images." Simone's laptop was already showing footage. "IPIP recently stormed into a school and shot dozens of young students to death."

Mike looked at the screen. Bullet holes riddled the plaster walls of a classroom. There was blood all over the floor. It had been a brutal massacre. He imagined the bloody, limp bodies of innocent children being carried out. Haunting memories whirled through his mind and his eyes teared up. The thought of young lives being ended so tragically touched a personal chord in him. He squeezed his eyes tightly shut and tried to force the memory of his accident from his mind. His teeth ground together. *Maybe this is how I can use my gift to improve the world.*

"OK, let's go." He turned to Simone.

"How do you transfer other objects besides yourself? You need to take us both to the other side of the planet," she asked.

"I'm not sure. I try and focus on the atomic bonds of what I want to transport with me."

"Does it hurt?"

"Not a bit."

"Let's practice. This is serious business and I don't want to make any mistakes."

"All right," Mike agreed. He easily channeled his mind and tried to include Simone as he bumped into her guest room, alone.

"Yoo hoo, forget something?" She laughed from the main room.

"I don't understand." Mike pondered the situation as he walked back down the hallway to where Simone was standing. Even in khakis she was alluring.

"Let's hold hands — touch," she suggested. Mike immediately felt the energy of her presence through their contact as they clasped hands. *This must be how I can bump my clothes with me: by physical contact.* This time both of them appeared in the back room of the apartment. *I wonder how much control I have over this?*

"Wow! You weren't kidding. I didn't feel a thing, just poof!" Simone was wide-eyed with excitement.

Mike took her hand again and bumped them back to the main room, except Simone was nude.

"Yaaaa! What are you doing!" she shrieked in surprise as Mike grabbed her and wrestled her tawny body onto the carpet.

"You're giving me rug burns!" she laughed.

"Payback for scratching my butt yesterday." He grinned.

"Mmmmmm. I've got more than that in store for you, my dear. But business before pleasure. It's late afternoon in Pakistan, so we need to get going." She pulled his lips down to hers and planted a kiss that made Mike's mind spin.

"¡Ándale!" she commanded and slapped his ass.

Mike lifted himself, reluctantly, off of Simone's inviting figure, then helped pull her onto her feet. She walked back to the guest room to retrieve her clothes, with Mike watching every receding step.

"How will I know where to bump us?" he called. "I don't want to end up at a Motishan campfire or something."

"I can sense other beings' connections to Continuum. We will drop into an area where I don't perceive anyone's presence."

Simone returned to the main room, clothed. She intertwined her fingers with Mike's. "Let's go see what we can do."

Mike focused deep into his mind and dissolved their bodies, and clothing, into their fundamental component of energy. They entered Continuum. Then, guided by

Simone's sense of where people's minds were active, they reappeared in a village near Persar, Pakistan.

The heat was similar to the Western Slopes of Colorado, a dry heat. The air smelled both sweet and acrid at the same time. The duo were standing in an alley. The plastered walls of the nearby buildings and the cream-colored gravel at their feet reflected the brilliant sunlight all around them, causing Mike to squint. They could see people walking nearby but no one had noticed their sudden appearance.

"Should we try and find the police station? Or a church?" Mike whispered to Simone as he put on his sunglasses.

"Let's walk out to the street and see if we can discover anything promising."

They walked to the end of the alley, which opened onto a narrow road. The main part of town seemed to be to the right, so they entered the street and headed in that direction. Mike noticed that the village was extremely clean. They looked around at the white buildings; most of them were very tidy, with flowers blooming in window boxes. But some also had bullet holes spattered on their walls. Many of the villagers were wearing the traditional shalwar kameez combination of light trousers and a tunic. The young children wore colorful T-shirts. It seemed to be just a normal day. But they immediately felt that they were drawing attention. A few people stopped what they were doing and turned their eyes on the American couple.

"Try not to look so white," Simone nervously joked.

Mike's arm was grabbed from behind. "Yah!" he cried out.

"Come, please." The stranger had a kind, and very urgent expression on his face.

They were quickly hustled into a doorway and through

a building, then out the back door. The man beckoned them to follow him and hurried through a narrow alley before he entered a small house about fifty yards away. He shut the door behind them and nervously looked out of the window. A woman and a young girl were working in the kitchen. They looked up happily at the man, but then seemed alarmed when they saw Mike and Simone.

"I am Javid," the man said. "Who are you?" He spoke halting but perfect English.

"I'm Mike, and this is Simone."

The three Pakistanis looked at them in wonder. "Where did you come from? Why are you here?"

Mike and Simone weren't prepared to answer such a question; the truth would be bizarre. They couldn't just say, 'We're here to take out a few Motisha, can you tell us where we can find some?'

"We're teachers from the United States. Our organization is trying to make a connection in this region so that we can ship used textbooks and supplies to areas that need them," said Simone, quickly fabricating a hopefully feasible lie.

"You must not walk around. It is very dangerous for you," Javid warned them.

The woman began speaking to the man in a language that Mike and Simone did not understand. She was clearly scolding his actions. The man continued to peer outside.

Javid waved the Americans away from the windows. "Westerners are not liked here. You must return to a different place."

"Why aren't Westerners liked here? Aren't we helping to rid your country of the Motisha?" Mike asked.

"It is not so simple. Most people believe that the United States has brought this suffering to our country, and that you are anti-Muslim. Sometimes your drones hit our buildings and kill our townspeople. However, I have traveled to England and studied there, so I have a different view of the situation. The local people will be suspicious of you, and the Motisha will murder you."

Mike and Simone were quiet.

"Thank you for bringing us into your house," Simone replied quietly. "Are you in danger for doing this?"

The man looked over at his wife and daughter, who were clearly frightened.

"One never knows. The Motisha can be anywhere, watching what is happening."

"Do the Motisha have a base around here?" Mike inquired.

"Yes, but they keep an eye on the whole area, they do not just stay in their headquarters."

"Can you tell us where they are located? … so we can avoid that area?" Mike pressed for more information.

Javid rubbed his forehead and grimaced. "You don't understand the danger. You must leave, there is no safe place for you."

Mike and Simone stood quietly, wondering what to do next.

"Come, I'll show you." Javid nodded towards the rear door of the apartment. The three of them entered the alley and quickly walked between a few buildings, avoiding the street. After several minutes they were on a narrow passage, closed on both sides by two-story walls. Javid motioned to stay close and hidden. They crept to the end of the buildings and peered into an open plaza. Javid pushed them behind two fifty-five-gallon drums and pointed to the square.

Mike and Simone raised up over the barrels and scanned the open area. Some people were milling around the edges, but in the middle was a post, driven into the ground. A body had its hands tied behind its back, around the post. The person's shirt was completely coated with blood. There was no head, only the ragged strands of connecting tissue hanging over the collar of the shirt.

Simone gasped and sat back on the ground. Mike covered his mouth with his hand and fought back the impulse to vomit. He turned away in horror.

"It's just a scare tactic," Simone said, trying to defuse their panic.

"They're good, very good." Mike was hoarse.

"Look, look." Javid pointed. "Jeans." He pinched Mike's pants at the knee and shook the fabric. "Look."

Mike peered through the barrels again and saw that the corpse had jeans on its legs. He also discovered the head, propped on a stone about ten feet away from the body. It had empty eye sockets.

"You do not blend in at all. You cannot walk among these people and not be detected. It is very dangerous for you, please go back."

Mike was touched by Javid's concern and willingness to face danger in order to protect them.

"Thank you, we will leave. Can you tell me where the Motishan headquarters is?"

Javid was clearly frightened and quickly pointed to the hills to the north. "They have taken over some buildings beyond that hill. There are about forty of them in that group." He rose to return to his home and motioned them to follow. Simone and Mike looked at each other. Simone took a deep breath and whispered, "Let's bump into the woods and check it out, then we'll move again from there. We can do this!"

Mike smiled as the thrill of danger began coursing through his body. The image of the bullet-ridden schoolroom steeled his resolve to retaliate against the extremists. He grasped Simone's hand and looked towards Javid. His back was turned as he worked his way through the buildings. The couple vanished and appeared, crouching in the woods above the village.

They cautiously looked all around them. The trees were spread out and did not provide good cover, but it was also easy for them to survey their surroundings. Simone scanned Continuum and tried to detect if anyone was nearby. "These people don't have a strong signature with Continuum. Perhaps they are so narrowly focused on their training that they have limited their ability to think about anything else." Simone rubbed her temples as she tried to analyze their situation. "It's difficult to tell, but I don't think anyone is in this area. However, there's more activity over there," she whispered and pointed.

The two of them walked through the trees, hunched over, and worked their way to the ridge of the hill where they could examine the terrain below them. Through the leaves the buildings came into view that the Motishans had occupied. Outcroppings of rocks protruded on the slopes of the hills in various places.

"Let's bump over there." Mike pointed to a cluster of boulders that offered a better view of the buildings. "I can vanish whoever I can see and then we'll get the hell out of here."

They held hands and bumped behind several large rocks. Crawling to the edge of the flat area they were kneeling on, they considered the situation. Mike pointed to a group of men standing around a truck. Simone peered over the …

"Oh no!" she cried.

CHAPTER 6

COMBAT

Simone whirled around. Mike looked up to see a rifle butt crash into her face. At the same time he was struck on the back of his head and collapsed onto the stones. He desperately reached for Simone's hand and she wildly reached for his, but a man grabbed her hair and jerked her away. Mike tried to rise but a heavy knee pressed on the side of his face and pinned him to the coarse rocks. His vision was distorted as he watched Simone being dragged to her feet. A black combat boot ground his fingers into the rough rocks.

"Wwwyyaaaa!" Simone shrieked. Her arm was cranked behind her back in addition to the savage tearing of her hair. Warm blood ran down her chin and neck. A third man stood in front of her and ripped her blouse open, revealing a rose-colored sports bra.

Mike struggled against the weight on his head. The militant in front of Simone grabbed her breasts and roughly squeezed and twisted them. Simone writhed in pain.

"Get your ass over here!" she screamed. The man wound up and punched her solidly in the mouth, causing her legs to buckle beneath her. Then he turned and barked orders to the Motishan soldier on Mike's head. Mike heard the metallic clacking of a gun being cocked, and felt the warm barrel of a pistol being jammed into his ear. BLAM! The bullet blasted a crater in the dirt where Mike's head had been. The soldier who had been kneeling on his skull toppled forward.

Mike instantly appeared lying next to Simone and her two capturers. He grabbed her bare ankle and they vanished, collapsing back in the pathway next to the fifty-five-gallon drums. The three Motisha on the hillside looked at each other in shocked confusion.

Simone leaned against a plastered wall and slid down to the dirt. Her knees were tucked up in a fetal position as she wrapped her arms around her tummy and aching breasts. Blood was streaming from her broken nose and her lower teeth had been punched through her lip.

"Aaaooooh," she moaned, sounding like she had a cold. Her nasal passages had already swelled shut from the trauma. *Angel, why do you do this to me?*

Mike's head hung limp. His ears were ringing and his vision was like a kaleidoscope. Multiple images twirled around before his eyes. He touched Simone's hand and repaired her injuries, just like he had mended the scratches on his butt.

Then he broke down his own cellular structure and rebuilt himself, healing his damaged body.

"Oh my God! I've never been in so much pain in my life!" Simone cried; her voice was coarse and barely audible. "This is not working out at all!"

"This place is a living hell. How can people survive here?" Mike turned in the dirt and sat up.

Simone's face, neck, and sports bra were soaked red with her own blood. Mike could feel rage building inside him. "I'm going back, and I'm going to kill those sons of bitches!"

"You are *not* leaving me here," Simone insisted.

"I'm *not* taking you back there!" Mike countered.

"That's not what I mean … what if you're …" Simone's voice drifted off. She looked at him, helplessly.

"Oh, I see, let's bump back to your apartment and then I'll return here alone. Now that you have guided us here I can find it again by myself."

Despite the great distance that they traveled, it was instantaneous. Mike and Simone were suddenly sitting on her living room carpet. She slumped onto her back, blood still coloring her face, neck, and top. Mike touched her tangled strands of hair. "I'll see you in a few minutes." Then he was gone.

The three Motishan fighters were still standing on the stones where Mike had left them. They were talking animatedly in Urdu, when they noticed the reappearance of Mike, about twenty feet away. The two armed men raised their guns. Mike vanished one; the man's rifle clattered to the ground on top of his clothing and boots. The two remaining men recovered from their astonishment and the second man leveled his pistol at Mike, but vanished as well. The third militant stood facing Mike, unarmed. His right fist was still glistening with Simone's scarlet blood. He showed no fear as he defiantly advanced towards Mike, yelling at him in words that Mike could not understand. Then he raised both of his hands and made a mocking squeezing motion, as if he were still wrenching Simone's breasts, and laughed.

I wish I could burn you alive instead of just vanishing you, Mike growled to himself. Fury built up in his chest as he prepared to eliminate the indignant brute. When they were six feet apart the Motishan spat in Mike's face.

I'm going to try something special with you, asshole.

Mike drew a shallow breath and held it. The Motishan reached his left hand for Mike's throat and cocked his right arm back in preparation to crush Mike's jaw with his leathery fist. As soon as he touched Mike's neck, they both vanished from the hillside.

Mike desperately ducked and leapt away from his assailant to avoid being punched. He landed thirty feet away in the scorching lunar dust. It was 210 degrees Fahrenheit. There was no air to breathe. Mike watched the militant swing a powerful punch that hit nothing. The astonished soldier gasped at his surroundings. He had about thirty seconds before he would become unconscious. Until that happened he would experience the pain of ebullism forming gas bubbles in his bodily fluids, and would be desperately straining for breath. In wonderment, he looked around at the fiercely hot moonscape. Two minutes later he would perish, 238,000 miles away from Earth.

Mike quickly bumped himself back to Pakistan. His body was shocked from the seconds that he had spent in space. He caught his breath and began to feel normal again, then he stole over to the edge of the boulders and looked at the buildings and grounds below him. This time he kept a careful watch for anyone approaching him from behind. There were about a dozen Motishans visible at their encampment.

All right, I'm going to clean this place out!

Mike tried to calm the rage that was reeling in his mind so that he could focus on connecting with Continuum. He vanished the group of soldiers that he could see standing around the truck. Raised voices could be heard as the disappearance of their comrades was noticed. More men came running out of the building to see what was happening. Mike vanished everyone in his field of vision, leaving piles of clothing scattered where the men had been standing. He stood up and spat triumphantly in the direction of the empty camp.

As he surveyed the clumps of clothing on the ground below him he assessed his powers. *I guess I can make any living creature disappear into Continuum, but I can't vanish inanimate objects unless I'm touching them. Strange, since I can bump anything through Continuum, as long as I have physical contact.*

Then he turned around and nervously peered at the surrounding hills. A glint of sunlight reflected off something in the trees above him. Binoculars? A scope on a rifle?

I'm outta here! He bumped back through Continuum to Simone's apartment in Colorado.

Mike crouched next to the bloodied woman as she lay on her back on the carpeted floor, her knees bent and raised, smiling at the ceiling. They were both covered with dust from being pinned to the ground, and Simone's sports bra was stiffening as the blood dried. Mike was still charged with adrenaline as he lay down and wrapped one arm around her midsection. "Are you all right?" he croaked.

"How many did you kill?" she quickly asked.

"I took out those three guys who jumped us, then I vanished about thirty more in their camp."

"Then I'm great!" She sounded victorious. "That was such a nightmare, but we prevailed!" Simone squeezed Mike's thick forearm. "You're a one-man army, but I'm realizing that we'll need more help if we're going to conquer that region for ourselves."

They both rose to their knees.

"What do you mean … conquer? I love an adrenaline rush, but that was lunacy!"

"Well, yes … that's what I mean too. I think we should try to bring peace to that region. Come on! You've got to admit that was a thrill." She sat up and looked directly at Mike. "You went to the moon, didn't you?"

"Yes, I bumped that asshole that punched you up there, and I left him to die."

Simone beamed. "I want you to take us to another planet."

"Another planet?" Mike squawked. "Your ideas get crazier and crazier!"

"Yes, another plant. I've been scanning Continuum and doing some research over the past few days. I can sense a population of life forms on an exoplanet known as Kepler 3-6. It's in a two-sun system, about 180 light-years away, towards the Orion constellation." Simone's eyes sparkled with excitement. "There's life up there, and four of those lives have a strong connection to Continuum. I want to see what technology they have developed and if we can use it to rid the Middle East of those murderous, raping animals. Now don't tell me that doesn't sound like an awesome adventure!"

Mike couldn't help becoming excited, but wondered how it could be possible. "How do we know if we can breathe up there?"

"Let's do what you did on the moon. Pop up there and quickly see what it's like. We can instantly bump back if it's toxic to us."

Mike looked doubtful.

"I'll take the first breath," she bargained.

Mike thought of the endless sea of stars that was always above him. He had spent so many peaceful nights looking up at the infinite expanse of space and wondering about extraterrestrials and their ships. *Would their planes be even faster than our fighters here on Earth?* Now he was standing on the threshold of traveling into the depths of darkness and seeing for himself. "Can you guide us that far away?" he finally asked.

She held the sides of his face and touched her fore-head to his. "Let me see if I can get you to visualize the location that I can see." Simone could get impressions of other people's thoughts, but she had never tried to instill any information into another person's mind. "Can you feel anything?"

I feel my dick getting hard. Mike smiled to himself as he placed his hands on Simone's curving hips.

"Try and focus," she scolded him.

They relaxed and Mike actually felt the awareness of this distant planet, and its location in space. "I've got it," he murmured.

"Give me a couple of days to plan for this." She stroked his hair. Simone could see that he was still doubt-ful about this idea; she was losing her control over him.

"I know what we need." She seductively placed her hands on his grimy neck and kissed him with an open mouth. "Let's have a little get-away and put the worries of this day behind us."

"Hmmmm, a little get-away?" Mike raised his eye-brows.

"Yessss," she gently hissed into his ear. "I know just the place."

Fifty minutes later Mike leaned on the steering wheel of his truck in front of the lobby of Red Bluffs Lodge.

"We're all set," Simone said happily as she pranced out of the office. "Unit three, right down there."

Mike drove to their suite and backed up to the en-trance. They gathered their bags and unlocked the heavy wooden door. Western themed paintings hung on the wall and the bedspread was a large, woven Indian blan-ket. The late afternoon light made the woodwork glow with warmth.

"This is gorgeous," Simone exclaimed as she dropped

her suitcase at the entryway.

Mike set his pack near the bed and went back outside to lock up his truck. When he returned, the bathroom door was closed and he could hear the shower running. The mental image of Simone, naked and washing the Pakistani dust out of her hair, sent Mike's mind wandering back to the pleasures at hand. Any concerns about traveling into space, or fighting Motishans, drifted away. He sat on the edge of the bed and pulled his boots off. Dirt spilled onto the floor.

Mike contemplated the mess. *That's a mixture of dirt from Pakistan and the moon.* He shook his head in amazement. *Next will be some planet in deep space!*

The noise of the shower ceased. Mike prepared to get up and rinse the dust and grit out of his hair, ears, and every nook and cranny of his body.

The bathroom door opened and Simone walked through the steam around the corner. Mike let out an audible gasp. She was wearing a mini terri-cloth bathrobe, solid white, tied at the waist. Her arms were raised as she wrapped a towel around her damp tresses.

Only heaven could create hips that swivel like that, Mike concluded as he admired her sultry gait. Simone's bare feet padded along the wooden floor. Her shapely, honey-colored legs were as graceful and smooth as wine bottles. "What am I thinking about now?" Mike teased.

"You'll just have to wait a minute, Dusty. It's your turn to freshen up."

Mike leapt to his feet, patted her ass as he slid by her, and started a shower for himself. In record time he soaped every part of his body and watched the water turn brown and gray at his feet. He let the warm stream flow through his hair as he brushed it. It felt good to scrub the grit and sweat off himself. He also felt the tensions of the crazy day swirl down the drain with the dirt.

Mike shut off the water and patted himself dry. Then he wrapped the towel around his waist and went back to the main room.

"I like the look of that," Simone commented as she eyed the bulge forming under Mike's towel.

"And it likes the look of you." Mike smiled as he wrapped his arms around her waist and kissed her smiling lips. She still smelled warm and damp from the shower: fresh, like soap and lotion.

Mike pulled on the dangling end of Simone's belt, untying the bow. Her robe draped open and he slipped his hands inside, one around to the small of her back, and the other between her breasts. Simone slid her fingers into Mike's towel and grabbed his crank.

"Oh yes." They smiled and laughed simultaneously. Mike tossed his towel aside and pulled Simone's belt clear of her waistline. They grappled each other onto the woven rug. Her robe lay open, revealing a complete view of her sultry figure. Mike pulled himself onto her warm body, still moist from her shower. Simone locked her legs around his hips. Their noses pressed together as they eagerly kissed and tasted each other's mouths.

"Just so you know, I'm on the pill," Simone whispered.

"Thank you." Mike bit and gently tugged on Simone's lower lip, then kissed her chin, and under her chin, then her smooth neck. He cupped both of her breasts and slid lower against her body. She moaned with expectation as he settled with his stomach on the soft wool between her legs. He took his time exploring each bosom with his mouth, rolling her nipples with his tongue. They reminded him of gumdrops as he gently pulled them with his lips.

"Hmmmmm, that's nice." Simone grabbed Mike's hair and squeezed. He shifted lower and tugged on her navel ring with his teeth. Then nibbled her soft tummy

… and shifted lower again …

"Ahh!" Simone jerked slightly as Mike flicked her most sensitive part with his tongue. He worked her soft folds until they shivered with anticipation.

"Ohhaaa, I want you in me." Simone pulled his face back up to hers, aligning his erection with her moist opening. After four years of incarceration, Mike devoured the opportunity to release his lust. He hooked his arm behind Simone's neck and banged her like a sewing machine.

Twenty minutes later they lay catching their breath on the sofa. Mike was facing up, with Simone on top of him, her head against his neck. He stroked her back and smiled into her tousled hair.

"I guess you'll have to brush this again," he noted. He felt her cheeks smile against his chest.

"I'm getting chilly, can we slip into bed?" she suggested.

They made their way into the king-sized bed. The mattress pad and comforter were as soft as clouds. Squooshed among the pillows, the lovers intertwined their arms and legs, then drifted into a peaceful sleep.

At the same time, in Pakistan, American intelligence operatives were reviewing video that the Pakistani military had taken earlier that day. As the images shone on the screen, the sergeant who took the footage narrated. "Two people, an Anglo man and a Latina woman, dressed as civilians, suddenly appeared out of nowhere by this outcropping of rocks above the Motishan camp that we were investigating. They did not notice the three soldiers who crept up and attacked them. After a brief struggle, the man and woman vanished as suddenly as they had appeared. Approximately three minutes later the man reappeared and confronted the soldiers. Two of the militants disappeared into thin air. Then the third soldier and the American man vanished together."

The intelligence and reconnaissance team stared intently at the screen, wondering if this was simply trick photography.

"The Anglo man reappeared and proceeded to watch the encampment below him where we witnessed the disappearance of approximately thirty Motishan soldiers. Then he vanished again."

The team of intelligence operatives studied the video carefully. "Did you get a sample of that saliva?" one of them asked as he watched Mike spit on the rocks overlooking the IPIP camp.

"Yes sir, we did."

"Let's do a DNA analysis of it and run it through our database."

"Yes sir, we have already begun that process."

"Very good. If he's an American citizen … we'll find him."

Six hours later Mike lazily opened his eyes. He was looking directly into a pillow, but he could tell that the morning light was starting to reach the valley walls around the lodge. He carefully moved so that his lips were against Simone's forehead and listened as she breathed. He felt her chest swell and contract, ever so slightly, while she slept. He dozed back to sleep.

Fifteen minutes later the Earth had rotated so that the morning light directly penetrated into the suite. Mike woke again. *Darned real life*, he grumbled to himself.

Slowly extricating his limbs, he rolled into a sitting position and contemplated the room. He tiptoed across the wooden planks towards the lower level.

"Nice butt," a sleepy voice came from the jumble of

covers and pillows.

"Are there any scratches on it?"

"Not yet."

Mike smiled. "I'll get coffee started."

"Mmmmmm," was the only response.

He prepared the coffee maker and walked into the bathroom.

Simone blinked her eyes and turned onto her back. She ached a bit from last night's exertions. Letting her eyes wander across the ceiling beams, she cradled her tummy with both hands. Pressing slightly, she smiled knowingly. Her face glowed as she gently rubbed circles around her pelvis. "I didn't say which pill, now did I?"

The toilet flushed and the coffee maker stopped bubbling. Mike walked back into the room and poured two cups. "What do you like in it?"

"You," she cooed mischievously.

Mike paused, then grinned at the green eyes sparkling back at him from the pillows.

"Cream, thanks," she answered.

He carried the mugs over to the bed.

"How about we have these in the shower?" Simone's sexy smile invited Mike as she sat up.

"I like the way you think."

CHAPTER 7
THE ALIEN

After the lovers parted on Monday morning, Mike drove to Salt Lake City so he could get an early start on Tuesday, and meet Major Brennevin.

He slept fitfully in his hotel room. A terrifying memory haunted his dreams. Mike recalled the greenish glow of the speedometer, showing that he was approaching ninety-five miles per hour. The headlights pierced the night, illuminating the dashed yellow stripes on the median as they flickered past him. The road was dry and he had driven this section dozens of times. He glanced quickly at his sleeping daughter in her car seat beside him.

Kalump!

Later reports would identify the pulverized remains of a coyote at the scene. That small collision was enough to twist the front wheels and trip the speeding car into a long series of devastating flips. Mike heard Jennie startle and cry, before his head went through the windshield and his world blacked out.

Two weeks later, his heart and soul drained to emptiness at Jennifer's funeral. The future didn't matter. His plans didn't matter. His four-year marriage couldn't handle the blame, prison term, and guilt.

Now, after fifty months in prison, Mike continued to seek danger and high speed whenever he could. He had nothing to lose, nothing to live for anymore. He couldn't bear the fact that he had survived, and Jennie had died.

Major Cody Brennevin had his own demons to deal with. He had replaced two decades of heroin addiction with alcoholism. Flying missions over Vietnam had been the most impressionable period in his life. Everything since then seemed pointless. The real world tortured him with its irrelevance.

Early the following morning Mike met Brennevin and left his truck at a Denny's. He hopped into Cody's 1978 Camaro. Together they drove through the security gates at Foothills Air Force Base. Brennevin's eyes were glassy and he smelled like a bar.

"What'd you have for breakfast, old man?" Mike joked.

The major belched his reply and wheeled his car to the end of the parking lot. They had been through this routine many times before. He and Mike donned old flight suits and helmets, then walked past the F-15 Eagles towards a pair of F-4 Phantoms. Brennevin smiled nostalgically as he climbed under the open canopy and squeezed into the pilot's seat. Mike had his own copilot's compartment, behind and above Cody.

"Ya know why this plane is like your mother?" Brennevin drawled as he clicked and tightened the restraining belts around his hefty midriff.

Mike had heard this joke many times. "No, why?"

"Because she's got a big cock pit! Haw haw."

"You know why your mother is like a highway?"

The major ignored him.

"'Cause she's been laid all over the country."

The friends locked their canopy and Brennevin lit the jets. Mike tightened his air mask around his face.

"Damn! This thing is armed!" Cody looked at his control panel. Mike peered out at the missiles that were mounted on the hardpoints under the wings.

"Maybe this isn't the plane your buddies want us to take up today?" Mike questioned.

"Tough shit." Cody taxied to the runway and gunned the powerful engines. Eleven thousand pounds of thrust pressed Mike back into his seat and he fought for breath as the G-forces compressed his internal organs. Soon they were soaring above the mountains of Utah, heading west.

There was still snow on the high peaks. The wooded mountains soon dissipated into an immense desert below them. Ancient geological rifts and formations were easily recognizable at their altitude. The barren Earth looked basically the same as it had over fifty million years ago.

"When you're done stretching yer frank back there let's see what you remember." Brennevin turned over control of the plane.

Mike made some subtle turns to refamiliarize himself with the Phantom and then accelerated to Mach 0.9.

"Hell!" the major bellowed as he noted the radar screen. "We're being tracked!"

Two other planes, F-15s, were tailing them, and closing fast.

"Gun it!" Brennevin yelled, his voice filled with excitement as he recalled his days of dogfighting over Nam.

Mike obeyed and pushed the plane above the speed of sound. The dry landscape roared by, five thousand feet below them. Without knowing it, Mike crossed into the Utah Test and Training Range, a live-fire range for the United States military.

The radio in their helmets came to life and a determined voice commanded them. "You have entered a restricted area in a stolen plane. Return to Foothills Air

Base or we will be forced to shoot you down."

"Lose 'em!" Brennevin hollered and took a gulp from a flask he had brought on board.

Mike yanked his controls and banked the roaring plane, causing his own body to jerk against his restraining harness. A loud thump resonated from Cody's cockpit. The Eagles followed precisely. Mike was no match for experienced pilots.

"What now?" Mike yelled. No answer. He looked into the pilot's cockpit. Brennevin's head was limp and twisted against the canopy. "Shit!"

"Turn your craft east and return to Foothills Air Base. This will be your final warning."

Mike panicked. *What can I do? Where can I go?* A shadow darkened his cockpit as one of the F-15s lowered itself sixty feet above him as they sped along at over nine hundred miles per hour. *I am not going back to prison!* Then he collected his thoughts. *Wait a minute, no prison can hold me, I can bump through Continuum and escape! That's it! Continuum!* Mike turned the jet evasively. Brennevin's helmeted head flopped over and banged against the opposite window. The Eagles backed off and lined up behind him, ready to shoot him out of the sky.

Mike focused his mind on the fifty-five-thousand-pound aircraft that he was touching, and the location of the dual-sun planet that Simone had inserted into his mind. The pursuing pilots fingered the controls of their air-to-air missiles, but stopped. The Phantom II was gone, leaving nothing but empty, blue sky over the Utah landscape.

"Yow!" Mike was astonished to find himself tearing through the atmosphere, just two thousand feet above the hills and valleys of a different planet, Kepler 3-6.

"Commander Zath! We have detected a new aircraft

on our radar. It came out of nowhere."

"Just one?" Zath peered at the screen in his command center above the city of Pacabria. The new plane was faster than anything they had ever seen. He quickly analyzed the trajectory of Mike's fighter. "Squadron B, get airborne! Operation Stranglehold," he barked into his radio, setting up an ambush for the unidentified flying object.

Mike slowed the Phantom down to four hundred miles per hour. "Cody! Are you all right?" he called desperately into his mask. Brennevin's head hung lifeless.

Mike glanced at the limp shoulders and helmet in the pilot's cockpit. *How the hell did I bump you through space without touching you? I thought I needed to touch a living creature in order to …* Mike's mouth dropped open as he realized that Cody was no longer living.

The strange landscape whizz by beneath him. Everything looked slightly peculiar. The colors of the cliffs were different, the shapes of the trees were strange. The sunlight was intense. Mike looked through his canopy and noticed that there were two suns shining in the sky. *I am a looong, damn, way from home,* he realized. *And I can't stay up here forever before I run out of fuel.* He looked around the cockpit for the lever to eject himself, and caught sight of his radar screen. He was being chased.

"No, no, no! I'm just visiting!" he accelerated and pulled away from Tyrandus's fighters. "Ha! Too fast for you?" Mike exalted.

Two other aircraft appeared on his left and closed in. They were huge, strange-looking craft, crude when compared to the Phantom, but they looked like they'd win in a demolition derby. Mike veered to his right to avoid a collision.

"Commander Zath, the markings on this plane are not from Kael."

"Is the ship attacking us?" Zath tried to analyze the situation from his command center.

"No sir, no signs of aggression at this moment."

"Herd him in. Let's see who it is."

Mike saw a city several miles ahead of him. Suddenly he was surrounded by the massive enemy fighters. One cruised directly above him and began lowering onto his dome.

Damn! They led me into a trap! The plane above him didn't slow down. Mike reduced his altitude and decelerated to avoid flying into the plane in front of him. *I can't eject either or I'll blast up into it!* As Mike was being forced down he saw a runway come into view. He had practiced with Brennevin coaching him, but could he land this sophisticated machine alone?

I could abandon this whole thing. I could bump out of here right now! Mike tried to consider his options as he lined up with the runway. *Where would I go? Into the trees? Back to Earth? And what about Brennevin? Is he still alive?* He slowed the Phantom to landing speed and prepared to touch down. *Let's see what these people are like*, he decided. The tires squeaked as they hit the surface of DuoSol. "One small step for man …" he muttered as he guided his heavily armed fighter into an open area next to some enormous buildings, becoming the first alien since Creation to land on a foreign planet.

Large trucks pulled up around the F-4. Massive scaly creatures with weapons surrounded the plane as Mike turned off the whirring turbines. One of the gigantic fighters had landed behind Mike and taxied up against his tail. He was cornered.

Looking beyond the trucks and squad of soldiers he noticed what appeared to be an officer, with his entourage, standing behind the crowd. *That's who I need to talk to.* Mike took one more look at Brennevin's lifeless body.

"Cody! Can you hear me?" He desperately refused to accept the truth. The cockpit was oddly quiet. The distinctive sound of breathing through the major's air mask had ceased. His friend was dead. Brennevin's head dangled from a broken neck.

"Noooo! What the hell happened to you?" Tears blurred his vision.

Mike's attention was torn away from Brennevin as the enormous Pacabrians clunked ladders against the Phantom fighter. Mike looked out at the troops surrounding his ship. "I'll take care of you, old buddy." He wiped his glassy eyes.

I hope I can breathe out there.

He bumped behind Commander Zath.

CHAPTER 8
DEAL

Zath and his two officers spun around and looked in amazement at the strange creature that had magically appeared behind them. Mike tentatively took his first breath of DuoSol's atmosphere and discovered that it had a mixture of nitrogen and oxygen that was similar to Earth's. He raised the visor on his helmet.

"This is not a Kaelite!"

"How did it appear here?!"

"Is it hostile?" The three Pacabrians exchanged astonished questions.

Mike held his hands away from his sides and spread his fingers, hopefully in a universal gesture that indicated non-violence. The thousand pounds of monsters in front of him were making deep clicking and guttural noises.

Zath noticed Mike's hands and made a similar gesture. "Who are you? Where did you come from? Why are you here?" he asked the smaller Earthling.

Mike shook his head. "Sorry, buddy, I don't speak lizard." He prepared to bump back to Earth if things turned unfriendly.

"Clearly his aircraft and powers are beyond our level of technology. If he was aggressive, he would have fired upon us by now," Zath suggested.

The three Pacabrians turned and looked at the Phantom II. Its sleek titanium structure and the array of missiles bristling beneath its wings were impressive, to any species. By comparison, the Pacabrian fighters looked heavy, bulky, and dirty. The entire area smelled of spilled fuel and exhaust.

Commander Zath turned to Mike and gestured that he follow the Pacabrians into the building. "Have this creature speak into the language-assimilator. Then bring him back to me. It might be possible to have this alien assist us when the Kaelites attack," he ordered his assistants.

Mike was led through several hallways. He felt dwarfed by the immense doors, furniture, and creatures that surrounded him. The group entered a room with several machines lining the walls. His escorts clicked and grunted to the attendants in the room. Everyone was curious about Mike, the visitor from outer space, as he watched, warily, to see what would happen next. After an exchange of vocalizations, one smaller Pacabrian, seemingly a female, gestured to Mike that he stand in front of one of the giant pieces of equipment and speak into a bulb that was mounted on it.

What should I say? Do they want some sort of explanation of why I'm here? Mike felt confused. Then it occurred to him that the machine probably needed a large sample of his language. Maybe it would decode the structure of English and hopefully interpret what was being said. He looked at the bulb in front of his mouth and began. "Once upon a time, Mike Kruger stole a fighter plane…" He continued talking for twenty-five minutes until the attendant indicated that he could stop. A small headpiece was handed to him. Mike placed the thin apparatus on his head, adjusted the earbud and mouthpiece, and listened.

"Can you understand me, My Cougar?" the female

technician asked him.

Mike was dumbfounded. *Ahhh, I get it. Mike Kruger becomes My Cougar. Whatever.* He looked up at the emotionless eye band of the assistant. "Yes, I understand you. And you may call me Mike." He heard both his own voice, and the Pacabrian translation coming from a small speaker in his headpiece.

"Very well, MyC. These guards will return you to the presence of Commander Zath."

Two Pacabrians in uniform entered the room and led Mike through the gigantic building until they reached a conference room, with Commander Zath seated at a massive table.

Mike felt like a child, walking among the furnishings of the room. Zath indicated a chair, which had three cushions on it so that Mike could sit comfortably at the table.

"We are to welcome you to our planet, DuoSol, and our great city, Pacabria," Zath greeted Mike. "I am Commander Zath, and this is my second in command, Estryk."

Mike nodded to both Pacabrians. "Thank you. My name is Mike. I entered your airspace by mistake, please forgive my intrusion."

Zath and Estryk listened to the translation coming from Mike's headpiece. "We mean no aggression towards your person. Our airspace must be protected. We are expecting an attack by our enemies at any moment."

A server brought a container and several smaller vessels to the table. He poured a clear liquid into a cup and set it before Mike. Mike sniffed it suspiciously.

Estryk drank from the same container and explained to Mike, "This is dihydrogen monoxide. It is one of the basic molecules that sustain life on DuoSol. We are hoping that it is also common to your planet. Please refresh yourself."

Mike nodded and smiled. He took a sip. It tasted like water.

"Your airship is very fast, and has many explosive devices. We are hoping to ask you to aid us in our battle against the attacking Kaelites," Commander Zath said, getting right to the point. "Since pre-history they have been intolerant of any civilization besides their own. It is impossible to coexist with them on the same planet, though we have tried diplomacy many times. They have created a new fighter plane, and we must destroy it before they use it against us."

Mike swallowed hard and tried to look important. He recalled that Simone had wanted to bring some advanced technology back to Earth to help in the Middle East. "We also fight against tyranny on Earth. Perhaps we can help each other? I would be glad to assist you against the Kaelites. In return I would borrow some of your mighty airplanes to fight with me against our enemy on Earth."

Zath and Estryk wrote some notes to each other, then responded to Mike. "This is a favorable proposition for us. We will request an audience with our Tsar, Tyrandus. A decision of this magnitude must be approved by him."

"Commander Zath, my copilot perished in combat on my way here. Would you permit me to bury his body in the hills above your valley?" Mike was suddenly melancholy, thinking of his good friend.

"We will make the arrangements, MyC," Estryk replied.

Two hours later, Mike had emptied the Phantom II of his belongings and was scooping a final shovelful of soil onto Major Cody Brennevin's grave. He looked around at the strange trees and the lovely view of the colorful, alien valley. "You taught me well, my friend. I hope that you like your final resting place." He looked up at the evening sky, just as a meteor streaked above the hills. "Wow! Did you see that!?"

Estryk, who was standing next to the grave, nodded. "It is not uncommon here. That was a small one."

I'd hate to meet a big one. Mike took one final look at the freshly turned dirt and set Cody's flask on top of it. "You might need this in the afterlife, old man."

The Pacabrians drove him back to Pacabria, and the royal edifice. Mike's flight suit and the contents of the Phantom II were taken to a guest room, then Mike was led to meet the Tsar.

Tyrandus and his counselor Kota were seated at a huge table. They faced Mike as he was led to a chair, stacked with cushions.

"I am Tsar Tyrandus, ruler of Pacabria, and this is my chief counselor, Kota. We have been informed of your arrival, and your suggestion to form an alliance."

Mike peered around the table and recognized Commander Zath.

"Yes, sir. If that is favorable to you." Mike tried to maintain an air of confidence. *Otherwise I'm taking my plane and getting the hell out of here!*

Kota leaned forward. "Our enemy has developed a perilous weapon: eight aircraft, with the intention of destroying our civilization. Two of these airships are ready for battle, and six are almost completed." Counselor Kota spoke with deep concern. "The first two fighter planes are superior to our aircraft. The remaining six, the Generation II fighters, are even more deadly than the first two. We are unsure of their capabilities, but we are learning that your aircraft also has great velocity and many explosives. If you are able to help us destroy these warships, we will commit ten of our fighters to assist you on your home planet. Provided you are able to transport them there and back to DuoSol."

"How do you plan to defeat these fighters?"

"We know where the first two ships are being housed. We will fly into Kaelite airspace and bomb these two planes in their hangar. That will hopefully give our spies enough time to determine where the Generation II planes are being completed. Then we will destroy that facility as well."

"I accept your terms, sir." Mike was not at all sure how this would work out, but he knew that Simone would be delighted that aliens were joining the fight against IPIP. "Tsar Tyrandus, my copilot perished in a dogfight. I need to transport myself to Earth and bring back a replacement. I will return in one day." Then he quickly added, "If that is acceptable to you."

Tyrandus and Kota needed time to understand the translation. "We wish to attack the Kaelites and destroy their warships before they have the opportunity to launch an assault against us. Be as rapid as you are able."

Mike knew that the Phantom II was securely locked. He slid from the chair and bowed slightly to the Tsar. *I might as well make a show out of this.* He clasped his hands in front of himself. *I feel like a genie.* He smiled, then bumped through 183 light-years to the main room of his apartment.

Tyrandus turned to Kota and Zath. "This is a very fortuitous development. If we can destroy the Kaelites' new warships, including the six under construction, we should be able to maintain peace between our two species."

Mike looked around his empty apartment and quickly checked his phone. He had two texts, one from Tina, one from Simone, and a voicemail from an unknown number. He called Tina.

"Michael, I would like to talk to you. About Jennifer."

Mike held the phone away from his face and looked at it in disbelief. "Jennie? My daughter?" he finally responded.

"Yes, may I stop by for a minute? I'll be quick. I can tell that you are in a hurry."

"Sure, come on over." He hung up and tried to remember if he had mentioned Jennie, or the accident, to Tina.

He called Simone.

"What have you been up to? I was getting the sensation that you were all the way in outer space, at Kepler 3-6!"

"I was. It has been amazing. You said that you wanted to see what technology was up there? Well, I met the commander of their military, and the tsar of the whole nation. They want me to help them fight their enemy, who has some new super fighter planes. Then they will help us to fight IPIP. I want you to go back with me, now, and be my copilot."

"New super fighters? It seems like we should be on the other side of the battle." Simone tried to analyze the situation. "But ... hell yes! Let's go!"

"I've got to meet somebody first, then I'll bump over to your place. We need to get back up to DuoSol ASAP, our attack could begin at any time."

Mike returned his attention to Tina's visit. Jennie's death was so personal, so agonizing to think about, that he usually suppressed the memory. He was sure that he had not told Tina anything about it, other than to mention that his daughter was dead.

He looked around at his messy apartment. Mike quickly gathered the dishes that were scattered about and set them in the sink. He looked at the piles of papers and magazines and began ...

Tap ta tap tap sounded on the door. He pulled it open and greeted …

"Simone!" Mike anxiously looked past her at the parking lot. No sign of Tina yet. "Long time no see, come on in." They kissed and he waved her into the room. "I thought I was going to come over to your place."

Simone helped herself to a chair. She leaned back and crossed her legs. "I was driving by when you called on my cell. Tell me about this planet, DuoSol, and the commander, and the advanced weapon that the other side has."

"I'm not really sure. But the plane I have up there is faster than what the Pacabrians have, so I guess it can destroy the Kaelites' new ships. Then they will help us in the Middle East. It's amazing! I've never had such an adventure in my whole life!"

"Pacabrians? Kaelites? You need to bring me up to date." Simone's eyes sparkled with excitement.

Another knock at the door.

I could just bump back to DuoSol by myself and hide, avoiding this whole scene. Mike cringed. He opened the door again. "Hi Tina, come on in." His forced smile betrayed his anxiety.

Tina slipped through the door and scanned the room. Her eyes stopped at Simone.

Mike made clumsy introductions. "Uhh, Tina … this is Simone, Simone … Tina."

"Hello," Tina said coolly, and with recognition.

"Well well, here we are at last. The three of us in the same room." Simone leaned back in her chair and narrowed her eyes into green slits. Her ebony hair flared around her head like inky tendrils.

Tina met Simone's glower with her own piercing glare.

"You two know each other?" Mike backed away from

the searing tension in the room.

"We both knew when you accessed Continuum, Michael, and we came to Grand Junction to find you," Tina explained.

Mike looked at the two women. They stared back. He could see that it was true. They each wanted to become his partner and use his capabilities.

"Well, it's awfully nice of you to drop by," Simone diminished Tina's presence, "but Michael and I already have plans."

Tina set her jaw and seethed through her teeth. "*You* have plans. Michael will decide how he is going to use his own powers."

"He already has. We have our own plans for improving mankind …" Simone cast a scornful eye on Tina's slender figure, "… Tinker Bell."

"Right. Well if boobs were brains …"

"… you'd be a cretin," Simone interrupted.

"This is pointless." Tina instinctively folded her arms beneath her breasts. "If we could set this bickering aside, the three of us could work together and bring peace to humankind."

Simone uncrossed her legs and sauntered through the room. "You take care of Neverland, Michael and I will take care of Earth."

She lavished a kiss on Mike and eased past Tina towards the door. "I'll see you in a few minutes, Michael. I need to pack for our little trip." She slipped out the door.

Mike turned nervously to Tina. "Hey, so … it's nice to see you," he ventured.

"Shut up!" she shouted crisply. "You're screwing that trollop at the same time that you're asking me to dinner?" She stomped across the room. "You ignorant, pussy-whipped jackass! Can't you see, Michael? She's seducing you. You are just a puppet to her!"

Mike helplessly searched for anything to say. Tina's eyes burned with wrath as she faced him. But she controlled her breathing and the anger slowly subsided. She looked at the ceiling and laughed and cried at the same time. Then raised both of her arms, in exasperation.

"OK, Michael, I don't chase anyone. If that's your choice, go right the hell ahead." She dabbed her eyes with the back of her hand and sat down. "I still want us to help each other as far as Continuum is concerned. You are just beginning to understand your powers, while I have been developing mine for many years."

"What sort of powers do you have?" Mike was intrigued by the possibilities.

Tina took several breaths and finally composed herself. "I can do everything that you can do: reduce matter into energy, travel through Continuum, heal my own flesh and anyone else's flesh too. Simone seems to have different abilities. I gather that she can get impressions of what other people are thinking. I can't do that." She sighed and assessed Mike. "But greater than that, I can reach into Continuum and communicate with beings who have entered that realm. I found the presence of your daughter, Jennifer."

Mike sank into a chair. The terrible image of Jennie's final seconds of life on Earth flashed through his mind. He held his head in his hands. Tina came over to him and put her arm around his shoulders.

"She is at peace. She feels no pain, only serenity, and she forgives you. That is what I came to tell you."

"How can you know? Can you show me how to see her myself?" Mike asked desperately.

"I can't … yet. I have been connected to Continuum for a long time, Michael. You will not be able to experience Continuum the way that I can until you develop your powers."

"Why do you call me Michael? My name is Mike. Is Tina your full name?"

"It's Christina."

"How long have you been connected to Continuum?"

"Over eight thousand years."

Mike was speechless. *This is unreal. This whole day must be a dream!* He looked at Tina; her eyes could tell him anything that he wanted to know. He could see that everything she had said was true.

Tina touched his hand. "You are capable of doing great things, Michael. Remember what I said: 'think about the possible good works that you can do.' Forgive yourself for Jennifer's death and join me in trying to bring peace to the Earth." She rose and walked to the door. "I know that you are leaving with Simone. I can't make these decisions for you. You're going to have to decide what's right and determine what your path will be." She quietly opened the door and walked out.

Mike looked at the closed door for several minutes. *Eight thousand years? How is that possible? But then, how is any of this possible?* He rose from his chair. "I *am* trying to bring peace to the Earth." He picked up a photo of Jennifer. "I would give anything to be able to see you again, my baby girl."

Mike quickly made a sandwich and sat down. This day had been very draining. Brennevin had died, he had been to another planet, Tina contacted Jennie in the afterlife, and now he needed to get back to DuoSol and try to fly the Phantom II in combat. He bit his sandwich and leaned back in his chair. "Ahh, peace at last." He looked wearily about the vacant room.

His phone rang. It was the same, unknown number that had left him a message, which he hadn't listened to yet. He decided to let it go to voicemail again and just listen.

"Hello, Mr. Kruger. I am Special Agent Bristol, calling from the Military Intelligence Corps of the United States Army. I am contacting you because we have acquired some amazing video footage of two American civilians who encountered several Motishan soldiers yesterday in Pakistan."

Panic seized Mike as he recalled the glint of sunlight in the woods behind him after he had vanished the militants. He paced the room as he listened to the rest of the message.

"You left a small sample of saliva on the rocks, which provided us with your DNA, which has been positively matched to information from your term in prison. We cross referenced the video with photos of you in our database, which leads us to this phone call, Mr. Kruger."

Mike tried to comprehend the significance of this; he was no longer anonymous. Any bizarre situation would likely be traced right back to him, such as vanishing fighter planes, or bullies that disappear in the parking lots of pubs.

"Please do not be alarmed, Mr. Kruger. We would like to learn more about your astonishing abilities, and join together to fight the extremists in that region of the world. I will try to catch you by phone later in the day. Goodbye for now."

"Arrgggghh!" Mike set the phone down. "This is getting out of control!" He peeked through the blinds on his windows, looking for agents wearing dark glasses and driving big, black cars. Nothing seemed suspicious.

He sat back down and slowly chewed his sandwich. There was no time to think about this now. Tina had made contact with his deceased daughter, and he was preparing to bump back to DuoSol with Simone. He set his plate in the sink, took one more look at Jennie's photo and bumped into Simone's main room. The pain of being reminded about Jennifer, and the fear of being discovered by military intelligence, raged in his chest. He needed to burn off the energy that ached in his body.

"Are you ready?" he asked, noting that Simone had changed into cowboy boots, a casual shirt, and black leather pants. She held a small bag.

"Yes, let's go see what kind of a deal you've made with these creatures."

CHAPTER 9
ATTACK

Mike and Simone bumped next to the building by the airfield, where Zath's headquarters and the barracks were located in Pacabria. Mike pointed to the intimidating Phantom II, shining in the light of two moons. The Pacabrian flight crew was filling the fuel tanks with their mixture of high octane fuel. "I came here with that plane. We're going to fly it together and try and destroy the new weapon that the Kaelites have."

Simone looked through the darkness towards the fighter, and the Pacabrian warships beyond it.

"Those creatures are huge! Who lives here? Jolly Green Giants?"

As if to answer her question, two guards approached. They recognized Mike, and seemed curious about Simone. Mike put on his translating headpiece.

"We will escort you to your sleeping quarters." The guards motioned them to enter the building.

"You're *friends* with these beasts?" Simone whispered. "They look like a cross between linebacker, chameleon, and metal shrubbery."

Mike chortled and entered their guest room. He felt like he had stepped into a scene from *Alice in Wonderland*;

the furniture, doors, window height, and light switches were all significantly larger, and higher, than normal.

"Wow! Do you think the beds are big enough?" Simone stared at the sturdy frames that supported a soft pad.

Mike's and Brennevin's flight suits and helmets were lying on a chair. There was water, juice, ice, and a bowl of unusual fruits on the tables next to each bed.

"We don't know when our assault will begin, so we better get some rest," Mike suggested, although he was wired.

"Are you kidding? I'm so excited to be here! This is crazy." Simone jumped up onto a bed. "But Michael, tell me about this other species, and their weapon. Maybe we're playing for the wrong side. We need the best firepower on our side when we return to Earth."

"I don't know much. The Pacabrians are impressed with the speed of the F-4 that I brought here. And they seem very nervous about the new aircraft that the Kaelites have developed, and they want to destroy them."

"I wonder why the Kaelites are attacking. I mean really, who are the good guys in this situation?" Simone dropped from the bed and took her bag into the bathroom. Mike checked the flight suits. Everything was intact and ready.

"A person could drown in here." Simone's voice sounded hollow through the walls.

Mike smiled and turned towards the bathroom door, just as it opened. Simone entered the main room, dressed in a light blue camisole. "We're on the verge of taking control of these alien ships and returning to Earth," she whispered suggestively as she reached for a switch on the light fixture. "I think we should celebrate." The room darkened and looked eerie in the dim light. The huge furniture surrounded the couple in massive, dark forms.

Simone peeled Mike's T-shirt up over his arms. He

held her shoulders and admired the lacy bodice.

"This is beautiful." He felt the strain of their situation leaving his mind.

"It's celeste."

Mike's brow furrowed. "It's what?"

"That's the name for this color, celeste. As in celestial."

"Very appropriate." Mike slipped his hands down and gently squeezed her breasts together.

"Errrrg …" Simone grunted. "Please be gentle, they're slightly tender today."

"Sorry." Mike carefully kissed each fleshy dome, as if to apologize. Simone undid his belt buckle and pushed Mike's pants down to his ankles. He stepped out of them and they lifted themselves onto a bed. They piled the pillows against the massive headboard and poured themselves two juices.

Simone smiled mischievously and lay her head against Mike's shoulder. She twirled her finger in her drink, making the ice cubes tinkle against the glass. Then she traced her wet finger along Mike's lips. He kissed the tangy drops.

Simone set her glass on the table. She took his juice and filled her mouth with the cold liquid. Then she slid down and enveloped his penis in the chilly fluid.

"Whoa," Mike gasped as her tongue gave him a fruity tickling. She carefully slid her lips off of his hardon and swallowed the juice. Then she smiled and gave him a wet kiss.

"You are a playful lady." Mike grinned as he rolled her into a reclining position and crawled between her soft thighs. He kissed her eyelids and carefully teased her nipples with his thumbs.

Mike pecked tender kisses along Simone's jawline, from ear to ear. Behind her head he slipped an ice cube into his mouth. He maneuvered himself so that he could kiss her neck and cleavage with his chilly lips. His strong hands carefully pulled the straps of Simone's camisole off of her shoulders, exposing her honey-colored bosom. Then he traced his cold tongue around her full breasts and enveloped a tip into his mouth. He rolled the ice cube against her rubbery nipple.

"Aaahhhhh." Simone squirmed and held Mike's head in her hands as he moved from breast to breast. He melted the ice at the base of her neck and let the water trickle through her cleavage and down to her tummy. He grasped her hips and pulled her flat onto her back. While he kissed her lips he fished another cube out of his glass with his fingers and then placed it in his teeth. He drew a wet path down her chin, neck, through her shining, wet breasts, and then to her triangle of curly black hair. He held her tightly as he massaged her pussy with the cold, wet rock.

"Ohhhh!" Simone arched her back and offered her folds to Mike's playful stimulation. He set the melting cube at the mouth of her vagina and pushed it in as deep as he could with his tongue. Then he slid back up so he was face to face and slipped his erection into the opening that was both hot and cold at the same time. The ice quickly melted and the chilly water ran out and down the seam between Simone's butt cheeks.

Simone grabbed Mike's ass and pulled him closer. They found their rhythm and writhed together until they reached the point of relief, first Mike, and then Simone a minute later.

After their lovemaking, Mike remained on Simone, like a human blanket, and they both fell asleep.

Breeuuuurp … breeuuuurp … breeuuuurp …

Mike's head shot up and he looked around at the dark, alien room. Simone sat up next to him. "That must be the alarm!" she said excitedly.

They slid off of the bed and quickly dressed, including the flight suits.

"This is definitely not my size," Simone complained; the one-piece suit hung on her figure like a deflated hot-air balloon.

The door burst open and Estryk clicked excitedly at the two Earthlings. Mike put on his headpiece.

"Get your plane airborne and follow instructions!"

Mike and Simone grabbed their helmets and joined the crowd of Pacabrian soldiers and pilots who were hurrying through the hallway. It was like running in a herd of buffalos.

"We might get trampled to death before we even get in the sky!" Mike tried to keep up with the flow of the huge aliens.

They ran across the tarmac to the Phantom II. The orange dawn glowed like a furnace and they had no trouble seeing their harnesses and instruments. The cockpit was filled with the rich smell of spilled scotch.

"Strap in and attach your mask to the oxygen flow," Mike directed Simone. He started the turbines and the F-4 powered up. The Phantom lurched backwards, bashing Simone into her control panel.

"Ouch! What the hell are you doing? Can't you drive a stick shift?" she yelled into her mask.

"Sorry, this thing is a beast."

"MyC, align yourself on the right side of our formation, second row. The Kaelites have launched their two SAWs and are attacking."

"What are they saying?" Simone could hear Commander Zath clicking through the radio in her helmet.

"Basically, he wants our plane to stay out of the way until we can join the fight."

The Pacabrian fleet roared into the air. Mike gunned the Phantom down the runway, set the ailerons, and managed to lift off.

"All right!" He was pleased with his successful take-off. Now he just needed to remember the basics that Brennevin had taught him.

"Wow! Look at those guys!" Simone peered through her canopy at the Pacabrian fleet aligning themselves into tight formation. "They really know what they're doing."

The Pacabrians established three rows of seven planes. They would meet the Kaelite attack in three waves, twenty seconds apart. Flight Commander Zath was piloting the plane in the center of the first row of fighters.

Mike matched their speed and stationed himself on the right flank of the second row as they sped towards the sunrise.

Ten minutes earlier and three hundred eighty miles away, Queen Cassilius oversaw the opening of the hangar and the takeoff of the two Generation I Strongforce Attack Warships (SAWs). As soon as the hangar doors began to open, Tyrandus's spies radioed to Pacabrian headquarters that the new warplanes were being deployed.

"They look beautiful," she complimented the chief engineer and contractor who had built the aircraft. "Let's see if they can annihilate the Pacabrian air fleet."

"As you are aware, my Queen, due to intense secrecy, the ships have never flown beyond our valley. But we will test them in battle." The chief engineer sounded excited and confident.

The queen watched the twin, dual-wing aircraft taxi to the open pavement in front of the hangars. They engaged the energy-engines which drew their extraordinary power directly from the atomic forces that were everywhere in Continuum. The SAWs were able to take off vertically, without a runway. Once airborne they accelerated and vanished over the horizon, away from the colorful sunrise.

Queen Cassilius turned and walked to the infirmary, where her son lay in the throes of death.

Mike made some slight turns and got comfortable with the controls of the plane again.

He covered the mouthpiece on his translator and called to Simone, "Don't worry, if things get bad I'm going to bump us, and this plane, back to the desert above Utah."

Simone looked at the bulkhead in front of her. "Like hell you will! You might be able to bump yourself and this plane, but you can't take me along unless we're touching! Can you reach back here?"

Oh yeah. Mike realized that she was right. He imagined the plane vanishing, leaving Simone hurling through the air at four hundred miles per hour, naked. "OK, bad idea. Do you see the ejector seat handle between your knees?"

"Yes."

"Whatever you do, don't touch it unless we absolutely need to. Your job is to watch your radar and help me to see these attacking ships."

"Oh my God! I see them." Simone was transfixed on her view over the front of the Phantom.

The larger sun peeked above the distant mountains and shot its first beam of yellow light into her eyes. Mike lowered his visor. The brilliant sunlight was immediately eclipsed by an X-shaped shadow, then another to the left of the first one.

The blue-gray warships rushed towards them. Their double-X wings were packed with missiles, pointing directly at Mike's Phantom II and the rows of Pacabrian fighters. The razor-sharp silhouettes grew in size as the attacking planes blazed towards the massive Pacabrian fleet.

"They're coming, and fast!" she said with dread in her voice.

"Arm missiles! First contingent, attack and flare off!" Commander Zath ordered from the vanguard of lead warplanes.

The Pacabrian fleet accelerated past the F-4. Their gray, smoke-stained bodies hurled towards the two enemy ships. Mike sped up and fumbled for the controls of his missiles.

The second sun broke over the horizon, making it difficult to see the incoming fighters.

The Kaelite ships accelerated to an incomprehensible speed, directly at the Pacabrians. Mike watched in horror as eight machine guns flashed from the two approaching fighters, sending a wall of high caliber bullets into the first wave of Pacabrian planes.

The first row of Pacabrians fired their missiles and split off in all directions. Defying physics, the Kaelite ships abruptly turned almost ninety degrees straight up. The Pacabrian missiles soared beneath the SAWs, hitting nothing.

"Follow them!" Zath commanded the second row as he sped under the Kaelite ships. "Spread your fire!"

"How the hell can they change direction like that?" Mike was astonished by the impossible turning ability of the SAWs. "The G-forces must be incredible on the crew!" He fingered his missile triggers and watched the Kaelite warplanes turn down towards his row of fighters.

The second tier of Pacabrian fighters reacted to the Kaelites' evasive maneuvers and rose to face the twin SAWs. This time the Pacabrians fired their missiles and machine guns in a wider pattern, anticipating that the

SAWs would try to dodge their warheads.

The Kaelites released six missile into the Pacabrian fleet and separated left and right to avoid the incoming Pacabrian projectiles. The left SAW cleared the attack, but the right SAW was clipped by machine-gun fire. It still functioned, but its aerodynamics had been compromised. Mike pointed the Phantom II at the wounded ship and fired a Python missile as he hurled past the damaged vessel, which missed. The SAWs were able to turn and accelerate so quickly that the heat-seeking missiles couldn't follow them. He banked hard up and right, pressing himself against his harness. Simone was slammed against the side of her cockpit.

"Yaaahh!" she screamed as her inertia bashed her helmet into the fuselage.

The SAWs' guns were targeting the Pacabrian fleet with amazing accuracy. The Kaelite ships were so fast and able to turn such extremely tight radii that the more cumbersome Pacabrian planes had no chance. Mike watched the bulky Pacabrian ships being blown out of the air and spinning towards the forests of DuoSol in flames. Eleven out of first fourteen ships had been lost so far.

Twenty seconds later the third wave of seven Pacabrian fighters arrived and split into two groups. Each honed in on one of the Kaelite war machines. Mike and the three remaining Pacabrian planes from the first two waves began circling around above the mountains to rejoin the fight.

The Kaelite ships abruptly dropped beneath the third tier of attacking Pacabrians and instantly rose up behind them to become the pursuers. Their cannons fired dozens of shells at the fleeing ships, disintegrating all seven before they even hit the ground. Only three Pacabrian ships were still airborne, plus Mike. Three more warships sat on the Pacabrian airfield, held in reserve.

Mike and the remaining ships completed their large arc and approached the battle again.

"Break off!" Zath ordered his three remaining fighters. "Retreat to base!" He knew that he was overpowered and decided to cut his losses.

Mike desperately dropped eight hundred feet in order to avoid the SAWs. His body lifted and strained against his harness. Simone rose from her seat as if she were in a roller coaster.

"Uuuurfff." She frantically raised her mask up and vomited violently onto her chest and the instrument panel in front of her. "You asshole!" she screamed at Mike, spitting chunks of fruit onto the canopy.

"Are your straps fastened?" Mike called back.

"Too late for that, neither of my boobs are still inside my bra!"

Mike blinked and shook his head. "I mean your restraining harness! Synch down the straps so you don't get thrown around!"

One SAW chased the three Pacabrians, and the damaged ship turned on the Phantom II.

"It's on now!" Mike hollered as he jammed the accelerator and felt the thrust of the fantastic engines hurling the F-4 up into the cloudless sky. Simone was slammed back against her copilot's seat, her head whipped backwards into her headrest.

"Ooooof! What the hell are you doing!!" she screeched.

Looking at his instruments, Mike watched as they hit Mach 1. The deadly Kaelite ship locked onto his trajectory, rapidly closing the distance between them. Smoke began streaming out of its damaged hull.

"Man! That thing is fast!" Mike kept accelerating. The SAW fighter caught Mike and cruised next to him for several seconds as the Phantom approached Mach 2.

"That ship is almost silent!" Mike realized. His own engines howled with power as he desperately tried to outrun the alien warship.

A single cannon extended from the shuddering Kaelite ship and pointed directly at Mike and Simone. The damaged SAW trembled violently at this speed, causing its cannon to wave around as it tried to aim at Mike.

"No no no!" Simone screamed as she looked into the cannon's barrel.

Blam! A single shell was fired at the F-4, but the erratic quivering of the Kaelite ship caused the shot to narrowly miss.

Mike rapidly decelerated to six hundred miles per hour and ducked behind the SAW.

Simone was crushed forward into her vomit-covered steering column. "You're so dead when we get out of here," she cursed Mike.

"Fire the machine guns! Squeeze the triggers and don't let go!"

Simone engaged the powerful guns and sprayed the SAW with bullets.

The Kaelites instantly slowed down as well and extended another four cannons from the rear of their ship towards the Phantom.

"Shit! We're going to eject!" Mike ordered. "Pull the handle!"

"My fingernails, your balls," Simone warned deliriously.

Blaaash!! The SAW's cannons fired and obliterated the Phantom's left wing. The mortally wounded F-4 spun out of control and flashed into intense flames. Simone desperately shot all the remaining missiles from their right wing.

"Eject!" Mike screamed, as the canopy blew off.

He pulled his own lever and was propelled out into

the rushing atmosphere. The drogue chutes stabilized their violent spinning and slowed them down until the main chutes deployed and carried the battered couple into the dense woods. The F-4 disintegrated upon impact as it drilled into the rocky forest floor.

Mike's back was broken from the force of being ejected. Before he slipped into unconsciousness he watched the Strongforce Attack Warship, gyrating, riddled with holes, and trailing heavy smoke, fly over the mountains towards Kael.

Mike's pilot seat struck the forest floor, but Simone's chair tore through several trees before striking the ground and turning onto its side.

"Shit! Whenever I'm with you I get beat to hell!" She struggled to unclip her harness with her one good hand and raised herself to her feet. She flung her helmet to the side and staggered over to Mike.

"I told you we were fighting on the wrong side!" she gasped at the lifeless body. "Are you listening?" She scraped a handful of vomit from her flight suit and splattered it at Mike. No response. She knelt down and raised his visor. Mike's eyes were turned up into his head, showing only the whites. "Oh no! Mike! You asshole! Wake up!" She shook his shoulder with one hand.

Mike groaned miserably, then in agony, as he regained his senses and could feel the deep pain of his injuries. "Oh God, I'm really broken up."

"Well, fix yourself, dim-wit," Simone demanded.

Mike cleared his head and concentrated on breaking down his body into its elemental components. As before, he was instantly renewed. "Thank goodness, that's better." He unclipped and rolled out of his pilot's seat. Removing his helmet he looked at Simone.

Her torn flight suit exposed her left arm, which had

a splintered bone sticking out of it. He touched her good hand and repaired her injured body.

Mike examined the barf on his flight suit. "What the hell is this?"

"You bashed me all over the place up there!" she accused.

"I told you to synch down your straps!" Mike yelled incredulously. Then he had an epiphany. *Tina was right. As long as everything's going her way, we're partners, but as soon as she gets pissed off, then I'm just her whipping boy.*

Simone brushed another gob of vomit into her hand and whipped it at Mike. "You drive like a lunatic!"

"It's a fighter plane! We'd be dead if it …" He choked on his words. Six Kaelite sentries emerged from the trees, pointing their weapons at the Earthlings.

The faceted eyes, scaly flesh, and curling horns on the aliens shocked Mike and Simone. As the troops advanced, Mike and Simone could look directly down the barrels of their frightening weapons. They clearly meant business.

The Earthlings raised their hands. Simone took a step towards Mike so that she could touch him, but the Kaelites reacted excitedly and raised their guns to her face. She looked at him desperately.

"Please don't leave me," she pleaded.

Mike spat a fleck of wet puke that had landed on his lip onto the ground.

CHAPTER 10
CAPTURED

The armed sentries closed in around Mike and Simone. Mike's earbud had become dislodged during the violent ejection from the F-4. He inserted it and listened to the melodic clicking of the small soldiers. The dialect was similar to the Pacabrians' language, and his translating headpiece worked.

"These creatures are not of DuoSol. Yet they are fighting for the Pacabrians!"

"How can they see out of those small dots?"

"Their flesh coating appears easy to puncture, or burn under the light of the suns."

"They stink like bile. Kill them and we will bring their bodies back for dissection."

"They seem to have the ability to heal their injuries. Queen Cassilius will be interested in speaking to them."

"Very well, separate these beings and transport them to the palace."

Mike looked towards Simone. "I think we're going to be OK. They're taking us to their queen."

"OK, let's find out what they want. Maybe this is the team we should be on anyway." Simone stepped warily towards the trees, arms raised. "Obviously they beat the crap out the Pacabrians."

The squad of Kaelites guided the couple through the

woods and into a transport vehicle, keeping them separated from each other at all times.

The truck was small and Mike and Simone needed to duck their heads to fit inside. The Kaelites were clearly nervous and kept their guns directed on the Earthlings for the duration of their drive to the city of Kael.

"Have these aliens speak into the translator and then bring them to the throne room," the leading sentry directed his subordinates.

Mike and Simone spoke into a language-decoding machine, similar to the one in Pacabria. They were fitted with headpieces, cleaned up, and brought to the throne room of Queen Cassilius, who was surrounded by her counselors.

"My guards inform me that you are aliens, fighting for the Pacabrians," the queen addressed them.

"Your Majesty, we come from a planet called Earth. We are here on your planet in order to form an alliance. Had we met your race first we would have joined your side in the battle," Mike tried to explain.

The room full of fly-like eyes peered at Mike and Simone.

"You have powers similar to those of our cerebrals. My sentries report that you are able to repair injuries and cure illness? Is this true?" the queen probed Mike.

What's a cerebral? Mike wondered, then replied, "Yes, I am able to heal injuries. I'm not sure about illnesses."

The queen and her counselors considered Mike's response. Mike decided not to reveal his ability to bump through Continuum, nor his ability to make objects vanish.

Cassilius turned towards Simone. "Have you similar abilities?"

Simone was still stunned by the shimmering appearance of the Kaelites. She also admired every detail of the fabulous throne room. The stonework, the tapestries, and the beautiful decorations were everything she had dreamed about for herself. *Now this would be a fine castle for me!* She smiled. "I have different abilities, your Highness. I am capable of identifying other beings who have special powers, and locating where they are in the universe." She considered it prudent to refrain from revealing her ability to get impressions of what other people, or aliens, were thinking.

Among the beings in the universe that she could detect through Continuum was a new person, her recently conceived child.

"You fired upon our warship. We will see if you can be useful to us. If not, we will terminate you for your aggressions against Kael." The queen motioned to her guards and Mike and Simone were directed to follow Cassilius through several halls until they were in a completely different-looking area of the expansive compound. Everywhere they went, Simone was awestruck by the castle and connecting buildings.

"This place is so wonderful!" she whispered.

They were brought into a room where a larger Kaelite lay on a bed, with tubes running into his appendages.

"My son, Prince Syndor, is unable to recover from this illness. He worsens with every cycle of the Great Moon. If you are able to heal him, perhaps we will trust your allegiance to Kael."

Mike approached the bedside. He had no idea what strange malady was killing the prince, perhaps some form of cancer. *All I can do is try.* He touched the scaly wrist of the comatose prince and concentrated on his molecular makeup. It certainly seemed strange, but Mike also felt the familiar forces and energy that everything in the universe inherited from the original moment of Creation. He reduced and aligned the atomic structure of the alien body before him and then released his control of those forces. He stepped back and eased himself closer to Simone. *If this doesn't work I'll make a quick jump towards her and bump us both out of here.*

The malignant cellular abnormality that was ravaging the prince was eliminated; however, Syndor was still weak from his extended period of sickness. His head turned and he made some tired sounds. Queen Cassilius approached his bedside and clasped his four-digit paw. Although she tried to maintain a regal presence, it was obvious that she was deeply moved to see her son regaining consciousness. She turned to her aides. "Show them to the SAWs." Then she sat on the bed as Syndor raised himself to a sitting position. "My son, my dear son, you have returned to my side."

Cassilius turned to one of her aides. "Radio Commander Mora and inform him that I am sending these aliens to the hangar. I want him to evaluate them and see if the male can function as a replacement for the cerebral that was just killed. The female might join the other cerebral that we hold as a hostage."

Mike and Simone were brusquely herded out of the building and into a vehicle which transported them to the enormous hangar.

"Michael, I'm sorry I was so testy. There's something I need to tell you." She cupped her abdomen with both hands.

"Shhhh." Mike tapped his headpiece, indicating that the Kaelites could understand anything that she said.

They ducked through the door into the hangar, walked past the front rooms, and entered the huge space where the two Generation I SAWs were parked. Repairs were already being made to the airship that was hit during the battle.

"I am Fleet Commander Mora. The damage to the hull will be repaired overnight. But the cerebral on that ship has died of her injuries. The ship cannot fly without a cerebral." The commander scrutinized the two Earthlings.

"We are pleased to meet you, Commander Mora." Mike bowed slightly.

Mike and Simone exchanged curious looks. *What's a cerebral?*

The fleet commander led the couple into the undamaged SAW. The fuselage contained the atomic powered engines, as well as well-organized rows of ammunition. The flight deck inside the front of the plane was strangely ovoid in shape. Two seats were set before the windshield, for the pilot and copilot, and two other seats were set in front of arrays of computer monitors and video screens. These were for the gunners, who could shoot cannons, missiles and machine guns in any direction from the warship. There was a solitary seat, placed in the center of the oval, surrounded by a sphere of sensors.

"This is where the cerebral sits. The ship is powered by the infinite Sea of Energy that permeates our entire universe. We can never run out of fuel, we access it continuously as the SAW moves through the atmosphere. The key element to the system is the cerebral."

Mike and Simone leaned forward, examining the small seat in the center of the sensors.

"A mechanical machine cannot be directly connected to Continuum. Only a brain can do that. So we need a Kaelite with the gift of access to transfer the astonishing force that is contained in the nucleus of an atom into the drive of the plane. Unfortunately, the cerebral in the other ship was killed. Now we only have two left. One to power the plane, and one that we keep in seclusion. No one else, to our knowledge, has the gift of access." He watched for Mike's reaction.

Mike smiled at Simone. *I understand, and I know that*

I can do this! She sensed his thoughts and smiled back.

Simone spoke to the commander. "Why isn't the crew killed by the G-forces when the SAW turns at high speeds?"

Mike already understood.

"The cerebral is capable of maintaining the ship's crew in a state of half energy and half physical form. This flight deck becomes a pod of energy when the cerebral focuses her powers. The crew's physical bodies cannot be affected by forces in this condition. The intense acceleration and sharp, evasive maneuvers do not damage the cores of energy that sit in these chairs for the duration of the flight. The crew is still capable of manipulating the controls of the ship, but are in enough of a fluid state so that they are not affected by the physical forces surrounding them." Mora looked at the empty cerebral's chair. "Unfortunately, the cerebral in the other ship was directly pierced by gunfire and died after the SAW returned to the airbase. We are learning that this system can be vulnerable."

Mike nodded knowingly. *They need a new cerebral, and I'm the only other being on this planet who is capable of filling that seat! I'm going to fly in this crazy ship!*

The commander led them out of the SAW and walked to the other damaged warship.

"It was a very unfortunate shot that penetrated the hull and mortally injured the cerebral in this ship. We will increase the shields around her chamber in these two SAWs, and in the six Generation II ships that are being completed," the commander informed the couple as they completed their tour.

Mike and Simone peered around the hangar. "Where are the other ships?" Simone asked.

"They are being constructed in another facility. The second generation SAW is already a superior warship as compared to these two Generation I fighters. They will have Continuum-pulse cannons and a protective energy-shield when completed. They will also be able to operate at higher velocities. One of these ships is almost ready, the other five Gen II warplanes will be completed in a few rotations of DuoSol."

Simone looked at Mike as he smiled vacantly towards the alien ship. She could tell what he was thinking.

I want to fly in these ships. I'll be the fastest human being of all time! Mike recalled the astonishing speed of the SAWs during the air-battle.

Simone smiled and covered the mouthpiece on her headpiece with her hand. "You are going to command one of these fighters. Then we will bring justice down on all of the evil men back on Earth. *Now* we are fighting for the right team."

Mike barely heard her as he walked over to the SAW, placing his hand reverently against the fuselage.

Simone turned and surveyed the giant hangar and the kingdom that she could see through the windows. She quietly spoke to herself. "Then we will return here and I will make myself queen of Kael."

CHAPTER 11
SYNDOR RISES

"What has transpired during my illness?" Syndor asked. Queen Cassilius brought her son up to date. "Our Generation I warships engaged the Pacabrian fleet this morning. We have destroyed eighteen of their fighters."

"Why did we cease our attack? Why did we not attack Pacabria itself?" the prince demanded angrily.

"One of our SAWs was penetrated. The cerebral was mortally wounded and has died. But we were able to return the ship to our airbase and it is being repaired."

"This is a gross vulnerability in the design of these ships. Have any other Kaelites been identified as having the gift of access?"

"No, my son. However, two alien beings have been captured, and they have powers. One of them cured your illness instantly and might be able to replace the cerebral that we have lost. They are examining the SAWs as we speak."

Syndor stood up and dressed in his robes. "They are examining the SAWs? I do not trust these aliens with such information. I will speak to them myself. Why are they here on DuoSol?"

"They say that they want to form an alliance. Their planet is called Earth."

"An alliance to do what? I am thinking that they will assist us in destroying the Pacabrians, then they will lead us to their home planet and we will conquer that as well."

"Perhaps some gratitude is in order," the queen suggested. "After all, the male alien just saved your life."

"That was his mistake." Syndor gestured for his attendants to follow him. He left the infirmary and rode over to the hangars to meet Mike and Simone.

As soon as the royal entourage entered the vast hangar, Mike recognized the prince, whom he had healed an hour earlier.

Commander Mora made the introduction. "This is Prince Syndor, son of Queen Cassilius, and first commander of all military branches in our nation-state."

"What are you called?" Syndor was several inches shorter than Mike or Simone, but his physical prowess and authority were unquestionable, even after his extended illness. The horns on his head curled completely around and then faced forward. He was clearly the dominant male of Kael.

"I am Mike, and this is Simone, your Highness," Mike quickly replied.

"Have you the gift of access to the Sea of Energy?"

"Yes, sir."

"We will test your capabilities in the SAW." Syndor spun and walked directly to the sleek ship that they had just toured.

Mike was jammed into the small cerebral's chair and the surrounding sensors were closed around him.

"Are you able to feel the connection that you are required to make?" the prince demanded.

Mike could readily access Continuum, but becoming the conduit between Continuum and the elaborate warship was a new sensation for him. Suddenly he was concerned. *What if I can't do this? If I fail to maintain my body in a suspended state, I'll be crushed by the G-forces.*

"Yes, Majesty, I can feel the connection. This is a delicate procedure and I'll need to meditate and focus on Continuum this evening, but I can sense I'll be able to align myself with the ship and power its engines, as well as safeguard the crew." Mike tried to sound confident.

"Very well, we will attack Pacabria as soon as both SAWs are operational again. Once we have broken the ability of the Pacabrians to challenge us, we will assist you on your planet, Earth." Syndor's eyes lingered on Simone. She caught her breath as she sensed his power and interest in her.

Syndor then waved at his attendants and marched out of the hangar, his robes and cape billowing behind him.

"I will take you to be settled in your guest chamber." One of the assistants ushered Mike and Simone into another vehicle, which carried them to a stark-looking building.

Once they were alone in their room, Simone headed for the shower while Mike sat on the edge of the small bed and pondered his impending challenge. *What if I lose my concentration? I could be killed. Why the hell am I doing this? I could just bump back to Earth and forget the whole thing.*

When Simone emerged from the shower she assessed the short beds. "Can we go stay with the Pacabrians for the night?" she joked and snuggled next to Mike, with only a towel wrapped around herself.

"Why am I doing this? We could just leave these creatures to fight it out amongst themselves and go back to Earth." Mike glanced at Simone's bare shoulders.

She kissed his cheek. "Do you remember the pictures of the school in Pakistan? The blood on the floor? That guy with his head chopped off? That part of the world is insane!" Simone directed her green eyes directly at Mike. "The children over there should be able to play, laugh, and grow up without the shadow of such terror hanging over their heads."

Her words had the desired effect on Mike. Images of Jennifer flashed through his mind and he blinked back the tears swelling in his eyes. He tried to never think about his daughter, it was just too painful. *She's right! We've got to see this through. I can still help improve the world for other guys' daughters.* Mike thought about the complex spaceship that he was supposed to merge with in two days. *Wait a minute! Jennie … Tina said that she had connected with Jennie in Continuum. Tina's powers are very advanced compared to mine. She can help me understand how to integrate with the SAW.* He relaxed and looked excitedly at Simone. "You're right. We have to do this and get those ships down to Earth where they can help us wipe the brutality out of that part of the world."

Simone smiled and stroked Mike's thigh. "Michael, there's something that we need to talk about." Her other hand rested on her tummy.

Mike stood up. "Not right now. I need to bump back and see Tina. She can help me figure out how to connect the ship with Continuum."

"What!" Simone shook her head in disbelief. "What! What kind of crap is that! You're here with me!"

"This is not about romance. I need her guidance."

"You don't need shit from that pixie! I'll wring her scrawny neck! She's just trying to break us up and destroy our plans to rid the world of evil. You keep the hell away from her!" Simone jumped up; her eyes burned like green lasers. "I'll take you down with the rest of those raping bastards!"

Mike leaned away from the verbal attack. "What the hell are you screaming about? Tina has powers that we don't have. She can help me integrate with the SAW, which will help us destroy the Pacabrians, which will commit the Kaelites to our cause on Earth. This is all part of our intentions."

He could practically feel the wrath emanating from the furious woman. *What a temper!* Mike briefly considered kissing her goodbye, but wisely decided against it. "I'll be back soon."

"You'd better be."

He bumped through the Orion arm of the Milky Way galaxy to Tina's front door.

CHAPTER 12
TINA

"Welcome to Earth. Do you want me to take you to my leader?" Tina smiled slightly as she opened the door. Their previous meeting in his apartment had not been entirely congenial. "I like your hat." She wondered at the translating headpiece.Mike stood in the evening air and tentatively explained, "I need your advice."

Tina stepped back and beckoned Mike to pass inside. "My advice? Dump that manipulative vamp and start following your own will." She gestured Mike into a chair. "Sorry, that's none of my business. I could sense that you were on an exoplanet. How exciting! What in the world are you up to?"

Mike wasn't sure where to begin. He pulled off the headpiece. "We're trying to make a deal with an alien race, on a planet called DuoSol. I'll help them conquer their enemy, and they'll come to Earth and help us bring peace to the Middle East."

"How will you do that? And how will they do that?"

"Their fighters are powered by Continuum. They are extremely fast and deadly. But they need a person, or alien, that has access to Continuum in order to connect the infinite energy to the plane's engines. They call this person a cerebral. One of them was killed during the air battle, so they only have two left. But for some reason they keep that one in seclusion."

"I wonder why," Tina mused, and waited for Mike to continue.

"I need to enter a state of half-energy so their fighter can draw power from the atomic forces in Continuum, through me. At the same time I will envelop myself and the crew in an environment of the same half-energy condition, so we're not torn apart by the G-forces of the plane's acceleration and maneuvers."

"Fascinating." Tina understood. "Continuum is certainly a source of unimaginable power. Is that what you need my advice on?"

"Yes, I'm not sure how to maintain myself in a state of half-here, and half-bumping through Continuum."

"When you bump through Continuum, you concentrate on the space-time coordinates, or location, of your destination, correct?"

"Yes."

"You don't need to maintain anything, just bump yourself to the boundary between this physical world and the surrounding ether."

"Where is the boundary?"

"That's an interesting question. Remember that Continuum is not two or three dimensional. There is no boundary, such as a line or border in the sense that we are accustomed to. Continuum is beyond the dimensions that we are familiar with, it is more of an experience, a state of being. You need to learn how to 'be' a half-object, a ghost, a phantom. Think about the stages that you take yourself through when you meditate. You gradually lose your awareness of your physical body, and become just a mind."

Mike could relate to most of what she was saying. "I

think I understand."

"Your powers will continue to develop, just like mine have. Explore and experiment. You will discover new passages and abilities in the folds of Continuum. Try to bump yourself to that zone in between the two realms."

Tina dimmed the lights and brought them each a glass of water. "Here, relax and try it. I'll just sit here and guide you if I can."

Mike sipped the cool water and closed his eyes. He could feel the evening breeze drift through the window and across the room. His mind relaxed and descended past the daily chatter of his thoughts. He settled on the core level of consciousness, where Continuum was directly connected to his brain. The endless peace and serenity flowed through him and he floated on that energy.

Then he felt it: the passage between his body, sitting in the chair, and the expanse of universal force that pervades everything. He bumped to that experience, and opened his eyes.

Tina was aware of his altered state. "Mike, I can't see you. Can you hear me?"

"Yes, can you hear me?"

"Yes, quite clearly. Can you pick your glass up off the table?"

The glass rose and tipped while Mike took a sip. From his perspective, the room seemed normal. Except that he couldn't see his arms or hands.

"I think you've done it," Tina observed. "You're invisible to me, but you're able to manipulate objects in the physical world. So the pilots can control the ship, but their physical bodies will be unaffected by forces around them. Can you return to your normal state?"

"Wait a minute. I'm invisible! This could be incredible!" Mike reached over to pinch Tina's thigh, but she accurately slapped him away.

"Yeah, well, just remember that I can detect where you are, whether you're invisible or not." Tina smiled.

Mike bumped himself back to his regular experience, sitting in the chair. He held his reddened hand in front of his face. "Now I can see myself!" He turned to Tina and continued. "One of the beings in this state died during battle. A bullet killed her."

Tina pondered this new information. "That's interesting. Somehow you'll be shielded from pure forces, such as the G-force, but you can still have physical contact with the controls of the plane, or a projectile. How sad. Is that the situation you'll be putting yourself into?"

"Yes, they had three cerebrals, one for each SAW and a third that is not used to power the engines. I'll be replacing the dead cerebral in the second warship. They said that they are holding the other cerebral 'in isolation,' I'm not sure why they don't just use her in the second ship."

"Hmmmm, that is curious." Tina wondered about the purpose of holding a cerebral in reserve. "Then the aliens are going to bring these ships to Earth and fight against IPIP?"

"Yes, that's the deal."

"It's so sad that violence breeds more violence. The whole thing sounds shaky to me."

"Well, we're going to give it a try." Mike settled into his chair and looked at Tina in the partial light. Her amber hair and delicate features were so pretty, and yet she showed the wisdom of all of her years of experience. "You say that you've been developing your powers for eight thousand years?" Mike changed the topic.

"Yes. Each body wears out, or is killed, and I pass completely into Continuum and join the other souls. But I've been able to return through the boundary between the realms and become the life force for another body.

I have been a man, a woman, a newborn, a carpenter, a pilot, but always I have maintained the knowledge of my previous lives."

"That's amazing," Mike said quietly. "And you've found Jennie in Continuum?"

"I have."

"Can you bring her back?"

"That remains to be seen. My abilities are also improving and expanding, just like yours." Tina sipped her water and smiled at Mike. "And I am a complete human, Michael, just like you are. I feel everything that a human feels, and desires."

Mike looked at her smile. It was genuine, and also wistful, maybe even sad. He suddenly felt the great peace and generosity that she was capable of. She was special in so many ways. He gazed at her lips. They looked soft and sensual. Before he knew it he was leaning towards her and placing his hand on the curve of her neck. They gently kissed.

Mike had never felt anything so wonderful in his life.

"You look tired, would you like to stay over?" Tina whispered.

"Mmmm, I'd like that."

Tina rose and walked to the hall closet. She tossed a pillow and blanket at Mike.

"Until you're ready for a mature relationship, you're riding the couch." She winked and entered her bedroom suite and quietly closed the door behind her.

"I can bump into your bed any time that I want to," Mike teased.

"I can turn you into a toad," came the voice from behind the door.

This is certainly a new type of relationship. Mike considered the partnership that was forming between himself and Tina, two humans with exceptional abilities.

He spread the blanket out on the couch and tried to get comfortable.

"Crap, what am I doing?" Guilt twisted his guts as his thoughts returned to reality, and of Simone waiting for him. *I should go back now.* He rolled to his side. *But she's kind of crazy, like a dual-personality psycho or something.*

Mike slept fitfully. His mind raced back and forth between the impending flight in the SAW, Simone's bare shoulders, and the lovely woman who was sleeping less than twenty feet away from him. He rose in the pre-dawn and fumbled around in Tina's kitchen, trying to make coffee.

"How about some bacon and eggs?" Tina walked in behind him. She was wearing gym shorts and a tank top.

"Yes, thanks. Can I help?" Mike's eyes were fixed on Tina's nipples, visible through the white, cotton fabric.

She kissed him lightly as she entered the room. "No thanks, I'll have everything ready in about ten minutes."

They enjoyed breakfast together, then Mike redirected his thinking to the task at hand: operating one of the two fastest warplanes in the universe. "I've got to go. I'm long overdue as it is."

"Wait a second." Tina held Mike's head in her hands and touched her forehead to his. "Let's see if I can pull the exact location of DuoSol from your brain into mine."

Mike concentrated on the position of the exoplanet. She focused through Continuum into his mind.

"I'm getting it. I could tell that you were deep in space yesterday, but now I know specifically where you are going." She pulled her head away from his and looked directly at him. "Be safe. This project of yours is not more important than your life. I want to see you again." She pulled his mouth to hers. He resisted at first, then wrapped his arms around her warm, feminine figure.

What am I doing? Simone would freak out if she knew

about this. "I want to see you again as well." He stood there awkwardly for a moment, remembering Simone's furious reaction to his consultation with Tina.

"Well, here goes." And he was gone.

CHAPTER 13
DESTRUCTION OF PACABRIA

It was still night when Mike returned to the guest room in the barracks in Kael. He looked for Simone on the small bed. She was not there.

"Simone," he called as he checked the bathroom. Nothing. He put on his translating headpiece and carefully opened the door to the hall. A guard stood by their door.

"Do you know where my friend is?" Mike asked the sentry.

"She has been taken to confinement, with the other sister."

"Can I see her?"

"She will remain isolated from you until you have completed your mission. I will take you to the hangar in thirty minicycles."

What the hell do you mean, confinement? Mike checked the room; there was nothing there but the furniture.

What the hell is going on? And how long is thirty minicycles? He was nervous and needed to pee. Then he returned to the hallway where the guard led him outside. Two of the three moons were shining brightly. Another reddish dawn was brimming over the mountains. Mike followed his escort into the hangar.

The crew of the first SAW was entering the sleek ship. Mike noticed that one of them was smaller — a youth, practically a child. Mike got nudged from his guard and headed towards the second SAW, which had been repaired. Fleet Commander Mora met him.

"Come with me." He pointed to a door at the side of the great hangar.

Mike entered the small room and immediately saw a large video monitor, showing Simone sitting in a cell with another small Kaelite, wearing her headpiece. They seemed deeply engrossed in animated conversation.

"Your friend will remain in confinement until you complete your obligation," Mora explained flatly.

"Bullshit!" Mike was furious at this betrayal. "We have an agreement based on trust. Bring her back here now or I won't do anything for you!"

Mora spoke calmly into a radio. "Remove one digit."

"Get the hell away from me!" Simone shrieked on the video screen. The small Kaelite next to her clicked frantically as four Kaelite soldiers entered the picture and wrestled Simone to the floor. She kicked and clawed desperately while they locked her left pointer finger into an apparatus that looked like bolt cutters and closed the jaws of the device.

"Yaaaaaaaaaa!" Simone wailed as her finger crunched and was severed. Blood instantly covered her hands as she clutched the terrible wound. She writhed on the concrete floor next to the slender finger with red nail polish.

"You were saying?" Mora was still emotionless.

Mike stared at the screen. His mind whirled as he considered his options. He didn't know where Simone was, so he couldn't bump to her and rescue her. He could vanish Mora if he wanted to. But that would only bring more torture and retribution onto Simone.

"Let's get going," was all he could think of.

Mike joined the other four crew members in the elliptical flight deck. He was crammed into his seat and the sensors were positioned close to him. He had a perfect view of the pilots and gunners … and their controls.

Mora's voice came over the speaker system as he monitored the attack from his command post in Kael. "Mike, engage Continuum and establish the energy medium for the crew."

Mike tried to put all of his other concerns aside and focus on bumping to the border between the physical and ethereal realms. The crew before him vanished, except for their uniforms, but the control knobs and switches were still being operated, seemingly by themselves. The atomic engines stirred behind the walls of the cockpit; the mighty ship trembled with power. Through the canopy, Mike watched his warship leave the confines of the hangar.

Actually, this thing seems less complicated to operate than the Phantom II, Mike noticed as he watched the invisible pilots manipulate the controls.

"Pilots!" It was Prince Syndor on the speaker. "We will carpet-bomb Pacabria until we engage their six remaining fighters. Destroy the air fleet and then concentrate on their military installation. Major Alyx, you are the primary commander."

"Yes, my Lord," the pilot in Mike's ship responded.

The dual SAWs rose straight up into the morning sky. Mike peered through the front canopy and noticed another meteor streak across the firmament. The engines hummed smoothly and the plane shuddered slightly. The mountains and clouds sped past in a blur. Mike knew that they were approaching Mach 2. He was unaware of anything physical. The extreme acceleration went unnoticed.

Brennevin would have loved this!

"Enemy aircraft are airborne. Pacabria is twelve microclicks away. Prime bomb bays," Commander Mora's voice ordered over their speakers.

The pilots' sticks were abruptly shoved forward and the view through the canopy showed that the SAW had suddenly taken a nosedive. Mike caught a glimpse of missiles and four Pacabrian fighters soaring overhead as his plane ducked beneath the active air defense of the Kaelites. Levers moved where the gunners were stationed.

"Carpet bombs away," the invisible gunners reported.

Mike saw the nation-state of Pacabria hurtling beneath them as the bombs were spread out across the dwellings. They were indiscriminately destroying the entire city. It took less than eight seconds to engulf Pacabria in flames.

"Reverse and pursue," Syndor ordered from his remote station in Kael.

Mike's eyes opened wide as the view through the canopy spun 180 degrees so the SAWs could chase down the four Pacabrian fighters that they had just evaded. The engines whined at a high pitch as the Kael warships mercilessly closed in on the scattering Pacabrians. The SAWs lined up behind the enemy fighters as they fled towards the high crest of the Shillus mountains.

The four Pacabrian warships vanished over the mountain ridge, just skimming the treetops. Mike's ship and the other Kaelite fighter followed close behind. Suddenly, the remaining two Pacabrian fighters appeared over the ridge, flying directly in the face of the SAWs, and firing a spray of machine-gun fire and missiles.

"Ambush! Split!" Major Alyx screamed into his comm.

The SAW's machine guns returned a blaze of fire as Mike watched the mountainside spin to the left. His fighter desperately banked to the right to avoid the incoming missiles.

"We're hit!" the other Kaelite fighter screamed from the speakers.

"Is the cerebral intact?" Syndor's voice demanded.

"Yes, sir, but both pilots seem to have been killed."

"Engage the emergency landing rockets. Stay with the ship and defend it!" Syndor commanded from his remote base in Kael.

Mike's ship immediately reversed its course and fired its cannons at the two Pacabrian fighters, bringing them down. The SAW abruptly turned and sped back over the ridge of the Shillus mountains, hunting the final four enemy warplanes. Major Alyx expertly closed in on each fighter and the gunners blasted them with a barrage of cannon fire. The last of the Pacabrian air fleet were demolished while they were still in the air. The remains spun to the ground in mangled, flaming wreckage.

"Hit the main military outpost and then get your ship back to base!" Syndor ordered Mike's crew.

The SAW wheeled around and powered its tremendous engines. Within seconds Mike saw the thick smoke and flames billowing from Pacabria.

That looks like the fires of hell itself. Mike watched, horrified at the total annihilation of the nation-state. *They were kind to us down there*, he lamented to himself.

"We have successfully landed in the woods," the other SAW reported.

Mike's SAW descended and bore down on the Pacabrian military base.

"Bombs off!" the gunners called out. Mike watched their controls being moved, seemingly by themselves.

The SAW looped around and made one final pass over Pacabria.

"Target hit and destroyed," Major Alyx informed Syndor.

Back in the control room in his palace, the prince raised his hands in celebration as he watched the video coming back from the fighters, showing Pacabria in flames. "How do you like us now, Tyrandus! You would never acquiesce to our terms and conditions, so now you are obliterated. You are the vanquished, and we are the victors!"

Mike watched the complete destruction of Pacabria pass under them as they returned to Kael. He also noticed the location of the downed SAW, in the woods. *I wonder who's still alive over there.*

Within nine minutes his ship had returned to the Kaelite airbase and landed.

Fleet Commander Mora met the crew as they exited the SAW. He directed Mike to the side while the pilots and gunners left the hangar.

"You performed well. We will prepare you to be trained in one of the Generation II planes in the following days. They are located in the large gray building with the red roof, on the other side of the airfield."

"There's no one left to fight, sir. Pacabria has been completely razed. It's gone." Mike was astonished by the effectiveness of the SAWs. They were not invincible, but they were extremely deadly.

"The Pacabrians have smaller military outposts in the surrounding forests. They are still potentially dangerous. But we have broken their ability to pose any major threat," Mora exulted. "We will search the remains of Pacabria after the flames have died out and enslave whoever is still alive."

"Speaking of enslaved. When are you going to release my friend?" Mike wanted to get to Simone and heal her severed finger ASAP.

"She will be incarcerated for the duration of your service to Prince Syndor." Mora turned his back to Mike and began walking away. "I must get ground troops to our downed SAW immediately, before the Pacabrians capture it."

Two armed guards flanked Mike and pushed him towards the door. *What the hell are my options?*

The missiles, bombs, and ammunition were already being replaced on the returned SAW as Mike walked past.

If we're going to use these ships on Earth, then I've got to get that other SAW back here!

"Commander Mora!"

Mora turned impatiently as he reached the exit.

"I'm going to bring back the downed SAW." Mike didn't wait for a response. He vanished and appeared in the woods about fifty feet from the warship.

The emergency rockets had done their job and lowered the SAW to the ground without any further damage. The front canopy was fractured by the bullets that had killed the pilots. The rear hatchway was open. A large Pacabrian soldier squeezed out of the exit, dragging the two dead pilots.

"There are five seats in there! Find the missing three crewmembers!" he called into the woods.

Mike crouched down as he realized that there were Pacabrian troops searching the forest all around him. Soon the two Kaelite gunners were discovered and pushed at gunpoint into the clearing around the SAW. The Pacabrian leader calmly walked up to the captives, raised two pistols at their faces, and blew their heads apart.

"Find the fifth one!" he bellowed.

Mike ducked lower and took several steps back until he stepped on something soft, that squeaked. The young Kaelite cerebral was hiding in the thick foliage. Mike quickly knelt down and held the small creature.

"It's OK, it's OK," he whispered. But the terrified youth struggled against Mike's grasp.

"I'm another cerebral," Mike said. "I'll get us out of here. We're going to take that ship with us. Give me your hand — uh, paw."

As soon as they touched, Mike bumped them into the empty ship. He set the young cerebral in her seat and went to close the rear hatch. The young Kaelite began melodically clicking at him in excited tones. Mike listened to the translation.

"Please help us! You can help us! My sister is held captive and is tortured if I do not obey Mora's commands to power the plane."

Mike remembered the small Kaelite in the cell with Simone. "Do you know where they are being held?"

"Yes, the mining compound in the high forest."

Mike thought quickly. He held the child's paw and bumped them both into his guest quarters in Kael. The room appeared just as he had left it.

"You must be silent and stay hidden. I'm not sure what will happen, but I'll come back here and we'll go get your sister."

The small creature slid under the bed and lay still. Mike checked his headpiece and bumped back into the downed SAW in the woods. He could hear the Pacabrian soldiers calling to each other as they searched the forest for the fifth Kael crewmember. He looked at the sensors around the cerebral's chair, and the pilot's controls six feet away.

Just for the hell of it, I'm going to see if I can do this. He focused his mind and bumped to the border between the realms. In this state he reached back and closed the rear hatch. The Pacabrians immediately reacted and fired their guns at the locked door. Mike turned the sensors surrounding the cerebral's chair so that they faced the front and then he sat in the pilot's seat. He engaged the engines and they hummed to life.

A scaly face with one eye band appeared in the shattered canopy. Mike vanished him and grabbed the controls with his invisible hands. He directed the thrust of the powerful engines straight down and lifted the airship above the trees. Then he carefully transferred the force of the engines to the rear and propelled the SAW forward, clearing the woods and rising above the gunfire from the Pacabrian squad.

Mike familiarized himself with the basics of the unusual plane. *This thing is awesome! When it's repaired I'm going to really floor it!* He found his way back to the Kaelite airbase and landed the fighter in front of the hangar. Then he transformed back to his physical self. The engines immediately shut off.

Fleet Commander Mora met Mike as he crawled through the exit hatch. "Where are the gunners, and the cerebral?" Mora demanded.

"They were captured and shot by a Pacabrian squad of soldiers. The bodies of the pilots were dragged from the ship and piled with the rest," Mike responded, unsure of what to do next.

"We have not finished eliminating this worthless species from DuoSol!" Mora fumed. "You will begin training in the Gen II SAW after the next darkness. We must repair this first generation ship again and re-arm it. This ability of our enemies to shoot through our fighters and kill the crew cannot be accepted. In addition to the energy-cannons, the new Gen II warplanes have an energy-shield that surrounds the ship. Nothing will be able to penetrate that shield." He motioned to the guards to lead Mike to his quarters. "One of our Gen II warplanes is battle-ready now. The others will be fully commissioned very shortly."

Two escorts guided Mike from the hangar. He cooperated and followed along.

Once in his room again, Mike carefully peeked under the bed and helped the frightened cerebral back to her feet.

"Can we go and get Quint now?" she asked.

"We have to wait," Mike tried to explain. "The SAW is going to be repaired and I am going to be trained how to fly the Generation II ship. Then we will steal the two SAWs and the Gen II ship that is completed, fully armed, and take them to my home planet, Earth. We'll have to leave the other five Gen II fighters here." Mike tried to comfort the young Kaelite. "My name is Mike, who are you?"

"I'm Kresta. I had two sisters and one brother. We all have the gift of access to the Sea of Energy. When Prince Syndor realized how he could use us to propel his new ships, we were captured, except Drake, our brother. He ran into the woods and is probably dead by now."

"You're all in the same family?" Mike queried.

"My sister Liza and I powered the ships. Our oldest sister, Quint, is held captive and tortured if we don't do what Commander Mora tells us. But Liza was just killed yesterday. Only Quint and I are left, and they hurt her every day, so I am forced to be a biological component of their engine."

Mike felt a sting of guilt as he realized that he might have shot Liza himself.

"We must go get them," Kresta implored.

Mike agonized over Simone and Quint in the cell. *How could we possibly wait for two or three more days while the SAW is repaired? I can't just leave them there to be tortured every day.*

The doorknob to the room twisted. Kresta quickly

crouched behind the bed while a guard brought Mike his dinner and left. The two of them shared the meal in silence.

Thirteen miles away Simone lay suffering on the cold floor of her cell, squeezing the stump of her finger as hard as she could to quell the flow of blood.

CHAPTER 14
QUIET INVASION

"**A** brother?" Prince Syndor listened to the speaker that was connected to a hidden microphone in Mike's room. Fleet Commander Mora stood next to him as they spied on Mike. "I believe that we can work this traitorous plot to our advantage. Wake the service crew up and have the damaged SAW repaired tonight. Fill the storage chambers of both SAWs with as much ammunition and spare missiles as possible. Then empty the storage chambers in the new Gen II fighter. Bring Major Alyx, sixteen assault troops in full battle gear, one doctor, one engineer, and two women from my harem to the red hangar."

"Yes, my Lord." Mora reached for his radio.

"Make that three women."

"Yes, my Lord."

Syndor's face brightened. "And find the brother."

"Yes, my Lord." Mora nodded again. "We will begin searching the woods immediately."

"Try the prison first. Meet us in the hangar."

"Yes, Prince Syndor."

"And Mora … you're coming too." Syndor left the Fleet Commander's office to explain his intentions to the queen and pack the equipment that he would be needing.

Mora relayed all of Syndor's orders and gathered his own battle gear.

Back in Mike's quarters, he tried to be patient and sleep. But all he could think of was Simone's finger falling to the floor. He stared at the ceiling for several hours, then rolled to his side and noticed Kresta, sitting in a chair, staring directly at him.

"To hell with the damaged SAW!" Mike stood up. "We'll take the good one and the second generation fighter tonight. We can't wait while Simone and Quint are suffering."

Kresta was clearly pleased, and relieved. She hopped up and held Mike's hand.

"Where is the mining compound in the high forest where they are being held?" he asked.

"Beyond the Rastyth fields, above the old Fastillion curllets." She tugged on Mike's hand, anxious to leave.

"Hmmmmm, OK. I'll get us out of here and you point me from there." Mike bumped them to the foot-hills surrounding Kael. In the light of two moons he could clearly see the barracks that they had just left, and the hangar with the SAWs. The other hangar with the red roof, where the Generation II fighters were located, was visible across the airstrip. "Now where?"

Kresta oriented herself and pointed to a group of buildings where the trees had been scraped away, leaving a scar in the high forest. Mike bumped them above the compound and the pair looked at the sturdy, concrete structures below them.

"There." Kresta indicated a well-lit building with guards chatting at the door.

"Stay close to me. This might happen fast." Mike held

her paw and bumped them into the building. The ceiling was low and Mike had to hunch over to avoid scraping his head against the rough surface. They looked up and down the empty, stark hallway. Creeping along the walls they peered around a corner and spotted a guard sitting in a chair by a door. Mike vanished the guard; his clothing and weapon clattered to the floor. Kresta ran ahead of Mike and eagerly clicked her vocalizations at the thick entry to the cell. Mike held her paw again and bumped them into the small, darkened room.

"Simone," Mike whispered. Kresta quietly called her sister's name.

"Mike! You found us." They groped in the dark until all four beings were touching each other. Mike quickly bumped the group back into the foothills above Kael.

While this was going on, Prince Syndor met with Queen Cassilius in her personal counsel chamber.

"The hour is late, my son. Why do you disturb my rest?"

"Forgive me, Mother. A situation has arisen very quickly, and I feel that we must take advantage of this opportunity."

"What is passing?"

"The aliens are planning to steal three of our war-planes and take them back to Earth with them. I request your permission to stowaway on one of those ships, with a small squad of attack troops, and travel to their home planet, Earth."

"To what end, my son?"

"I wish to conquer their planet, so that the Kaelites can colonize it and establish ourselves as the dominant race in the universe."

"That seems overly optimistic, considering that you will only have a small squad of soldiers," the queen said, strategizing with her son.

"Yes. However, this planet seems to have many beings with access to the Sea of Energy. First I will capture Mike and Simone, then we will take control of a part of their planet and acquire more cerebrals. We will force them to return to DuoSol where they will transport the remainder of our Gen II fleet, and more troops, back to Earth."

Syndor respectfully touched the queen's paw. "It is imperative that you complete the five Gen II fighters that are under construction. They are only days away from being ready for battle. Then we will have eight warships and a small army on this alien planet. With our superior technology we will be able to dominate these complacent Earthlings."

Queen Cassilius considered her son's plans. "You are very ambitious, Syndor. And what of the population of civilians on this planet? There must be thousands of beings living there."

"I intend to move across Earth like a juggernaut, eliminating or enslaving most of the natives and taking control of their resources. The Kaelite nation will then rule two planets!"

Queen Cassilius moved to her window and breathed the fresh air that was blowing in from the surrounding woods. The same woods where Mike, Simone, and the two small Kaelites were hiding at that very moment. A few small meteors streaked across the star-filled sky. "Our people have eliminated the brutish Pacabrians from DuoSol. Perhaps you are correct. It is time to take our proper place as the superior race in the universe."

"I must be on my way, Mother. The aliens might begin their escape at any time." Syndor knelt on one knee and kissed the queen's golden ring, the ring bearing Cassilius's family crest, signifying that she was the supreme ruler of Kael, and now DuoSol.

She grasped her son's hand and kissed one of his many rings, which also bore the royal family's crest. "Fare well, my Prince. I look to your return."

Syndor bowed and hurried out of the chamber, over to the red-roofed hangar that housed the operational Gen II fighter, with its empty storage compartments.

Syndor and Mora met the sixteen Kaelite soldiers and Alyx in the massive building. The doctor, engineer, and three women stood to the side. The prince addressed his group of warriors and settlers.

"It is imperative that all of us touch each other's flesh. I am confident that this is how the Earthling transfers other beings. Fleet Commander Mora and I will be located at the air vents beneath the gunners' chairs. The entire mission depends on our ability to reach through the vent and touch one of the conspirators." He looked up at the fantastic Generation II warship. The first two SAWs were painted gun-blue, but this ship was coated in daring red. Its dual wings were loaded with missiles, and bombs. The energy cannons were retractable and were not visible at this time. "The Earth beings have no idea of the hell that is about to invade them tonight."

Mora listened to his radio, then relayed a message to Syndor. "My Lord, the sentries have verified that Mike's chamber is now empty, and a guard has been killed at the containment building. The dark-topped Earthling and the cerebral's sister have escaped."

"Has the SAW been repaired?"

Mora spoke into his radio. "Yes, my Prince."

"It is time to seclude ourselves in the storage compartments," Syndor commanded his troops.

Simone collapsed into the grass in the woods above

Kael. The throbbing pain that she had endured had exhausted her. Mike quickly held her and reorganized her body's elemental components so that her severed finger was healed. She breathed deeply and looked up at the dual moons illuminating the valley.

"That was horrible." She gasped as she wiggled her new finger in front of her face. "I've changed my mind, the Kaelites suck balls. And I need my nail polish."

Quint and Kresta were delighted to be reunited and clicked their musical language excitedly as they touched and hugged each other. Simone still had her headpiece, so the four of them could communicate.

Mike looked at the red-roofed hangar. "Here's what I am thinking. I'll bump us down into the flight deck of the new Gen II fighter. That is the most powerful warship that they have. All of us will bump together with the ship to Earth. I'll leave you there and come back for another plane, the undamaged SAW. I'll bump that to Earth. Then we'll have two ships, and we can figure out how we're going to use them to fight the extremists in the Middle East."

"What is 'bump'?" Quint asked.

"That's what we did to get out of your cell. We'll disappear from one place and appear in another. But we need to be touching each other. "Now," Mike continued, "we need a remote place to set these machines. It can be anywhere on Earth. But I don't want to start a panic by having an alien spaceship appear in a Kansas parking lot or something."

"Panama." Simone looked at him. "In the jungle. I know where to go, we backpacked and camped there when I was a child. It is very secluded, with open places to set the planes among the thick woods."

"That sounds great. Your job is to guide us there."

Down in the red hangar, the last few soldiers were fitting themselves into the storage compartments under the floor in the Gen II fighter. A guard entered the hangar and ran across the huge space towards the Gen II, pulling on the arm of a younger Kaelite.

"Prince Syndor!"

Syndor wheeled angrily at the noisy intrusion.

"I have found him, my Lord."

Mora joined Syndor at the rear hatch of the plane and looked at the shabby Kaelite youth.

"We're on a mission to rescue your sisters from alien invaders. Will you help us?" the prince addressed the teen.

Drake was visibly stunned and frightened, but nodded and was quickly guided into the crowded compartment. The covers were slid over the storage chambers, and the troops waited silently.

Mike looked down from their hiding place in the woods at the red hangar and tried to focus. "Here we go." The four beings held hands.

Suddenly, they were in the darkened elliptical flight deck of the Gen II fighter.

"Wow! This is amazing!" Mike noticed the lower ceiling, a result of the plane's shallower exterior profile. The controls were basically the same as those of the SAWs. *I'll figure out where the energy-shield and cannons are when we get this thing back to Earth.* He motioned Simone and the sisters into chairs. The girls scowled at the cerebral's seat in the middle and sat together at one of the gunners' stations. Quint and her younger sister Kresta squirmed with nervousness and hugged each other close. In their excitement they did not notice Mora's scaly hand reach out from the dark vent and carefully touch Kresta's leg.

They all held hands while Mike concentrated on the massive machine and its contents. Simone focused on the location of the grassy area where she had camped as a child. Together they bumped the entire ship out of the hangar on DuoSol and set it in the jungles of Panama, 183 light-years away. Sunlight streamed in the canopy as the group let go of each other's hands and peered out at the lush landscape. Three sloths lumbered into the dense woods.

Mike climbed out of the rear hatch and examined the clearing. "This isn't big enough for another ship. I'll set the second one down there on those flat rocks."

"OK." Simone and the sisters explored their new situation, and Mike bumped back to the other hangar in Kael. He quickly ducked behind some machinery and checked to see which was the damaged SAW. *They're both fixed! I'll come back and get the second one too!* He popped into the closest fighter and effortlessly transferred it across space to the level stretch of flat rocks, two hundred yards below the first plane. He exited and looked up towards the Gen II and his group. They were hidden behind the trees. There was no room for the third plane on the flat rocks.

I've got to be quick! He spotted an open area in the forest about one mile away. *It will have to do.* He bumped to the second SAW, back in Kael, and brought it back to Earth, setting it on the next ridge over from the first two planes.

That was almost too easy! He smiled with satisfaction as he looked out of the canopy at the rich flora of remote Panama. *Hello, Earth, it's great to be home again!*

Mike climbed out of the fighter and breathed the fragrant, humid air. The sound of birds singing and monkeys chattering drifted from the lush foliage of the rainforest. The first two planes weren't visible from this distance. Mike peered across the tree-covered hills and tried to locate their position. He saw the first grassy area and bumped over to it.

The Generation II warship, Simone, and the sisters, were gone.

CHAPTER 15
REUNITED

Mike looked around the grassy park, completely bewildered. *It has to be here!* He carefully examined the soil and found the depressions that the wheels of the Gen II had made. *How could they move it? Simone doesn't have the ability to bump anything. They have two cerebrals, but no pilot. And* why *would they move it?* Mike looked around again in disbelief and sat down on a boulder. He leaned back and put his hand on something soft, wet, and warm.

"Jeeez!" He jumped up. It was Simone's finger. Mike clutched his hair. "Syndor! But how?"

A flock of birds chattered and flew from the trees two hundred yards below him. Mike peered at the disturbance. The sleek, gun-blue SAW rose above the forest, its atomic engines breaking the peaceful noises of the rainforest. It sped over the treetops, vanishing behind a ridge in the mountains.

"Oh no!" He looked back where he had just parked the second SAW, one mile away. Mike quickly bumped into the warship and locked the hatch. Every available space in it was packed with ammunition and replacement missiles. Peering out of the canopy he spotted Mora and several armed soldiers rushing along the ridge, in his direction.

Where the hell can I hide this thing? He thought of the vast spaces in Colorado and Utah where he frequently hiked. *Not good enough, people are always camping and hunting in the back country.*

The flaming red Gen II soared into view from beyond the mountains and hovered over Mike's SAW as the troops began entering the clearing. Mike took a shallow breath and bumped the pressurized fighter to the Bay of Rainbows on the northern hemisphere of the moon. China's Yutoo rover was one and a half kilometers away, gathering lunar rock samples.

Syndor appeared on the monitor in front of Mike. "You got that one, Mike, but I've got the Gen II, and the other SAW. Thank you for bringing us to Earth. It looks like a fine place to establish Kael's first interstellar colony. If everyone is as easy to kill as your friend, we should conquer this planet in just a few cycles."

"I'll have your head on a pole!" Mike screamed at the image on his monitor. Then he recoiled, shocked at his own vicious emotions. He unplugged the screen and quickly bumped himself back to the Panamanian rain-forest, at a safe distance from the troops.

The Gen II landed and picked up Mora and the Kaelite soldiers. Then it soared beyond the mountains, where the SAW had disappeared just minutes ago.

Mike flopped down onto the forest floor. "What the hell do I do now?" He looked at the blood on his hand from Simone's finger.

Twelve minutes earlier, Syndor lay under the floor of the Gen II listening to Mike. "This isn't big enough for another ship. I'll set the second one down there on those flat rocks." Commander Mora and the sixteen troops rapidly slid the floor panels open and rushed Simone and the cerebral sisters, standing on the grass.

"Run!" Simone screamed at the three young Kaelites while she faced the attacking troops. She launched a solid kick to the groin of one of her attackers. As soon as the tip of her boot crushed into the Kaelite's crotch, he cried in pain and collapsed. "What do you know?" She smiled with satisfaction. "These things have dicks." Immediately a baton was pulled across her throat from behind and she choked as her windpipe was compressed to the breaking point.

"Oh no! Noooo! Not again!" Two soldiers held her down with their knees while a third clamped the cutters around her left pointer finger.

"You slimy bastards! Get off of me!"

The cutters were pinched shut and Simone's new finger dropped onto the grass.

"Yaaaaaa! Damn it, Michael. Where the hell are you!?"

She was thrown through the rear hatch where she collapsed onto the floor, holding her bloody hand. Outside, her mangled finger was placed on a large rock.

Prince Syndor, Commander Mora, and Major Alyx split up. A knife was pressed against Drake's throat in order to force Quint and Kresta to power the engines of the SAW and Gen II, which were quickly moved into the next valley.

All that remained was for Syndor to guess where the second SAW would appear and to get a pilot and soldiers over there. They guessed correctly.

The troops on the ground ran frantically towards the third plane when it appeared while the Gen II returned to provide a cerebral for the engine. But Mike got there first.

"Damn!" Syndor bellowed when the SAW vanished.

He landed and picked up his soldiers and Mora. "Connect me to that SAW! I want to talk to that Earthling!"

The Gen II flew back over the mountains to the SAW they had captured. Kresta was transferred back into the Generation I fighter, leaving Quint in the Gen II. The two planes flew over the vast rainforest, searching for a suitable location for their headquarters on Earth, leaving Mike sitting alone among the trees after he had returned from the moon.

Mike wiped the blood from his hand on the grass and stood up. "Damn! I need Simone's powers in order to locate her in Continuum." He looked around and found the highest peak that he could see. He bumped to the summit and scanned the endless treetops that extended in every direction. This was one of the few places on Earth where a person could stand and see the Pacific Ocean to the south, then turn and see the Atlantic Ocean to the north. "This is so beautiful! But somewhere down there is an invasion of aliens, with two warships. One of those ships is capable of unimaginable destruction." He looked helplessly at the thick rainforest. "And I brought this terror to Earth." He agonized over his blunder. "How can I find them? How can I fix this?"

Eighty-six miles away, the blood red Gen II hovered over a coffee farm. The SAW circled the perimeter.

"Prepare the energy-cannons," Syndor ordered the gunners in the Gen II.

"Yes, sir. We have three options: the Bio-beam, which will annihilate all creatures within its radius, or the Harmonic-beam, which will destroy any structures, but leave the life forms. The third choice is a combination of the two."

"The Bio-beam," Syndor directed.

The retractable cannons extended from the hull of

the Gen II. On the farm below them, the workers and their families fled into the buildings as the terrifying ships threatened the compound.

Syndor tightened a chain around Drake's neck. Quint maintained her focus as the gunners fired the Bio cannons across the farm. The warship recoiled and shook slightly from the powerful impulses that were blasted from its guns.

Prince Syndor looked through the canopy. The terrified families that had been running for shelter were gone. The screaming had stopped. There were no bodies. The people, dogs, livestock, and birds had been reduced to energy and absorbed by Continuum.

"Land the ships. Troops, ready your weapons. Search the buildings for survivors, and kill any that you find." The prince admired his new headquarters. It had everything that they needed. It was remote, there were crops growing in the fields, and several buildings to suit his various needs.

The warships were huge, compared to the one-story structures. The soldiers disembarked and systematically searched the buildings. Syndor selected the main house for himself and delegated other buildings for the doctor, harem, soldiers, and pilots. He chose a metal granary as a prison for the two cerebrals and Simone. Drake was kept in a separate location, as a security measure against any escape attempt or disobedience.

Commander Mora joined the prince on the veranda of the house and together they surveyed the hacienda. "From here we will learn the weaknesses of the Earth civilization. We will exploit them and gradually take over and colonize this planet for ourselves!" Syndor exulted. "Bring a woman," he ordered his assistant as he retired to his quarters. "No, bring two."

Simone sat on the floor of the granary and tried to

nurse her wound. Kresta and Quint considered their new situation.

"This is worse than it was on Kael!" Quint exclaimed. "We have found Drake, but he is going to be used to force us to drive the engines." They slumped to the hard floor.

"It is worse," Simone agreed. "Everything is worse. Every time I try to accomplish anything with Mike I get beat up, or mutilated!" She lay back in frustration and held her throbbing hand. "I need his ability to bump us out of here! And he has no ability to locate me, the worthless shit." She rolled her head and looked at the sisters.

"So, what powers do you two have?" she pried.

Mike watched the afternoon sun reflect on the Pacific Ocean. *What have I got? A fighter sitting on the moon. But I can't fly it, connect to Continuum, and fire its weapons at the same time. The Gen II and the other SAW are so fast that they could be anywhere — in another country, or continent. I could never find them by just randomly bumping around looking for them. Or ... I could just sit and wait and see what they do, who they attack, and find them that way.*

Mike distressed about Simone and the two Kaelite girls. *Poor Simone! She gets injured everywhere we go!* He thought about her thick, black hair and her enchanting green eyes; they had shared some exciting and intimate adventures together. *She can certainly be temperamental at times, but damn! She's a lot of fun. And compared to Tina ...*

"Tina!" Mike stood up. *She has the ability to locate other people who are strong with Continuum.* Mike made a mental note of his present location in Panama and bumped to Tina's front door.

She answered his knock with a mysterious smile on her face. "Michael, come on in. We're about to have dinner."

Mike quickly entered the room and noticed a teen-aged girl sitting at the dining table. He had never seen her before, but somehow felt like he recognized her.

"Daddy!" The young lady leapt from her seat and rushed across the room to embrace him. Mike wrapped his arms around the unfamiliar child. It had been over four years since he had heard those words spoken to him. The girl looked up at Mike's face. She was in a different body, but her eyes were the windows to her spirit and soul. It was truly Jennifer.

"Jennie!" He squeezed her tightly. "Oh my God! Can this really be true?"

He collapsed to his knees and tightened his embrace, tears soaked his face.

"But how? You're older?" He stammered and tried to stop crying.

Jennifer looked at Tina. "She knows."

They sat down at the table. Mike couldn't let go of Jennie's hand while he looked at Tina for an explanation.

Tina was clearly pleased that she had been able to bring Jennifer back to the realm of life. "Jennifer left her physical body four and a half years ago. She was four years old. As you know by now, her sprit, her soul, the energy that is her being, went into Continuum. She became part of the endless Sea of Peace. She was everywhere, and nowhere. She was herself, and she was everyone."

Tina sipped her water and continued. "I have crossed into Continuum and returned many times. Only once did I return in the same body, the rest of the time I always found a new body to enter. After I encountered Jennifer I began trying to understand how to bring her back to the physical side of life. Sadly, a cruise ship sank in the Mediterranean Sea this morning and several people were lost to the depths. The moment the spirit of this girl left her body, I brought Jennifer back from the ethereal realm and gave her this new form."

Tina smiled at Jennie and looked at Mike. "She entered Continuum as a four-year-old, but has gained years of wisdom by association with the souls on the other side. Now she returns in the body of a fourteen-year-old."

Mike looked at the pretty girl. She had light brown hair, the same as him, but brown eyes. Jennifer had had blue eyes in her previous body. She was in the awkward in-between stage, between a girl and a young woman. Slim and lanky, yet showing signs of developing into a woman. Mike pulled her close and hugged her shoulders. "It's a miracle," he said quietly. Then he became more serious and sad. "Jennie, it was me — I killed you. I was driving carelessly, I was so reckless and foolish." He lowered his eyes in shame.

"I know, Daddy. I don't remember it, and I understand that it was a mistake. Everyone makes mistakes." She smiled a smile filled with daddy-daughter love. "I forgive you."

Mike felt as if a massive weight had been lifted off his chest. Since the accident he had felt no real reason for living, but now his precious daughter had returned. He was going to be a father again.

"Thank you, Tina. How can I ever begin to thank you? I've got a life, and a reason to live again."

"Seeing you two together is thanks enough."

Mike suddenly looked up and remembered the reason that he had bumped here in the first place. "The planes! Simone! There's an invasion. I need your help." He turned anxiously to Tina.

"Whatever it is, we will help you to the best of our abilities." She tried to soothe Mike.

He looked at Jennie. "Do you have access to Continuum too? Any special powers? You're my daughter, you might have inherited some of my abilities."

Jennie looked confused.

Tina explained, "Michael, Jennie doesn't have any experience to compare to. She had those four years as an infant and child, and today she's been alive for less than five hours. Jennie has a very strong connection to Continuum, just like you. But we need to discover what she's capable of. She doesn't understand what is normal and what is special."

"OK." Mike sat back and looked at Tina again. He cleared his throat. "I've got a bit of a situation."

"It sounds like it," Tina acknowledged Mike's concern. "The last time you were here you were going to bring some fighter-ships and aliens back from space to help bring peace to the Middle East. Has something gone wrong?" Tina became quiet and concentrated on Continuum. "I can sense your friend, Simone. She is in Central America. There are three other beings with access to Continuum near her. Are they all right? What are they doing?"

"We thought the Kaelites were going to be our allies, but we were double-crossed. So I stole three of their warships and brought them back to Earth with us. But somehow they stowed aboard and have taken control of two of the fighters. I don't know where they are." He looked cautiously at Jennie. "They cut one of Simone's fingers off. They are cruel beyond belief and intend to take control of Earth and colonize it."

Tina looked disgusted. "Did you ever think about just staying in bed and not messing with anything?"

"Ahhhgg, I know!" Mike rubbed his forehead. "I want to help make the world a better place, but I keep screwing up."

"I told you before, you need to begin thinking for yourself. Feel in your heart what is right." Tina smiled slyly and poked Mike's chest with her finger. "By the way, your heart is located up here, not down there."

Mike nodded. He straightened up and looked at Tina. "I've got to fix this. But I need your ability to locate them. If we can free Simone and the young Kaelites, and steal those two ships back, we'll have more than enough cerebrals to power our three planes. But we need more pilots."

He stroked Jennie's soft hair, his angel that came back to Earth.

An ear-to-ear grin spread across his face.

"Can you bring Major Cody Brennevin back from Continuum?"

"Who the hell is that? And how can he help this situation?" Tina looked doubtful.

"He's a balls-to-the-wall fighter pilot, an Ace during the Vietnam war. He's very patriotic and would love the opportunity to mix it up with the Kaelites." Mike remembered Cody's burial on the hills of DuoSol. "And he's a good friend."

"I'm not so impressed with your other friend, she seems like nothing but trouble."

"Cody is a hundred percent dedicated to protecting freedom and fighting tyranny. And we need a pilot."

"I'm a pilot," Tina pointed out. "I flew the San Francisco to Honolulu route for eight years. Compared to you I'm a professional and you're a rookie."

"I agree. But compared to either of us, Cody is the real deal. He's a seasoned combat veteran."

Tina gathered the dishes from the table. "I'll see what I can do while you two get reacquainted." She set the plates on the kitchen counter and retired to her suite in the back.

Mike and Jennie spent the rest of the evening catching up with each other. At ten o'clock Tina emerged from her bedroom. "I found your friend in Continuum. But it might take a while to find a body for him." She turned on the TV to the news. "Jennie, are you ready for bed? I've fixed up the guest room for you."

"You have a guest room?" Mike feigned being annoyed. He kissed Jennifer goodnight.

Tina led Jennie down the hall and tapped her fingernail on the linen closet door as she passed by. She gave Mike a knowing, sideways glance.

"Yeah, I know, I know." Mike shook his head. He'd be riding the couch again.

After a few minutes Tina returned and sat next to Mike on the sofa. She suddenly gaped at the TV screen. "Does your fighter plane have two sets of wings?"

"Yeah. How do you know?" He turned to look at the TV. There were blurry images of his plane, sitting on the moon. "Holy shit!"

The Chinese's lunar lander was sending back video that the Yutoo rover had taken of Mike's alien craft. The news commentator was describing the significance of the find: "Here we have the first, solid evidence that intelligent life exists elsewhere in our universe."

"I don't think that they're talking about you," Tina chided.

"Very funny." Mike gently elbowed her. "I also left a body up there, I hope they don't find that!"

"This could really freak everyone out. It could be like *War of the Worlds* all over again." Tina leaned forward. "It could start a global panic."

"What if I go and get the plane? I could find another place to hide it. Then people might think it was just a hoax."

"You would think that the moon would be a great place to hide something," Tina mused. "Well, where did you land it on Earth to begin with?"

"The jungles of Panama."

"That sounds pretty remote. Are you concerned that these Kaelites will find it there?" Tina tried to picture the situation.

"I guess not. They've moved on, probably setting up a headquarters somewhere."

"If they're settling in Panama, that's where we will eventually need the fighter anyway. You might as well hide it there."

"OK." Mike lifted himself off of the couch and looked at the image of the alien warplane on the TV screen. He took a few breaths, hoping that the cabin was still pressurized in the SAW. Then he bumped from Tina's apartment.

Tina returned her attention to the news as the commentator continued. "These live images are being sent to us via …"

The plane on the moon vanished.

"… uhhhh, we seem to be having technical difficulties with the video feed at this time."

Tina turned the TV off and stood up. She walked to the hall closet and pulled out the same blanket and pillow. Moments later Mike re-appeared in her living room.

"OK, it's sitting in a large clearing in the Panamanian rainforest." He turned to face Tina as the blanket and pillow hit him in the chest.

"Goodnight, cowboy. We've got a big day ahead of us tomorrow."

Mike glumly pulled his shoes off and settled into the couch. *We're coming, Simone. Just hang on.*

CHAPTER 16
FIRST ATTACK

In their cell, Simone and the Kaelite sisters tried to settle down for the night. Simone scanned Continuum to see if Mike was trying to rescue her.

"What the hell! That asshole is back in Colorado!" Exasperated, she turned to Kresta and Quint. "Let's try it again. We know that you can transfer yourselves to the edge of Continuum in the fighter planes. Try to think of the garden outside and blend into the Sea of Energy so that you can bump yourselves out there."

The sisters entered the state of mind that they were familiar with when they drove the energy-engines. They straddled the boundary of Continuum, becoming invisible. Both Kresta and Quint could feel the possibility of bumping through it, but actually doing it still evaded them.

"Ugh!" Simone groaned with frustration and pain, holding her mutilated finger.

The door was unlocked and two armed soldiers entered the small space. They set dinner and water down for Simone and grabbed the two cerebrals. "The prince is moving you closer to the planes." The girls were roughly pulled outside and the door was locked behind them.

"That's just great." Simone lay back on the floor. "I hope those two come and get me when they figure out how to bump out of here." She ate her dinner and washed her wound. "Damn you, Michael," she said to the stained walls, and fell into an exhausted, pained sleep.

Before he opened his eyes, Mike smelled coffee brewing. "You're a wonderful person," he muttered weakly in the direction of the kitchen.

Tina walked around the corner and kissed him lightly. "Good morning, and yes, I am." She smiled and returned to the kitchen.

What a cute butt.

Jennie walked down the hall in oversized pajamas. Mike sat up and greeted her. "Good morning, Sweet Pea."

"Hi, Daddy."

The first sips of coffee cleared Mike's head. "I've got to get back to Panama. There's no telling what Syndor is planning. And Simone must be suffering terribly."

"I need clothes, Daddy."

Mike hesitated. It was imperative that he return to the SAW and locate Simone. "Can you help me to locate her?" he asked Tina.

"Of course."

"OK. I still have a box of hand-me-downs at the apartment from your cousins," he said, addressing Jennie. "Let's bump over there and get you dressed, then we'll come back here and I'll get my ass back to Panama and figure out how to stop Syndor and rescue Simone."

"In the meantime, I'll see if I can locate your pilot friend in Continuum." Tina kissed Jennie on her forehead and patted her towards her father.

"I still can't believe that you're back." Mike smiled

and held his daughter. Then they vanished.

Syndor was already up when the morning sun began shining through the windows of his new residence in Panama. Fleet Commander Mora sat at the table with him.

"We need to do some reconnaissance this morning and see what the population is around here. Then demonstrate our power and authority," the prince directed Mora.

"Yes, my Lord. Should I use the Gen II or the SAW?"

"The Gen II. Scout out the area. If you can find a large city, test the Harmonic-beam on a building. We need to let these creatures understand that a new force has moved in." Syndor carefully eyed Commander Mora. "And we need to test the military power of these Earthlings."

"Yes, sir!" Mora eagerly excused himself and went to round up his flight crew, and a cerebral.

"You sent for me, my Lord?" The engineer entered the room.

"Yes, examine these devices and see what you are able to learn from them." Syndor gestured to the TV, computer, and dish washer.

Quint was pulled from the new quarters she shared with Kresta and placed in the Gen II. Mora sat in a pilot's seat while his copilot and two gunners filled the flight deck.

"Engage the engines. Establish the energy medium in the cabin," Mora commanded Quint.

The video display in front of Quint showed Drake, hanging by his wrists. She ground her teeth and patiently followed orders. Soon things would be different. The invisible crew took the controls and the magnificent ship rose straight up above the treetops. Mora began flying in huge circles, expanding the diameter each time in order to scan the Earth below him. Syndor watched the video of the flight from his main room.

Several other farms were discovered in the jungle. Then larger pueblos, and finally the great expanse of Panama City came into view. Mora slowed the Gen II down and cruised over the multitude of towering skyscrapers. The variety of architecture and the height of the buildings was like nothing he had ever seen on DuoSol. The blue-green Pacific Ocean lapped at the white sands along the shore.

"Can you see these buildings, my Lord?" Mora spoke into his radio.

"Yes, Commander Mora. It is stunning. Make sure that everyone can see the Gen II, then select one of those tall buildings along the coast and blast its foundation from under it."

Mora circled the vast city one more time. He could see the people on the ground pointing at his warplane. The sight of the scarlet ship, slowly orbiting the city, was causing pandemonium. Everyone rushed to their windows to see the UFO.

The Air Force Command was notified and two F-16 Fighting Falcons were deployed to the scene.

Mora guided the Gen II to the coastline and hovered in front of the twenty-five story Casa de Sueños Hotel. Colorful towels fluttered on the balcony railings and the suntanned residents stopped drinking their iced coffees as they gaped in horror at the roaring warplane hovering in front of them.

The gunners extended the cannons and set the charge to the Harmonic-beam. The Gen II shook as the powerful guns fired their pulses at the base of the building.

The concrete, glass, and steel disintegrated and the first five floors crumbled into rubble. The tremendous weight of the higher floors brought the entire building down within ninety seconds. The dust cloud rose to three times the original height of the hotel and billowed into the streets and onto the beach. Intense flames erupted from the fractured gas lines.

"Ya ha!" Syndor stood up and raised his arms in triumph. "Excellent work, Commander!" he called into his video feed.

"Thank you, my Lord." Mora burned with satisfaction, watching the pain and destruction that he had inflicted.

"Airships approaching." Mora's copilot pointed to the radar screen.

"Take them down!" Syndor clenched his paws.

Mora revved the energy-engines and charged directly at the incoming fighters. Before they could react, the Gen II rose above the F-16s and sharply reversed its course so that it now followed the jets.

"Switch to Bio-beam," Mora ordered.

The two Fighting Falcons separated and arced off in different directions, one over the Pacific Ocean, and the other over Panama City.

Commander Mora pursued the plane over the ocean first. The Gen II rapidly caught up to the F-16. The front Bio-cannons were extended and fired at the hot exhaust of the fighter. The crew was instantly killed and vanished. The Fighting Falcon hurled and twisted above the blue-green water, crewless, for half a mile before it sliced into the rolling waves.

"Where's the other one?" Mora turned his attention back to his copilot, and the radar.

"Circling over the city to attack us, sir."

"How valiant," the commander scoffed as he reversed

his direction and bore down on the remaining Falcon. "Set front cannon to Harmonic-beam."

The F-16 released two heat-seeking missiles at the Gen II, then arced up and back over the city.

"Fire the cannon!"

The Harmonic-beam struck the incoming missiles, reducing them to harmless dust. Mora pursued the Falcon over the coastline and the city.

"Switch back to Bio-beam and fire at that ship!"

The Gen II was only a quarter mile behind the F-16 when it fired the cannon. The crew vanished and left the speeding fighter to spin erratically until it plowed into the buildings and streets of Panama City. The fuel in the plane ignited in a fireball, setting the surrounding buildings on fire.

All emergency departments were routed to the two scenes of destruction. Mora took one more pass along the beach, admiring the two towering plumes of black smoke: the hotel, and the scene of the plane crash. Then he accelerated to fifteen hundred miles per hour. The Gen II streaked across the sky, back to the recesses of the rainforest.

In less than ten minutes, home videos of the attack went viral on the internet.

"What the hell was that?" United States President Feynman addressed the Joint Chiefs of Staff in the Pentagon. "Considering this bizarre hovering aircraft in Panama, and the video of the other ship on the moon … what else can we conclude? Earth is being invaded by aliens from space!"

"We are certainly being attacked, sir, but I would not consider one or two ships to be an invasion," the Secretary of Defense counseled the President. "I suggest that we deploy air support to Panama, hide our planes in Costa Rica, and seek out the location of their basecamp."

The Joint Chiefs nodded in agreement.

"Anything else?" The president wanted to be thorough.

"I also suggest moving anti-aircraft vehicles to the outskirts of Panama City, in case the alien plane returns."

"Very well. Let's get on it," Feynman concurred with his staff.

The United States Air Force mobilized a squadron of six F-15 Eagles and placed them in Costa Rica, Panama's neighbor to the north. Anti-aircraft tanks were positioned west of Panama City. Intelligence operatives began infiltrating the Panamanian countryside, seeking any clues to the whereabouts of the Kaelite stronghold.

At the same time in Colorado, Mike and Jennie rummaged through a box of clothes in his apartment and successfully discovered some outfits that fit.

"These are cute!" Jennie was pleased.

"I'm glad, Sweet Pea. Now we've got to get back to Tina's place." He hurriedly stuffed some of his own clothes into a daypack.

Mike pushed the box back into the closet and heard a knock at the door. Jennie opened it to see two men standing on the walkway.

"Good afternoon, young lady, could we please speak to your father?"

"Daaaaad," she called to the back of the apartment.

Mike walked down the hall and stopped short when he saw the two men. One was dressed in a dark suit and the other was wearing an army officer's uniform.

"Hello, gentlemen." Mike tried to not sound nervous. "Jennie, would you please go check your room and see if there's anything else that you want to bring along?"

Jennie headed for the back of the apartment while Mike met the men at the door. "What can I do for you?"

"Hello, Mr. Kruger. Please let me put you at ease. As our voicemail message indicated, we have positively identified you as the man who was in Pakistan a few days ago who, with a young woman, performed some extraordinary feats. I am Special Agent Bristol, of Military Intelligence, and this is Lieutenant Forbes, U.S. Joint Chiefs of Staff. Could we please ask you a few questions?"

Mike considered just bumping out of there and avoiding this conversation, but with Jennie in the back room he couldn't abandon her. Plus, maybe something good could come out of this meeting. "Come on in." Mike motioned them towards the chairs. "Could I offer you some water?"

"No thanks." Bristol sat down. "As you are aware, Mr. Kruger, there are factions of extremists all over the world that seem to have no regard for human rights. This is a growing problem and frankly, the United States government is exploring any means possible of containing the threat of terrorism."

Mike nodded.

"We reviewed the video of your actions many times, and the entire Chiefs of Staff are both perplexed and intrigued. As unbelievable as it seems, you apparently have the ability to disappear at will, and make your enemies vanish into thin air. Am I correct?"

Bristol and Forbes focused intently at Mike.

"Ah, yes, that is correct. I'm able to disappear and appear anywhere on Earth, instantly." Mike refrained from discussing his travels to DuoSol at this time. "And yes, I can make anyone vanish, which kills them, at will."

"Obviously the United States military is very interested in your powers. Conventional military operations are having limited success against these terrorists." Agent Bristol was direct.

Mike nodded again.

Lieutenant Forbes leaned forward. "Mr. Kruger, are you aware of the attack in Panama City that just occurred minutes ago?"

"Oh no." Mike gasped. "What kind of attack?"

"A fantastic fighter plane, like nothing we have ever encountered, destroyed a hotel and shot two F-16 Fighting Falcon jets out of the sky," the lieutenant explained.

Mike stood in stunned silence. He impatiently looked down the hall. *I need to get Jennie and get back to Panama!*

"We are interested to know if we can recruit you and your powers. We ask you to fight these terrorists, and whoever is targeting Panama City."

"We are planning to do that very thing," Mike replied with determination.

"We? Are you saying that there are other people who can already do what you can? Perhaps that dark-haired woman who was your companion in Pakistan?"

"She can't do what I can do," Mike answered truthfully. "We went together to explore the possibility of fighting the terrorists over there."

"Excellent, that is exactly why we are interested in teaming up with you, Mr. Kruger." Bristol smiled. "Perhaps you can also train some of our agents to develop the same powers that you have."

"I don't think that is possible, sir. There seems to be a genetic component that favors accessing these abilities."

Jennifer walked back into the main room of the

apartment. She carried a stuffed tiger in her arms. "This is the only thing that I found, Daddy."

"Your daughter?" Forbes scrutinized the young teen.

"Yes, this is Jennifer. Jennie, this is Mr. Bristol and Lieutenant Forbes."

"Pleased to meet you." Bristol nodded.

"Hello." Jennie peered from behind her father.

"Well, Mr. Kruger, this has been most instructive. It is imperative that we have you meet with our science expert. We will make arrangements immediately. Thank you again for your cooperation and hospitality."

Mike ushered the men to the door. They shook Mike's hand and left. He closed the door behind them and looked at Jennifer, the inheritor of his genetic blueprint. "We need to get back to Tina's place! The Kaelites are attacking us, and Simone is in the middle of it."

"OK. Those men were scary."

You ain't seen nothing yet. Mike thought of Syndor and his alien troops.

They held their belongings and each other's hands, then bumped to Tina's front door.

Mike paused, but Jennie went ahead and opened it.

They entered the apartment and found Tina sitting quietly in a chair, clearly in a state of deep concentration. Mike held Jennie as they stood still and watched.

"Daddy!" Jennie whispered.

"I feel it too, Sweet Pea."

Continuum was extremely dense in the apartment. Mike and Jennie could feel the pressure of the concentrated energy. The light in the room in front of Tina was bending and created an opaque blur before her. A hazy, out of focus form began developing. It seemed to be moving slightly. Then the bright image crystallized and became the body of a man. The intensity of Continuum slowly returned to normal in the room. Mike and Jennifer stared at the naked person standing before Tina. It was a young man, about twenty years old, of Asian descent. His lean, muscular figure moved slightly as he examined his arms and hands. Then he looked across the room at Mike and Jennie.

"Mad Mike! What the hell are you doing with that jailbait, ya creeper!"

CHAPTER 17
NEW ALLIANCE

The Gen II landed back at the hacienda after its attack on Panama City. Quint was returned to her confinement shack with Kresta.

"Well done!" Prince Syndor commended Commander Mora as he entered the main room of the house.

"Thank you, my Lord. The Gen II is much faster and more maneuverable than the fighters that are possessed here on Earth. However, we must be prepared for greater numbers to engage us in combat." Mora looked around the large room and noticed the soldier sitting at the computer. "Also, sir, eventually our location will be discovered and we will need to defend this compound."

Syndor agreed. "We must find a way to hold these creatures hostage. There must be hundreds of thousands of them on this planet. It would be impossible to dominate them by physical force. We need to control their lifelines." Syndor turned to the engineer at the computer. "What have you learned?"

"This machine is connected to a worldwide network of communication. Much of the transfer of information flows through this matrix, which is called 'internet.'"

"Really? Can it tell you how many Earthlings reside on this planet?"

"Just a moment, sir. Yes, just over seven billion humans."

"Billion!" Syndor and Mora were both shocked. "How can a planet have enough natural resources to sustain such a population?" "We will need to eradicate a large percentage of this infestation," Mora suggested.

"What have you learned of this region of the planet?" Syndor asked the engineer.

"That is more difficult, my Lord. The translating headpiece does not function with some of the entries on this machine. There seem to be several languages that are used in different parts of the planet."

"How ineffective," Syndor surmised. "However, this could work to our advantage. If the Earthlings are divided into many factions, they will be easier to conquer." The prince considered the challenge of the language barrier. He turned to his attendant. "Bring me that female Earthling. But first take her to the medical quarters to have her finger wound attended to."

"Yes, my Lord."

"And she needs to bathe."

The soldier bowed and left, heading towards the granary where Simone lay in misery, scanning Continuum.

"Damn you asshole, Michael." She confirmed that he was still in Colorado, instead of searching for her. "You and that scrawny chick, Tina. Whoa, who is the third person with access? Where did she come from?"

The lock rattled at her door and it swung open. A Kaelite guard pointed a weapon at her and motioned her to follow. He took her to the small building where the doctor had set up his office. Salve was applied to the injury, which immediately numbed the pain. The doctor cleaned and stitched the opening, then injected a long-term anesthetic. Simone was led to a shower stall, where she welcomed the opportunity to get cleaned up.

After bathing, she was led to Syndor's private chamber.

"Welcome, Simone," Syndor greeted her as the guard left them alone. "How is your finger?"

"Well, this one is gone." She held up the short stump on her left hand. "But this one is doing fine!" She stabbed the air in front of him with her middle finger.

"Excellent. I would like for us to discuss our present situation, and see if we can assist one another."

Simone crossed her arms on her chest and scowled at the alien man.

Syndor continued, "It seems to me that your companion, Mike, has been a terrible disappointment. You came to DuoSol seeking an ally. You wanted to defeat your enemies here on Earth. My guess is that you have aspirations of conquering a nation for yourself. Am I correct?"

Simone considered the prince standing before her. "Yes, you are right. I have been victimized and dominated all that I can tolerate. I want to be the ruler from now on. I want to control the miserable people that surround me."

Syndor's powerful jaw smiled. "I admire your attitude, and your fortitude under the severe circumstances that you have endured these past few cycles. Unfortunately, cruelty and threats are a very effective way of controlling other beings. Please understand that." He took a step towards her. "I propose that we work together from now on, become allies, and function as a team." He waved his hand around the room. "As you can see. I am very capable of conquering and dominating other nations and species, unlike your pathetic friend, Mike. He has some very unusual powers, but clearly he is too much of a coward to use them effectively. He has abandoned you."

Simone shifted on her feet. The wonderful surge of domination burned in her chest. She realized that she was being offered an extraordinary opportunity. "What kind of an alliance do you have in mind?"

"A complete partnership. I am the prince of Kael, and I will be the king of Earth. You will be my queen as we establish our control of this planet." He stepped directly in front of her, watching her chest rise and fall as she took each excited breath.

"What do I need to do?" She skeptically looked at Syndor. Although he stood a full eight inches shorter than she was, his shoulders and arms were broad and muscular. He was a prime specimen of his species.

"Can you speak this local language?"

"Yes, I speak fluent Spanish and English. These are two of the three most common languages used on Earth."

"Excellent. Are you able to deny your own species and swear allegiance to the Kaelites?"

"I have no friends, and my family abandoned me. But I might want some human companionship from time to time."

"That is understandable, it is obvious that you are a healthy and desirable female of your species. Do you have a fertilization canal?" Before she could answer he abruptly reached out and honked one of her breasts.

"Yowch!"

"You have a strange body," Syndor observed.

"Seriously, dude, your pillow talk and foreplay need some work." Simone rubbed her breast and assessed the alien. He was powerful both physically, and status-wise. Still … he was kind of a shrimp.

Syndor removed his top, revealing his muscular torso. Simone noticed that he had no nipples.

"Are you sure you're up to this? You don't seem to know what you're doing." She unbuttoned her blouse. A sly smile turned up the corner of her mouth.

"When we are finished, I will still need to visit my harem," the Prince boasted.

"We'll see about that." She removed her blouse and peeled her black leather pants onto the floor. "Hmmm, I always did prefer the bad-boys."

Syndor removed his leggings, exposing his male organ. The shaft was extended and had three bulges along its length.

"That thing actually looks like it would feel good." Simone smiled and removed her panties. She coiled her arms around the prince, reached around his head, and grabbed the thick horns curling from his skull.

Syndor considered Simone's full breasts, which were on either side of his nose.

"OK, Moon-man, show me what that lumpy cock of yours can do."

They wrestled onto the bed and spent the next hour experimenting with the first inter-planetary coitus.

At the same time, in Tina's apartment, Mike stood in astonishment trying to comprehend the return of Major Cody Brennevin.

Mike tossed his bag to Cody. "Here, find some clothes."

Jennie stared wide-eyed at the naked man as he walked to the back of the apartment to dress. "Don't stare too long, youngster, I'll spoil you for life." Brennevin strode to the bathroom, his manhood in full view.

Tina sat in her chair, slowly emerging through the extreme levels of mental concentration that it had taken to bring Cody back from Continuum.

"Where is he?" Tina opened her eyes and looked around.

"Dear God! What have you people done to me?" Cody bellowed from the bathroom. He peered at the reflection of the Asian man looking back at him. "Every time I look in the mirror I'm going to want to shoot myself!"

"It's time you got over that." Mike frowned. "The war ended forty years ago. Anyway, all nations need to pull together against a common enemy now."

Brennevin walked back into the main room where he spotted Tina. "Hey, Sugar."

"This is a friend of mine. Tina," Mike introduced her.

"I'm sorry to hear that." Cody leaned towards Tina and cocked his head in Mike's direction. "You can do a lot better than him." He winked.

"Excuse me, Major Banana-van, or whatever your name is. I brought you back from the dead, and I can send you there anytime I want to." Tina was clearly insulted.

Cody became serious. "Ma'am, I spent the last twenty-five years of my life trying to find a way to die. I did not enjoy living. Wherever I just came from was the best experience I have ever had. I was in a bath of peace and contentment. My enemies forgave me and I forgave them. I wasn't really me, but somehow I was there, a part of everything. It was gentle and serene." He looked at Tina. "Any friend of Mike's is a friend of mine. I apologize that I offended you. But please, when I die again, leave me there." He nodded politely and looked at Mike and Jennie. "And who are you, cupcake?"

"This is Jennie, my daughter."

Cody looked in amazement. He knew the story of the accident and of Mike's depression and suffering. "Well, what do you know? I'm very pleased to meet you." He shook her small hand and then turned to Tina. "You must be some kind of miracle-worker."

Tina relaxed and smiled at the bawdy man. "You might say that. I have developed some powers beyond what ordinary people are capable of. So has Mike, and Jennie will too. We brought you back to help us with a situation. We need your special talents as a combat pilot."

Brennevin looked around the room and wriggled his hands and fingers, as if he were getting used to his new body. Mike went over to where Tina was regaining her normal physical senses. "Are you OK? Where did you find a body for him?"

"There was an accident in a factory in Japan. This young man died of multiple head injuries. As he left his body, I took it and repaired the damage to his brain."

They both looked at Cody, who was bent over, sniffing a cactus plant.

"Maybe I missed a few things." Tina grinned. "Yes, I'm OK. Thank you. It is very intense to bring someone back to the physical world. But I'm ready to discuss what we are going to do about this alien invasion, and rescuing Simone."

It was nearing midday in Panama. After their sexual adventure, Syndor and Simone reposed on the large bed, catching their breath.

"It is my duty to impregnate the three women that we have brought with us to Earth. We must begin procreating and building our population. I wonder if I will be able to impregnate you.""No, you won't." Simone propped her head up.

Syndor looked at his new mate. "Do you have a malfunction of your child-development organ?"

"I'm already pregnant. Mike is the father." Simone lay back and caressed her tummy. "I am hoping that the child will inherit both parents' abilities to access Continuum."

"That could be a very powerful combination. I will permit the child to continue to develop."

The royal couple cleaned up, dressed, and entered the main room of the house. The Kaelite engineer who had been exploring the internet looked up. "I am ready to present my findings, my Lord."

Prince Syndor assembled Fleet Commander Mora and Major Alyx to hear the engineer's report.

"First of all," Syndor began, "I am presenting my new Life-Partner, Simone, of Earth. When we conquer and control this planet, and I become king, she will rule by my side, as your queen." Syndor selected one of the rings on his digits and removed the smallest one. "This ring bears the crest of the royal family of Kael. Simone is now the new princess of our great nation." He tried to slide the ring on her fingers, but it was so wide that it only fit on her thumb.

"My Prince!" Commander Mora instantly reacted with alarm.

"Yes, Commander." Syndor paced his words; clearly he would tolerate no objections.

"Yes … let me be the first to congratulate both of you, and the kingdom of Kael, on this glorious union." He practically choked on his words and slumped into his chair.

"Thank you, Commander Mora. I believe that you speak for everyone here." The prince cast his blank, black eyes across the table. Mora, Alyx and the engineer bowed their heads and acknowledged their new princess.

Simone felt the thrill of power and authority as she nodded back and acknowledged their genuflections.

"You may present your report." Syndor sat down next to his princess.

Simone adjusted the translating headpiece that she wore.

"My prince, it is my opinion that human civilization is approximately six days away from returning to the age of stone tools, and complete anarchy. This will be followed by widespread starvation, illness, violence, and death." The engineer paused.

"As you have directed, my Lord, I have been analyzing the lifelines of this civilization, and I find that it is very fragile. This is a result of specialization and loss of connection with the source of life-sustaining nutrients."

Syndor folded his paws under his chin. Mora smiled at the realization that their small military force, with only two warships, would be capable of controlling the enormous population of Earthlings.

The engineer continued. "Here at our base on Earth, we are surrounded by fields that yield fruits and other foods. Fresh water flows in the mountain streams. We killed the cattle, goats, and chickens when we arrived; however, we could easily replenish these and be self-sufficient. Most Kaelites have the ability and knowledge to harvest grains, vegetables, and livestock. But very few humans are able to do this."

Simone knew that this was true. Even if there was a dead deer in front of her, she would be unable to correctly butcher it. Much less hunt and kill a live one.

"In the large cities, humans are completely dependent on food items being delivered from rural areas. Much of this food must be kept cold to inhibit the growth of toxic microorganisms. These large cooling boxes run on electricity. If we sever the electric supply lines, the food will spoil within days, the alarm systems will not function, lights will not function, and computers will not operate. The populations will revert to survival instincts. They will plunder, loot, steal from each other, and destroy themselves. Only the self-sufficient farmers will survive, and they will be attacked by starving people fleeing from the cities."

"Control the neck and we control the animal." Commander Mora clearly approved of this strategy.

"Will we render the planet unusable to ourselves?" Syndor did not want to ruin his spoils of war.

"I suggest that we leave our area untouched. If we begin by targeting the largest cities, we will do the most amount of damage, and kill the greatest quantity of Earthlings. The leaders of these various nations will quickly recognize our authority and yield to us." The engineer bowed his head and sat down.

Syndor considered the logic of the plan. He had only two ships and about twenty military personnel, including himself. It was imperative that he create leverage and establish the greatest threat possible, with his limited arsenal. "Do you have a city in mind, engineer?"

"I do, my Lord. Los Angeles. The United States of America has the largest economy, and military, of any nation on Earth, and Los Angeles is the second largest urban area in the USA. It is a direct path from here, four thousand miles up the coastline. There are only ten sources of power that provide most of the electricity to the 18.6 million people that live in that metropolis. The Gen II needs to loop through the neighboring states of Utah and Arizona in order to destroy one nuclear power plant and two fossil-fuel plants. It can be there in slightly more than two hours. Then it will enter the Los Angeles area where it will obliterate four wind farms and three natural gas plants. Including the return to our base, the operation will take five hours."

Commander Mora addressed the engineer. "Are you able to adapt our equipment in the Gen II and SAW so that it is compatible with internet?"

"Yes, we will configure the pilots' consoles so that they have access to the internet. The Global Positioning System in our fighters is already aligned with the system here on Earth. This software will aid us in locating any target that we choose. We will be ready by pre-dawn of the next brightness."

"Very well." Syndor leaned forward. "Commander Mora, select your crew for the Gen II and prepare for this attack." He took Simone's hand. "My Princess, are you familiar with the functioning of this device?" He pointed to the computer.

"Yes, my Prince, would you like me to assist you?" Simone tried to sound erudite.

Mora left the room to make arrangements for the attack. Simone led Syndor to the computer and they sat down together in front of the monitor and keyboard.

In their cell, Kresta and Quint continued to explore their abilities. As sisters, with similar genomes, they were developing identical powers. They were now both capable of bumping out of their confinement and back in again, with their clothing. "We need to learn how to bump with another object. Mike is able to do it and take the entire SAW ship with him. We need to understand how to bump into Drake's cell, and bump back out with him. Then we can get out of here," Quint explained to her younger sister.

"But where is Drake?" Kresta wondered.

"Yes, we need to figure that out." Quint pondered the problem.

As afternoon became evening in Colorado, Mike brought Brennevin up to date on the Kaelite invasion, and his own powers.

"The plane never runs out of fuel?" the major was asking.

"That's right. It draws its power from the forces and atoms around us. This energy extends throughout the universe and is a part of everything."

"All right. This Super-Duper plane, or SAW, is very fast and can turn sharply." Cody reviewed what Mike had explained to him.

"Yup."

"And they have two planes and we have one?"

"Yup."

"And one of their planes is even more advanced than ours?"

"Yup."

"I almost feel sorry for them." Brennevin grinned and looked around at Tina and Jennie. "Well, ladies, we're off to check out this fancy-pants plane. Don't wait up for us."

Mike reached for Brennevin's hand. He quickly withdrew it. "Hey! Not in front of your girlfriend!"

"We need to touch skin to skin in order for me to bump us through Continuum."

"Did I ever tell you that I only turned down one offer of sex in my life? That was a little boy scout, I had to turn him face-down. Haw haw …"

Mike grabbed the major's hand and the two of them bumped to the isolated clearing in the Panamanian rainforest. The streamlined SAW sat waiting, with birds perched on its dual wings. Every hard point had a missile or bomb attached.

"Damn! I never saw anything like that before." Cody was both awed and impressed. "Let's see what you can do with this thing."

Mike opened the rear hatch and the two men climbed inside the small flight deck.

Bonk. Cody rubbed his head.

"What the hell?" he bellowed.

"The Kaelites are a bit shorter than we are," Mike explained.

"No kidding." Brennevin frowned at Mike.

"Just crouch and duck."

"You'd like that."

"Just pay attention."

"Easy for you to say. I've got a skull. You've got a rock for a head."

Mike checked that the sensors were aimed at his pilot's chair. "For now I need to be both the cerebral and fly the plane. Once you can fly it I will move over and handle the gunner's position. I can only do two out of the three jobs on the ship." Mike took one of the pilot's seats while Brennevin hunched into the other.

Mike concentrated and accessed Continuum, firing the engines. At the same time he created the bubble that held the crew in a state of half-physical and half-ethereal existence.

"Hey, where'd you go?"

"We'll be invisible while we operate the SAW. This is what protects us from the G-forces while we maneuver the plane."

"OK, just keep your hands to yourself, ya fruitcake."

Mike's controls moved and the SAW rose directly up. When it was a thousand feet above the forest he directed it forward and accelerated. The warship rocketed over the jungle towards the Pacific Ocean.

"Man! This thing hauls ass!" Cody approved.

The coastline rushed below them and the SAW headed out above the blue expanse of the Pacific Ocean. The sky was turning orange over the vast surface of shimmering water.

"OK, I'm going to reverse us now." Mike threw a lever and wrenched the steering stick. He was a bit clumsy, but the plane abruptly spun around and was shooting back towards the mainland, without losing any speed. Normally the G-forces would have ripped their internal organs apart, but in the state of half-energy, the two men felt nothing.

"OK, rookie, let me try my hand at this thing." Brennevin took control of the airship while Mike watched the master get a feel for the alien craft.

"Hey! Ya know why this plane is like your mother?" Cody hollered with enthusiasm.

Mike stared dully at the canopy in front of him. "No. Why?'

"Because it's got a big cock pit! Haw haw …"

Mike turned to the major. "Do you know what a beautiful woman says when she's totally satisfied sexually?"

Brennevin's invisible hands familiarized themselves with the controls. "Ahh, no."

"I didn't think so." Mike smiled an invisible smile.

"You are a cruel and insensitive bastard."

Cody rose and descended, turned ninety degrees and reversed direction. Then he took the plane up to 45,000 feet and punched it. He pushed the SAW to its maximum speed of 1800 miles per hour. Both oceans were visible at this altitude and the strip of land soared underneath as they neared Costa Rica.

"Ahhh flying, my second favorite thing to do." Brennevin's voice was oddly content.

He caught a blip on his control panel and quickly reversed direction, dropping to the level of the treetops.

"Someone is watching for us over there," Cody warned. "Let's get this sleek lady back to that clearing and put her away."

The GPS guided them right back to their hiding place and Brennevin expertly set the powerful ship on the ground.

"You're right," he agreed with Mike. "The basic functions and controls are similar to the Phantom II. Have you shot any of the cannons yet?"

"Not yet."

"We need to figure that out."

The two men examined the controls for the gunners and tried to understand the procedure for firing each of the armaments.

The shadows started getting long.

"Let's camp here and think about a plan tomorrow," Mike suggested.

"All right, but I'm sleeping in the plane. I have an allergy to jaguars."

"That's nothing compared to what we'll be up against tomorrow," Mike cautioned.

"I'm not afraid of munchkins," Cody stated flatly.

"Well, these munchkins aren't afraid of anything."

CHAPTER 18
A CHINK IN THE ARMOR

"**B**y tonight, this planet will be in chaos!" Prince Syndor stood outside before the Gen II and breathed the morning air. "The screaming voices of millions of humans will herald my conquest of Earth."

Simone peered out the window through the pre-dawn light and smiled. Her own rise to power was also beginning.

Kresta was placed in the Gen II and engaged the engines while the crew took their positions.

"Destroy the nuclear reactor first," Syndor directed Commander Mora through his comm link.

"I will not fail." Mora's intensity was tangible. "Establish the energy medium around the crew." The pilots, gunners, and Kresta became invisible as the blood-red ship rose vertically, fifty thousand feet above the compound. Hell had come to Earth, and was being unleashed.

Mora took the warship to the Pacific coastline and instantly accelerated to 2200 miles per hour. They streaked through the morning sky. The countries of Central America, and then Mexico, soared beneath them.

The Rio Grande River came into view and then flashed underneath the Gen II, marking their entry into United States airspace. Mora checked his instruments, then closed in on the Palo Verde nuclear reactor in Arizona. The ship blazed across the clear sky and covered the distance within minutes.

"There it is. Gunners! Prepare to attack!"

The ship descended and hovered around the three cooling towers like a hummingbird. The Harmonic cannons were extended and a barrage of pulses were directed towards the immense, concrete structures. The colossal mass of the giant towers required several minutes of cannon fire as the Gen II circled around and around. But eventually the structures began fracturing and collapsed, releasing a 5000 degree Fahrenheit inferno and a cloud of deadly radiation.

The Gen II regained altitude and tracked down the first coal-fired generating station, also in Arizona. The Harmonic cannon blasted the facility to rubble. Large sections of L.A. began experiencing electrical blackouts.

"Two down." Mora smiled a tight smile as he turned from the destruction and headed north into Utah. "Engage the ship's energy-shield."

A film of energy encased the Gen II like a well-fitting glove. Anything fired at the ship would now be repelled.

The United States Air Force reacted immediately to the invasion. Four F-16 Fighting Falcon fighters ripped into the sky from Foothills Air Base. The same base in Utah that Cody and Mike had borrowed the F-4 Phantom II from. The F-16s raced south to meet the alien plane.

Commander Mora picked up the incoming jets on his radar. "Rise to fifty thousand feet. Accelerate to 2100 miles per hour! We'll pass right over them." The Gen II instantly responded and soared above the clouds, crossing over the oncoming Falcons as they traversed the Grand Canyon. The F-16s wheeled around and headed back north to give chase.

Following his GPS, Mora guided his fighter towards the coal generator and angled down towards the structures. "Extend front Harmonics and prepare to release conventional bombs." The crew followed his orders exactly. There was no time to hover around the facility with the four fighters on his tail. Mora fired the cannon as he turned the nose of the Gen II directly towards the generator and then released his bombs. He pulled back up and regained high altitude. The generating station blew apart, erupting like a volcano.

The four F-16s, flying north, closed in on Mora and his warplane.

"Don't outrun them!" Syndor commanded from his remote post. "Their weapons cannot penetrate the energy-shield. Face them and shoot them out of the atmosphere! We must demonstrate our superiority!"

"Love to." Mora turned south and scanned the sky ahead of him. "Switch cannon to Bio-beams. Keep the front guns extended."

When the F-16s were just eight thousand yards away, Commander Mora accelerated towards the fighters. His cannon fired their pulses as the five planes closed in on each other. The F-16s each fired two AIM-9 sidewinder missiles. The infrared-guided missiles tracked into the Gen II and the eight warheads exploded against the alien fighter.

The invisible crew on the Gen II were nearly rocked out of their seats by the impact.

"The energy-shield has been overloaded and compromised, Commander!"

"That's impossible!" Mora checked the instruments himself.

The Bio-beams struck the F-16s and killed the pilots of the four planes. Just like the two planes above Panama City, the four Fighting Falcons spun, crewless, towards the Earth, drilling themselves into the desert.

Commander Mora looked sternly at his console, indicating that the energy-shield had been damaged. "Hopefully it will replenish itself from Continuum. As long as we can shoot the enemy before they fire at us, we will be fine. Keep your attention on that radar screen!"

Sweat poured down Kresta's forehead. Tremendous amounts of energy were flowing through her body as she powered the plane, energy-shield, and cannon.

Syndor and Simone followed the progress of the Gen II on their video screen. "Success!" Syndor gloated. "Now finish the job."

Commander Mora turned west. The Gen II roared into California and the outlying hills of Los Angeles.

He dropped the plane to eight hundred feet and cut his speed to four hundred miles per hour. The warship swept over the center of a massive wind farm. The cannon fired their Harmonic pulses across the entire field, disintegrating every windmill into crumbled debris.

Within seconds the Gen II was cruising at forty-thousand feet and honing in on the second wind farm, which was destroyed. Mora checked his GPS and wheeled his warship around to annihilate the third and fourth wind farms.

Over seventy-five percent of L.A. was without power.

The commander turned his attention to the three natural gas generators in the area. He sped between them and then hovered above the structures while bombarding them with the Harmonic cannon. The buildings crumbled, crushing the workers inside, and severing the flow of electricity.

Over ninety percent of Los Angeles was now without electricity.

"Ya ha!" Syndor leapt into the air in celebration.

Every target had been destroyed. He leaned towards his monitor to watch as the Gen II turned south to head back to base.

Mora flew up to 55,000 feet and cruised at 2200 miles per hour, back across the Mexican border and over Central America. As he approached the hacienda, he decelerated and reduced his altitude.

"Look at that!" Brennevin exclaimed as the brilliant, red ship streaked overhead like a shooting star.

"That's the Gen II!" Mike recognized the distinctive double wings and color. "I wonder what it's been doing?"

"They didn't just go out for coffee, I can tell you that." Cody watched as the alien fighter disappeared over the hills. "It could have just run a sortie. We need to figure out how to operate these armaments and get into the action!"

The American squadron in Costa Rica caught the Gen II on their radar as the Kaelite ship returned to its base. The pilots scrambled for their F-15 Eagles, but were told to stand down. News of the destruction up north, and the four fallen Fighting Falcons, had reached their commander.

"Engaging this warship in the air is pointless. The damage has been done. We are not going to lose any more pilots or fighters today. We need to develop a strategy to destroy this alien force at their home base."

Reluctantly, the pilots and crews returned to their briefing room, and watched the large screen TV. The crisis began unfolding in Los Angeles.

CHAPTER 19
APOCALYPSE: DAY ONE

Two hours earlier, at 7:08 a.m., Carter Hess sat at his desk on the thirty-ninth floor of an office building in downtown L.A. He could see the ocean through the large, plate glass windows. As an aspiring investment analyst, he liked to get an early start to his work day. He looked at his Rolex and compared the time on his watch with the digital clock on his computer screen. The screen dimmed slightly as it switched to battery power. The lights in the office went out. The ubiquitous humming of the ventilation system ceased. He looked around the empty office. "What the heck?"

Julia Espinosa was jogging in the foothills above L.A. She enjoyed starting each day with some exercise and fresh air. The expansive wind farm to her right made quiet whooshing sounds as the gigantic blades were rotated by the mountain wind. Her running shoes gently tapped along the pavement. A powerful, deep sound grew behind her. She turned and looked up as the speeding shadow of the Gen II rocketed over the wind farm. A shock wave crushed her to the ground. Then, in an instant, the plane was gone. Julia sat up and assessed her skinned elbows. She looked at the field next to her and gasped. There was only disintegrated, twisted wreckage, as far as she could see. The wind farm had been destroyed.

Wendy Winthrop pulled a frying pan out of the cupboard in her kitchen, located in the suburbs of L.A. She could hear her two young sons moving around in the back of their house. Suddenly, the coffee pot stopped gurgling. The morning news on the TV went dark. She opened the refrigerator to get some eggs but something was strange: the little light did not come on. "Darn, and we just bought all these groceries."

Weston Purcell was finally asleep after partying all night with his gang, the Scepterz. His phone rang over and over until it drew him back to consciousness. "You're dead." He answered the phone and looked at the digital clock beside his table. It was dark.

"Yo Wes, something's going down." The voice in the phone sounded urgent.

"You wake me up again and something's going down on you!" He powered his phone off and returned to his slumber.

In a small office in the Pacific Natural Gas and Electric Company, Chuck Ellison sipped his coffee. His night shift would be over in less than an hour. The deep rumble of thunder could be heard outside as the Gen II approached the facility. He stood up and looked out of the window at the clear morning. "That's odd," he muttered. The building started to shudder. "Earthquake!" he yelled and ran for the doorway. Within seconds the two stories of building disintegrated above him and collapsed, crushing him to death.

Doctor Stacy Warmuth leaned over the operating table in the Emergency Ward in Redwoods-Sinai Hospital in L.A. The patient had been struck by a hit-and-run driver and suffered multiple fractures. Warmuth had the victim's leg wide open and was beginning to set the fractured femur when the lights went off in the windowless room. The machine that was breathing for the patient stopped functioning. The heart monitor went black. Then the lights flickered as massive generators started up and provided temporary electricity for the hospital.

"We better stabilize this patient for now and see what is happening." The doctor sent an attendant to investigate.

President Feynman watched the multiple video screens in his control room. The Secretaries of the Interior, Defense, Homeland Security, and Energy were in attendance, as well as the Vice President.

"Let's focus on the facts," began the Secretary of Defense. "The ship can travel at close to Mach 3, it cannot be damaged by missiles, it has the capability of destroying gigantic structures, such as the cooling towers at the Palo Verde nuclear plant, and it has maneuverability that defies the laws of physics."

"Do we know where they have established a base on Earth?" asked the Vice President.

"More or less," the Defense Secretary responded. "They are in the jungle, west of Panama City. We have six planes nearby, in Costa Rica, but at the moment we are evaluating the best strategy for attacking them. So far, six allied fighter planes have been shot out of the air. The aliens clearly have superiority in this sort of confrontation."

"We must attend to our immediate crisis. Greater Los Angeles is without electricity. Basic life support is needed for millions of people, not to mention the threat of looting and rioting once night falls," the Secretary of the Interior urged.

"These are not just severed cables," the VP agreed. "The sources of power themselves have been eradicated. There is no re-routing of the supply of electricity, or backup. Los Angeles is running on battery power and generators. Soon the batteries will die, and the generators will run out of gasoline. Then all they will have are candles, and fires."

"At the very least, mobilize the Army Reserves from the surrounding states to try to maintain law and order. Have the Army assess the situation and bring basic supplies, water, food, and fuel into the area to support our troops," the president directed. "We will continue to develop our emergency plan as the situation develops." He turned to the Secretary of Homeland Security. "We must consider the possibility that they will do the same thing to other cities."

"We are already coordinating the major cities and their sources of power with the nearest air bases."

"Very good. We will meet again at seventeen hundred to update each other."

The cabinet members stood up.

"One more thing." President Feynman interrupted their dismissal. "Coordinate the F-22 Raptors that we have on the east coast. Washington might be next." The Commander in Chief referred to the fifth generation U.S. fighter aircraft. It had no equal on Earth. He would see if it could take on the Gen II fighter from outer space.

By mid-morning in Los Angeles, laptop batteries were depleted, but not before the news of the attack had spread. The only form of communication was cell phones, and they were running out of power as well. People turned the faucets on in their houses and no water came out. The toilets wouldn't flush. The food was spoiling in their refrigerators.

Hordes of citizens flocked to the grocery stores to buy water and non-perishable supplies. But the stores were dark and the cash registers wouldn't work. Uncontrollable stealing began.

Many families loaded their children into their cars

and attempted to drive beyond the blackout into Nevada, or Arizona. When they tried to fill their vehicles up with gas, the fuel pumps didn't work. The ATM machines were off. The major highways became overloaded and the traffic could barely move. Then cars began running out of gas and the freeway became hopelessly clogged. People abandoned their vehicles and walked.

The reality of the situation began creeping into people's minds. The basic necessities of life were no longer being provided to the millions of households. Everyone would soon be competing with their neighbors for food and water in order to stay alive.

Julia Espinosa jogged back to her home in the outskirts of L.A. Her husband, Martin, rushed out to meet her.

"We've been attacked! All the power plants were destroyed." He hugged his panting wife.

"I know, I saw a plane swoop down and wipe out the wind farm. Everything up there is wrecked. It happened so fast. Who's attacking us?"

They looked around their four-acre farm in the countryside. Their two young children were walking to tend to the six goats that they milked and raised. The chickens clucked and pecked at the feed in their pen. The leaves and stalks of the vegetables in their half-acre garden fluttered in the morning breeze. Young fruits were developing on their orange and apple trees.

"The news thinks that this might be aliens, from outer space! The power grid is down in L.A., but our solar panels and batteries are operating," Martin informed Julia. They walked past the barrels that collected rainwater, and the trickling mountain stream that bordered their property. "We'll be fine. But everyone in Los Angeles is going to have a tough time until the power comes back on, if it comes on at all."

They held each other and surveyed the humble farm.

Yesterday their family was considered poor, but this morning they had what anyone in L.A. would pay a king's ransom for: water, food, and electricity.

In Panama, the Gen II returned victoriously to the hacienda. Kresta was returned to her confinement and the engineer examined the damaged energy-shield.

Prince Syndor and Princess Simone welcomed Mora and his crew back to base.

"Prepare the Gen II for another mission tomorrow," Syndor ordered the soldiers. "Remove all exterior missiles, I want her as streamlined as possible. And activate the radar in the SAW. Assign someone to monitor it around the clock. We need to know if anyone is trying to attack us."

The soldiers scurried to obey.

"That was excellent!" Syndor congratulated his Fleet Commander. "You are truly one of the two best fighter pilots in the universe!"

Commander Mora bowed his head and smiled a weary smile at his prince. "The Gen II is an amazing war-machine, my Lord. The energy cannon functioned perfectly, and the energy-shield was able to withstand the attack from the Earth-fighters for quite some time. However, the extreme release of energy from the Earthlings' missiles has damaged the shield. I doubt that it could withstand another attack like that," Mora reported, then added, "We have established our dominance over this pitiful race of inferior creatures."

Simone pursed her lips and narrowed her eyes, expecting Syndor to admonish Mora for insulting his mate.

"Yes, Mora, our conquest of this planet has begun very well. And we have five more ships being completed on DuoSol. When we can figure out how to bring them here, our military dominance will be secured. Tomorrow I will conclusively show the world that we are the ruling power on Earth." He took Simone's hand and led her to his private chamber. He felt like celebrating.

Kresta knelt down in their cell. Quint came over and hugged her excitedly. "I did it!" she whispered. "I bumped and took something else with me. It's not much different than taking our clothes with us. You just need to think about what you want to travel with, and create a bubble of energy around it, sort of like we do in the planes." She could see how exhausted Kresta was from her morning in the Gen II. "After you rest, we can work on it together."

"Where will we meet? What if we bump out of here at different times? Where will we meet?" Kresta looked at her older sister as she lay down on the dirt floor.

"The tallest mountain, the one with the rocky top. We should be safe up there."

"But we need to find out where Drake is. We can't get him unless we know where he is," Kresta repeated. "And what about Simone? She was nice to us, maybe we can go with her too?"

"That would be wonderful, she could help us here on Earth," Quint agreed. "But Drake is the most important."

"And then where will we go?"

Quint was ready for this question. "It doesn't matter, as long as we are out of here. Maybe we can make friends with the Earthlings, or maybe we can figure out how to get back to DuoSol."

"OK, you can show me how after I rest." Kresta put her head down and passed out.

In Colorado, Tina and Jennifer watched in horror

as the news showed the destruction and chaos that was happening in Los Angeles.

"Is that where Daddy is?" Jennie asked.

"No. Your dad and Major Brennevin are in Panama, trying to figure out how to stop the people—uh, aliens, who did this."

"Do they need our help?"

Tina was silent. Her primary responsibility was to take care of Jennie. But the situation had become much worse since Mike had left. "We'll see." She comforted the young teen, then she called Mike.

Mike answered his cell phone. "Tina, how is Jennie?"

"We're fine. Have you heard anything about what's happening in Los Angeles?"

"No, the Gen II flew over us a while ago, from the northwest. What's going on?"

Tina tried to summarize. "That red plane destroyed most of the electric supply to Los Angeles. Millions of people are running out of water and fresh food. Looting has begun and it's turning into a war zone."

Mike tried to imagine the chain reaction that had been started. "Damn that Syndor! With just one plane he could be killing half the population of California. And he might do it again in another city!"

"Four fighters tried to shoot the Gen II down, but it has some sort of a force-field that deflected the missiles. The Gen II shot the Air Force planes down. I don't know what you'll be able to do with just one plane, even the SAW."

"I don't know either," admitted Mike. "But Cody and I will figure something out."

"All right, good luck." Tina added, "We both want to see you back here."

"So do I." Mike had both affection and determination in his voice. He hung up and updated Brennevin on the crisis in Los Angeles.

"Let's attack their base camp when that Gen II plane leaves again. All they have is another SAW like this one, right?" Cody suggested.

"That's right. You're probably as good a pilot as any of theirs, and the SAWs are an equal match. Plus, I can bump us in and out of any situation that comes up. I think we can take 'em!"

"Probably as good?" Cody corrected Mike. "I can fly knots around those maniacs. Let's check the radar on our SAW and monitor what flies in and out of their head-quarters." They headed for their warplane.

It was now mid-day in Los Angeles. Nursing moth-ers were having difficulty feeding their babies. Fire and police departments were trying to conserve the batteries on their radios. Alarms did not function. The National Guard was organizing and trying to patrol the streets, but L.A. is simply too big to have more than minimal coverage. Many people rallied together and helped each other, while the criminal element began to take advan-tage of the situation.

The streets were clogged with deserted cars, and some people had loaded camping equipment onto their bikes and were heading to the rivers, lakes, and the Los Angeles Aqueduct System. Fresh water and separation from the mounting chaos was becoming a priority. Most families holed up in their homes and hoped that the power would come back on soon.

The afternoon waned and the western sky became bright red as the Earth turned away from the sun. Night enveloped the skyscrapers, apartments, and suburbs of L.A. Fires could be seen glowing in trash cans and bar-beque pits. Civilization had been set back 150 years.

As darkness descended over Panama, Mike expressed

his concern to Brennevin. "Tina thinks we might not be able to challenge the Kaelites with just one fighter."

"Can you bump us to their base? We could do some reconnaissance and decide our best means of attack, instead of just flying in blind and shooting up the place. We don't want to hurt your friend."

"That's a good idea. Now?"

"Now."

"I need to get Tina to direct me there. I'll be right back." Mike bumped to the front door of Tina's apartment.

Jennie opened the door. "I knew it was you even before you knocked." She beamed. "I'm developing some powers, just like you and Tina." Then her countenance betrayed grave concern.

"That's good, Sweet Pea." Mike hugged his daughter, then turned to Tina. "What's wrong?"

"Los Angeles. It's horrible," she began. "People are dying all over the place. Large sections of the city are on fire. The looting and violence are out of control." Her face was streaked with tears. "The Kaelites don't need to attack us, we are attacking ourselves." She looked desperately at Mike. "We have these powers. But what can we do?"

"Brennevin and I are preparing to attack the Kaelite base camp. We need to bump there and scope it out first. Can you direct me to find it?"

"I should be able to if I concentrate on Simone's signature with Continuum." She tried to calm her emotional state and focus.

Jennie walked next to her father. He laid his arm across her shoulders.

"There are four beings with access to Continuum at the same location. That must be them." Tina approached Mike and placed her hands on his shoulders. "Let's see if I can transfer this information into your mind."

They were quiet for a moment. Mike felt the intrusion of information into his brain. "OK, I'm getting it."

Tina opened her eyes and looked directly at Mike. "This madness must end. The apocalypse will be next if we can't stop these creatures."

Mike was silent.

"Maybe we should go with you." Tina was serious.

Mike looked at his daughter. He had lost her once.

"Not yet." He kissed Tina, hugged and kissed Jennifer. Then vanished.

Brennevin had pulled on a coat as nighttime covered Central America. "Well? Do you know where to go?"

"Yes, we'll aim for the nearby woods and creep up on the place."

"You're the creeper."

The two men held hands and vanished from the side of their SAW. They appeared in the thick, dark jungle, a hundred yards from Syndor's compound.

"I can't see a thing," Mike complained.

"There's lights over there." Cody grabbed Mike's shoulders and turned him towards the hacienda. "Let's get closer."

They stumbled in the pitch darkness, crunching undergrowth and snapping twigs beneath their feet.

"Do you make this much noise when you're having sex?" Brennevin scolded. "Quiet. I need to listen."

The woods were full of sounds, wind, rustling leaves, and the distant hooting of owls.

"OK, come on."

They peered at the compound, noting the large open area in front of the main building. The two warplanes sat in the dim moonlight. Each had several sentries patrolling around them.

"That building over there, with the guard, that's probably where Simone …"

Crack! A stout branch smashed across Mike's head, knocking him out. He collapsed into the bushes.

Cody felt something shove past him and run for the lights of the house. "Oh no you don't!" He scrambled after the shorter biped, who began clicking loudly.

They raced towards the lights, and sentries, at the compound.

"Gotcha!" Brennevin caught their attacker by the collar and pulled him back.

Major Alyx spun around and swung blindly at Cody's eyes, striking him across the face.

"You little shit!" Cody wrestled the writhing alien and tried to cover its squealing mouth before the guards were alerted.

Alyx relentlessly thrashed against Brennevin's face with his eight claws until Cody maneuvered behind the Kaelite and wrapped his arm around the creature's thick neck.

The clicking stopped as Brennevin used his new, young arms to choke the flow of blood and oxygen to Alyx's brain. He looked anxiously at the guards in the clearing. The closer ones had heard the scrambling in the bushes and were calling into the dark jungle.

"Die, you little hornytoad!" Cody hissed and strangled the alien as hard as he could. Alyx went limp. Cody reached around and grabbed his victim's chin. With one strong jerk he wrenched the alien's neck, snapping his spinal bones.

"Gotta go." He dropped the Kaelite in a heap and silently ran in the direction he had come. "Mike," he whispered, feeling his way in the near darkness.

The guards discovered their dead comrade and their tonal clicking rose to an excited cry. Flashlights pierced the forest. The soldiers moved further into the woods, looking for the murderer of their major.

"Mike! Where the hell are you?"

"Errrrrr," Mike moaned to Cody's right.

"Come on! Bump us out of here!" Brennevin grabbed Mike by his jacket and tried to sit him up.

Gunshots fired behind them. Cody threw himself flat on Mike and tried to squeeze into the jungle floor. "Wake up, dipshit!" He slapped Mike's lifeless face. "You can rest when you're dead!"

Mike's head rolled to the side.

Syndor's soldiers closed in on the two men.

Something clutched Cody's neck from behind. He spun around and strained to see his attacker in the darkness.

It was Tina.

CHAPTER 20
STRIKING THE HEART

"This better be important," Syndor growled at his guards after they woke him. He exited his bedroom and quietly pulled the door closed behind him, leaving Simone asleep.

"Major Alyx has been killed, my Lord."

"How?"

"Someone strangled him and broke his neck in the forest."

"That sounds like military training. Soldiers must have discovered our location." Syndor analyzed this new situation. "Wake up Commander Mora. Have him fly over the surrounding jungle and fire the Bio-cannon. He is to kill every living creature around this compound."

"Yes, my Lord." The guards hurried to obey their orders.

"Damn! There goes one of my pilots." Syndor silently opened the door and entered his bedroom. Simone was sprawled out, breathing deeply, pretending to be asleep.

Minutes later, the sound of the SAW rising into the air brought a smile to the prince's face. "In a few hours I'll show the world who is in command."

Simone silently scanned Continuum. Mike, Tina, and someone else were together, about twenty miles from her location at the compound.

Was that you, Michael? Are you finally coming to rescue me? Old feelings were renewed in her chest.

A scaly paw slipped around her waist as Syndor crawled back into bed. "Wake up, my Princess, exciting things are happening, and I'm feeling energized."

Twenty miles away, on the ground by their SAW, Tina touched Mike and healed his concussion. Then she reached for Brennevin, touched him, and repaired the multiple scratches across his face.

"Much better." Cody wiped his bloody cheeks with his sleeve. "How's your head, Douche?" He checked Mike in the dim light.

"Fine now. What happened?"

"You were cold-cocked from behind. I killed the alien that ambushed us. Then Tina bumped us outta there right before the guards caught us."

"So they know we were there?" Mike rose in alarm.

"They know somebody was there. They might not figure out that it was you," Tina suggested.

Mike looked at her. "Thank you. We'd be dead if you hadn't been watching over us."

"You're welcome. What's next?"

While fires burned in Los Angeles, the sun had already risen over Washington, D.C. The mood was tense as the world watched to see what would happen next. President Feynman was in constant contact with the Joint Chiefs, and watching the news as it developed.

In Panama, Syndor and Simone emerged from their private chamber in the pre-dawn.

"Shouldn't I be at your side?" Simone asked the prince, hopefully. "We can show the world who their new rulers will be."

"This is still a military mission, my dear. You will translate from here." Syndor didn't slow down. "I couldn't risk you being injured, now could I?"

Simone seemed doubtful.

"We are on the verge of attacking the command center of the greatest military force on this planet. Our coup will place us as the new rulers of Earth!"

Simone's eyes widened. *At last! It is my turn to dominate mankind. Instead of being overpowered.* "I will monitor your conquest from here, my Lord."

It was Quint's rotation in the Gen II. She was brought to her position in the flight deck as Syndor took the pilot's seat.

"My Prince," the engineer reported, "the energy-shield has not been completely repaired. It is functional, yet compromised."

Syndor looked at his copilot. "You must be extremely vigilant. It is imperative that we are not be taken by surprise, we must get the first shot off."

The copilot nodded sternly and faced his controls.

Quint looked at the monitor, showing Drake hanging by his heels. She turned her head, unable to watch her brother suffer. But then she quickly looked back. There was a small window on the wall behind him. Through the window she saw a Panamanian flag, blowing in the breeze. "I know where that is," she said under her breath.

When the rest of the crew were assembled, Syndor ordered the energy engines to be engaged, and the energy envelope in the cockpit to be established.

The prince's controls moved and the terrifying ship rose to 9500 feet and soared northeast over the Caribbean Sea. He was immediately picked up on radar in Cuba, the Air Combat Command of the United States, and by Major Cody Brennevin.

"Hey! Mad Mike! That ship is leaving their base. He's heading towards the Caribbean."

After Tina had left to take care of Jennifer, Mike had been unable to completely fall asleep. He jumped up and looked at the radar screen. "Lord help whoever he's after today. But we'll return to their base and destroy that other SAW. And pick up Simone."

"Don't screw up a good thing with that Tina gal. She's a keeper," Cody advised as he took his position in the pilot's seat.

"I know, but I can't just leave Simone with those animals." Mike sat in the gunner's position and bumped to the Continuum boundary. The engines hummed to life as Mike and Brennevin went invisible.

The commanding officer at U.S. Air Combat Command monitored the alien ship speeding out over the sea. "Track 'em! And alert Tyndall."

Tyndall Air Force base in Florida, home of the world's first F-22 Raptor squadron, got the call. Two pilots climbed into the cockpits of their Raptors and fired their engines.

"Where's he headed? Dallas? Cuba? Miami?" the U.S. commander pondered, watching the progress of the Gen II on his radar.

Syndor headed straight for Cuba for twenty-five minutes, then changed his course and pointed the Gen II at Washington, D.C.

"Engage the Raptors, and alert the President. Alien attack is imminent."

As the Gen II neared the coastline of Louisiana, President Feynman was hurried into Marine One, his personal helicopter, and rapidly flown to his secondary command post. The entire White House staff was evacuated.

The two Stealth Raptors were ordered into the sky.

Their streamlined, black bodies appeared no bigger than a bumblebee on enemy radar, they were essentially invisible to Syndor's copilot as he scanned the control panel. With a maximum speed of 1400 miles per hour, the Raptor had no chance of catching the Gen II in a race. But the stealth fighters had the advantage of being capable of approaching the alien warplane without being detected on radar. If they could engage the Kaelites and fire air-to-air missiles, they might succeed at blowing Syndor out of the firmament.

The F-22s headed northwest on a trajectory to intercept the Gen II as it soared over the southeastern U.S. at over 2200 miles per hour.

The Gen II seared through the clear sky above the clouds at 35,000 feet. The prince felt the thrill of power as he clutched the controls of the fighter. "We'll reach our target before anyone can even get airborne to fight us." Syndor checked the empty radar screen. "Earth will meet its new leader today."

The copilot confirmed that the radar showed no other planes in the area. He turned his head around and did a visual check of the surrounding atmosphere. There was nothing but blue sky in every direction, except two telltale puffs of white exhaust coming from the rockets of two AIM-9 sidewinder missiles being fired from one of the Raptors.

The infrared guidance system on the missiles directed them towards the Gen II at Mach 2.5 miles per hour. Syndor's copilot slammed the steering stick and their fighter plunged into a steep dive.

"What the hell are you doing?" Syndor snarled.

"Incoming missiles!" the copilot sputtered as he continued his evasive maneuvers.

The heat-seeking sidewinders followed the Gen II as it twisted through the sky.

"Outrun them!" commanded Syndor, who took back control of the plane.

The second Raptor closed in from the east and released one more missile at the Gen II.

Syndor turned his warplane straight up and pierced the sky as he rocketed towards outer space. The three sidewinders turned together, converged, and pursued him.

"Extend rear Harmonic cannon!" Syndor barked as he squeezed the controls. "Ready ..." He waited until the missiles were three hundred yards behind him. "Fire!"

The mighty ship shuddered as it recoiled from the impulses of the cannon. The three incoming missiles disintegrated into particles as the Gen II arced through the clouds and continued to close in on Washington. "Where did those ships come from?" Syndor demanded. "I told you to be vigilant!"

"Yes, sir, somehow they are invisible to our radar. This is a technology that we have not experienced before."

"Damn! We must see them first! Find those planes." Syndor bore down towards the nation's capital.

The copilot anxiously watched the surrounding sky. "There!" He indicated below and to starboard.

Syndor redirected his warship and pursued the Raptor. "Watch out for the other one! Gunner, keep the cannon on Harmonics."

The F-22 Raptor roared underneath the Gen II, trying to gain an advantageous position, but the Kaelite fighter could turn sharper and soon had the fighter in its sights.

"Fire when you've got him!" Syndor commanded.

The Gen II recoiled again and the Raptor disintegrated, leaving the pilot hurling through space at over 1100 miles per hour.

"Yaaa!" Syndor enjoyed killing the pilot in this manner. "Watch for the other one, we are returning towards our target."

The Gen II approached Washington, D.C. and reduced its speed. But it passed over the National Mall and lowered itself towards Arlington, Virginia, and the Pentagon.

"I see the other fighter on our left flank!" the copilot reported.

"Ha! Shoot me. I dare you." Syndor smiled as he lowered the Gen II into the pentagonal courtyard at the center of the Pentagon Building. "Extend all cannon, combination mode."

The Raptor roared overhead and began circling the greater Arlington area.

Seventeen energy-cannon extended from the hull of the Gen II in every direction, pointing at the five sections of the Pentagon. The massive building began frantically evacuating.

"Set up the camera and video feed on the internet," Syndor ordered his copilot. He adjusted himself so that he was in front of the camera. "Keep the engines running but remove the energy-envelope in the cabin so we are visible," he ordered Quint.

Prince Syndor's image soon appeared on the world wide web. Within minutes it had gone viral and people were scrambling to get to their computers to see the alien, including President Feynman.

Syndor's smooth, scaly flesh, large eyes, and horned head had most of the inhabitants of Earth sitting in shock and disbelief. The screen was split and Simone appeared on the other half.

"I am Prince Syndor," he began, while Simone, who was wearing her headpiece and earbud, translated. "As the new ruler and commander of this planet I will be culling most of your population very shortly. We have already begun this process in the port city of Los Angeles."

Syndor turned to the gunners. "Fire forward Harmonic cannon."

The ship shuddered as the four cannon blasted their pulses at the five-story building. The northern wall of the Pentagon collapsed on itself, creating a massive plume of dust and debris.

"As I was saying," Syndor spoke to the camera. "As your new Lord, I order the military forces of your various nations to ground your planes and disarm your soldiers."

"Like hell!" Feynman thundered at his monitor. "What do we have in the area that can destroy that ship!"

"We have an F-22 Raptor circling that location. He has been ordered not to fire at the alien because we do not want to harm anyone in the Pentagon."

"Is everyone evacuated yet? If this bastard is going to blow the building up anyway then let's destroy him!"

"Yes, Mr. President. I will check on the progress of the evacuation and inform the Defense Secretary."

The walls of the Pentagon behind the Gen II were blown to rubble as the president returned his attention to the screen. "Send in the Raptor!"

Syndor glowed with power as he listened to the wall collapse behind him. The dust cloud billowed higher and wider, completely surrounding the Pentagon and engulfing the warship sitting in its center. The Raptor circled around and lined up with the burning building, which was obscured under the cloud of smoke and debris. It fired an air-to-ground JDAM missile at the base of the massive, black plume of smoke.

BLOOOM! The noise was deafening as a missile missed the Gen II and struck the Pentagon. The eastern walls were obliterated by the powerful explosion. The shock wave rocked the Gen II, but the failing energy-shield still protected the plane.

Syndor turned off the camera. "What the hell was that! We're heading back to base! Activate the energy envelope!" Syndor grabbed his controls and raised the ship clear of the smoke and into the sky above Virginia.

The Gen II rose to forty thousand feet and roared in a direct path towards Panama. The Raptor had anticipated this and aimed to intercept the Gen II as it fled. Syndor powered his ship up to 2200 miles per hour, too fast for the Raptor to keep up, but the F-22 was on a converging trajectory and would have one chance to fire its remaining sidewinder at the Gen II, with its damaged energy-shield.

A red warning light went off in the Raptor. It had been airborne long enough that it had depleted its fuel supply. There were only five more minutes of flight-time left. The pilot needed to withdraw from the chase and get to the nearest runway.

In the pilot's seat of the Raptor was Major Tam McGinnis. He looked at the warning light, then he checked his radar. His timing was spot on. He would cross paths with the Gen II in fifty seconds. He knew that he was invisible to the enemy aircraft's radar.

A blaring alarm filled the Raptor's cockpit, increasing the urgent message that the fighter was about run dry of fuel. Then it would simply be a 43,000 pound hunk of material and plummet to the Earth.

The speaker in his helmet came to life. "Major McGinnis, abort your mission and direct yourself and the Raptor to Radisson landing strip!"

McGinnis looked at the photo of his family that was taped to his control panel. He kissed his gloved hand through his oxygen mask and placed his fingertips on the image of his wife. "This is for you, my love."

He gripped the control stick and placed his thumb on the missile trigger. The radar showed the planes were close to having visual contact.

"There's the other fighter!" Syndor's copilot excitedly pointed to port.

McGinnis pressed the trigger and the AIM-9 sidewinder was instantly deployed from its internal bay and fired off of its trapeze. The rocket engines blazed to life and the infrared guidance system locked in on the Gen II.

Syndor pulled his fighter sharply up to evade the oncoming rocket, but it followed the heat signature of the Gen II and closed in.

"Extend the harmonic cannon!"

The prince banked sharply left, but the sidewinder struck the fuselage below the tail fins and exploded.

The Gen II spun completely around from the immense release of energy of the missile. The energy-shield was destroyed, but it had protected the warship one final time.

Syndor regained control of the spiraling plane and pointed for Panama.

"The energy-shield has been completely destroyed, sir," the copilot confirmed.

"Very well, if we encounter any more enemy ships, we must attack them first with our cannon. Is that fighter still after us?"

McGinnis pointed the Raptor towards Earth and found an empty road in the corn-country of Kentucky. He landed the fighter on fumes. His fuel tanks dried up when the three tires screeched against the pavement. He brought the fearsome warship to a stop and opened his canopy.

McGinnis spied a farmer, chugging through his field on a Farmall tractor. "Which way to Florida?"

The amazed man pointed south.

"Much obliged."

Syndor hurtled towards his basecamp, where all hell was about to break loose.

CHAPTER 21
ROUT

Two hours earlier, soon after Brennevin detected that the Gen II was leaving its headquarters, Cody and Mike engaged the engines of their SAW. Mike connected to Continuum and manned the guns, while Major Brennevin took the pilot's seat. The sleek, stolen plane trimmed the treetops as it attempted to fly undetected, below radar.

"If we can catch the damned SAW on the ground we'll blow it up there!" Cody instructed.

"We can't risk hurting Simone," Mike insisted.

"Commander Mora! We have an incoming airship, moving very fast."

"Get that cerebral out here!" Mora ran to the SAW. "Gunners!"

Simone walked to the veranda and watched the Kaelites prepare for battle. She scanned Continuum and immediately detected Mike, approaching fast. She ran back into her bedroom, stopping at a large mirror.

"Angel," she addressed herself. "What are we going to do?" She leaned closer to the glass; her eyes were filled with fear and confusion. "What if Prince Syndor doesn't return? I'll be alone. I should go back with Mike." She nervously twirled the thick ring around her thumb. "But Angel," her reflection replied, "if Syndor is killed, I'll become the heir to the throne of Kael, and the sole ruler of Earth!"

The sound of boots running and troops yelling brought Simone back to reality.

Frantically, she rummaged through Syndor's belongings, finding what she wanted. Then returned to the front of the house and observed the action through the windows.

Kresta was dragged into the plane and set in her chair. The gunners and Mora scrambled into their seats.

"Engage the engines and activate the energy envelope!"

The crew turned invisible and the SAW rapidly ascended into the air.

"I've got a visual!" Brennevin bellowed. He bore down on the Kaelites' SAW while Mike prepared to fire at the enemy plane.

Mora detected the incoming fighter and blasted towards the east over the foothills.

"I can't catch him," Cody realized. "We've got twin planes." He chased the aliens over the hills and valleys towards Panama City.

They roared over the jungle until the capital city appeared in the distance.

Suddenly tracers shot up from the rainforest. The Panamanian government had set up mobile anti-aircraft guns to defend themselves after the previous attack along the beach. Mora began turning erratically to avoid the flack that was being fired at him.

"Oh yes!" Mike cheered as he watched Mora being

attacked. "Oh no!" He quickly realized that they were flying an identical ship. "They think that we're aliens too!"

Explosions of light flashed in the trees below them as both Kaelite ships were targeted. Brennevin pulled up hard and tried to take advantage of the situation to get a shot off at Mora. But the Kaelite SAW turned south, straight out over the Pacific Ocean. Cody pushed the accelerator until metal hit metal; he was maxed out.

Mike extended the front cannon, expecting that Mora might reverse his course and fly directly at them. But the Kaelite ship continued its flight out to sea.

"This isn't working," Cody decided. "I'm going to turn around and head for their home base. That should lure them to follow us." He tipped the SAW to the right and made a beautiful arc in the sky, reversing his course and heading back to the mountains along the coast.

"We have left our compound undefended," Mora realized as Mike's warship soared back into the northern horizon. Mora rapidly reversed his course and sped over the open water, back towards the mainland.

"Let them catch up to us," Mike advised Cody.

"We are gaining on them, Commander." Mora's co-pilot watched the radar, and then made visual contact with Mike's SAW as the beach came into view, twenty miles ahead.

"OK." Mike readied the forward machine guns. "Reverse the plane and I'll bump right into their face and fire these guns."

Cody grasped the two controls. "Here we go!"

The view from the cockpit instantly spun 180 degrees. Mike used his ability to bump the entire ship forward three miles, towards Mora. Suddenly the SAWs were face to face, just a quarter mile apart. Mike was ready and unloaded a barrage of shells. Brennevin pulled up hard, turning their ship skyward to avoid flying into the enemy's SAW.

"Fire!" Mora hollered at his gunners as he pulled his ejection lever. But the crew could not react fast enough. High caliber shells tore into the fuselage of the SAW, setting off an explosion that blew it apart. All of the Kaelites aboard, including Kresta, were killed in the explosion. The burning wreckage spun into the ocean and sank beneath the slate-gray waves, settling on the bottom, fifteen miles off shore. Commander Mora hurled through the air in his pilot's seat for fifteen seconds before his chutes deployed and lowered him into the Pacific.

"Yes!" Mike exulted. "That's how you do it!" He was unaware that they had just killed one of their new allies, young Kresta. Neither Brennevin nor Mike noticed that Mora had ejected.

"Yaaa!" Brennevin cheered with satisfaction. He thrived on the thrill of battle.

"Let's go get Simone and destroy their base camp before the Gen II returns," Mike directed.

Cody watched his radar and returned over the rainforest to the aliens' mountain stronghold. He hovered over the trees and reviewed the layout of the buildings. Kaelite soldiers ran into the open grounds, weapons in their paws, unsure which SAW had returned, Mora's or Mike's.

"Blow those bug-eyed rats to bits!" Cody snarled as he lowered the powerful plane and landed in front of the main buildings.

Mike extended the machine guns, scattering the soldiers. Simone ran out of the main house.

"Holy handfuls!" Brennevin admired Simone as she sprinted across the courtyard.

"That's her!" Mike was pleased to see her alive and running towards him. "I'll go get her."

"No!" Brennevin argued. "You keep this ship running

and man those guns. I'll go bring her in."

Mike looked at the soldiers aiming their weapons at the plane. They had taken positions behind trees and buildings. Simone continued to run towards the fighter.

Something seemed strange to Mike as Cody crawled out the rear hatch of the plane. *Why are those soldiers just letting her pass in front of their guns?*

Cody ran under the dual wings and extended his hand. Simone looked confused to see the strange man, instead of Mike.

"Come on, Sugar! Let's get you aboard ..."

Simone raised a handgun and shot Cody. She hit him on the right side of his chest, fracturing his scapula and tearing a hole through his torso. He was twisted by the impact and spun to the ground.

"Bitch!" he cursed as hydrostatic shock immobilized his major organs. Cody collapsed onto the Earth, draining his blood into the dust.

"Whaaa!" Mike went into a rage as he watched through the canopy of the SAW. He instantly bumped to Cody's side and bumped them both back into the flight deck. But Simone had anticipated Mike's move and quickly shot him too, striking him in the pelvis. Both Cody and Mike appeared on the floor of the cockpit. The atomic engines were no longer running. Mike repaired himself and held the major.

"I'd stick with Tina if I were you. She's much easier to get along with," Cody advised as he grimaced in pain.

Mike focused on Brennevin's core structure and repaired his damaged body. Cody sat up. "I'm gonna kill that witch!" He returned to his pilot's seat and looked outside. Simone had fled.

Mike grabbed the controls for the machine guns and fired a blaze of bullets into the Kaelite soldiers, wounding and killing several as they returned fire with their rifles.

"Incoming!" Cody looked at his radar. A ship was flying directly to their location, very fast.

"The Gen II!" Mike concluded. "Let's get out of here and land so we're not on their radar." He ignored the engines and instantly bumped the SAW back to their clearing in the jungle.

Brennevin continued to monitor their radar and tracked the Gen II as it returned to the hacienda.

"Welcome home, jackass," Cody taunted as he examined his bloody shirt and marveled at his repaired body.

Syndor landed the Gen II and cautiously looked through the canopy at the bodies strewn about the compound. The space was empty where the SAW was normally parked. "Commander Mora!" he frantically barked into his radio.

Several soldiers emerged from their cover in the forest.

"Is this attack over?" he wondered out loud. Simone ran from the main house towards the damaged Gen II. Syndor ordered the engines turned off and headed for the rear hatch. "Return her to confinement." He pointed at Quint.

"What has happened here?" he demanded as Simone approached him.

"Mike attacked us with the other SAW," Simone began. "Commander Mora launched our SAW and they chased each other over the jungle and disappeared. The fighter with Mike in it returned and fired at our soldiers. I shot Mike and his companion, but they vanished, just minutes ago."

Prince Syndor scanned the property once again. "The other SAW, with Commander Mora, has it communicated with us yet?" he demanded furiously.

Quint listened to this discussion as she was taken across the yard to her cell. She looked around and found the fluttering Panamanian flag. She remembered the view from the window behind Drake and evaluated the location of the small buildings on the property. Most of them were constructed of wood, but one was made of concrete blocks. Its placement fit perfectly with the orientation of the flag. She made a mental note of her brother's location and entered her own one-room structure. Kresta was not there.

At the same time, in Costa Rica, the commander of the small squadron studied their radar screens. "I don't know who that was, but someone just routed the base camp of those aliens. Let's get our pilots on full alert. Contact the Panamanian ground troops and we'll see what develops."

Back on the ground at their hideaway, Cody removed his ragged shirt and wiped the blood off of his healthy young body with a wet cloth.

"Hey, Mad Mike. Even with your power to bump our fighter around in space it's going to be tough to bring that Gen II down in a one-on-one fight."

Mike was already nervous about facing the astonishing warplane. It was just as maneuverable as, yet much faster than, the SAW. And the energy cannon were much deadlier than the missiles in his ordnance. His own weapons would be ineffective against the energy-shield. "What are you thinking?"

"I want a fighter. I want an F-4 Phantom II." Brennevin was dead serious.

Mike knew that the Phantom was Cody's favorite

plane, his baby. "Why not a later generation of fighter? An F-15 Eagle, or an F-16 Fighting Falcon?"

"The F-4 is like an extension of my body. That's the plane we need."

Mike considered the logistics. They could go steal a plane easily enough; he could bump anything, anywhere. "But how will we drive the SAW? I can't do all three jobs at the same time while you're piloting the F-4."

Cody smiled knowingly. "How about that pretty gal that saved our asses last night?"

"Tina?"

CHAPTER 22
THE NIGHT BEFORE

Prince Syndor surveyed the carnage around him. The wounded were being carried to the doctor's quarters and the numerous dead were being covered up. His second ship was missing and his squad had been reduced to a handful of soldiers.

"Continue trying to contact Commander Mora. I want two ships when we hunt down Mike," the prince ordered his assistant. He spoke to his engineer. "Is it possible to repair the energy-shield?"

"The internal coils were burned by the extreme overload of energy that it deflected. I'll see what can be done. But we do not have any replacement parts here on Earth."

"We need it to be functional."

"Yes, my Lord." The engineer bowed and went right to work.

"Your mission was a success!" Simone congratulated Syndor as she took her place at his side. "The world knows who we are and the headquarters of the U.S. military has been destroyed."

"Yes, that is going well," Syndor agreed as he looked around the compound. "But our own military power has been damaged and reduced. I must hear from Commander Mora soon or I will assume that he has been shot down and the SAW has been lost." He looked directly at Simone. "The other five Gen II warplanes must be complete now. I need to get them from Kael! Are you able to transfer them across the galaxy?"

"Only Mike knows how to bump an object like that. Maybe his friend Tina can do it too."

"That doesn't help our situation at all!" Syndor growled.

"We're so close. So close!" Simone clenched her fists in exasperation. "You and me, the king and queen of Earth." Her voice had a maniacal tone to it.

"Their missiles are so powerful." The prince looked at the damaged Gen II, still radiating heat from its searing flight through the atmosphere. "But if we had all six Gen II warships, we would be undefeatable. We could continue choking the lifelines of the major cities around this planet and secure our dominance." He thoughtfully analyzed his situation.

Syndor turned and addressed one of his soldiers. "Monitor the radar!" He went inside to check the news updates on the computer.

The internet focused on two stories. The attack on the Pentagon by an alien spaceship, and the crisis in Los Angeles.

Five lives had been lost during the destruction of the Pentagon. They were all Marines who refused to leave the building and kept their rifles trained on the spaceship, in the event that anyone, or anything, emerged. They perished in the explosions.

In Los Angeles, it was the second day with no electricity. Vandals, thieves, and murderers drove terror into the residents of the great city, and warred amongst themselves. The police, National Guard, and fire departments worked around the clock, trying to secure and safeguard the property and citizens of L.A. But they were grossly outnumbered and without basic essentials themselves. Fires burned and looters walked freely through the streets, openly carrying stolen property in their arms.

Prince Syndor swelled with satisfaction at the mayhem and chaos that he had inflicted. Soon the death toll would rise as people perished from lack of water, or were casualties of the violence. He was a world-wide sensation as his image flashed on computer screens and newscasts around the globe. But he had one obstacle to overcome: the other SAW.

Major Cody Brennevin faced Mike as they stood in the grass beside their Kaelite fighter. "What's first? The Beauty or the Beast?"

"Let's go get the beast," Mike replied, referring to the F-4 Phantom II fighter that they needed to steal. "Is Foothills Airbase our best bet?"

"Yes, they keep several there for combat practice. In fact, there was one parked next to the one we flew the other day."

"I'm already in enough trouble as it is, why stop now?" Mike sounded remorseful, yet determined.

"Let's go, Mad Mike. By the way, do you know why your mother is like a city street?"

Mike shook his head and grabbed Brennevin's hand. They bumped behind the hangar at Foothills.

"Because she's got a big man-hole! Haw haw … Hey! What happened to my Camaro?" Cody looked at the empty parking space where he had left his car, just days ago. "Well, damn. If they're going to jack my ride, they owe me a plane! Fair is fair."

They were quickly picked up on security cameras and Air Force Guards ran towards them from all directions. Cody began to run.

"Don't run! I'll bump us right into the cockpit." Mike reached for Brennevin's hand and they appeared in the fighter. Mike placed Brennevin in the copilot's seat and bumped himself into the pilot's cockpit.

"Hey pal! I'm the captain of this ship!" Cody hollered from behind Mike.

"Save your strength for when we need you to fly this thing, Gramps." Mike bumped the Phantom to the Panamanian rainforest, right next to the SAW. "Now we've got our own Air Force!"

"Not even close," Brennevin corrected. "And watch that Gramps shit. In case you haven't noticed, I'm now younger than you are … Pops." Mike looked at his friend, a grizzled veteran in a young man's body. "Yeah, it's kinda weird." "Anyway, now we can team up against that Gen II. Get out of my seat! And sorry to say, but I need a flight suit and helmet."

"You couldn't have mentioned that when we were back at the airbase, Mr. Alzheimer's?"

"I was worried about my car, ya self-toucher. You were the one in such a big rush."

"Anything else?"

"Yeah, what happened to my flask?"

"I set it on your grave, on DuoSol."

"A lot of good it's doing me there."

"I'll see what I can do," Mike grumbled and vanished.

Brennevin stood beside the fighter and affectionately patted its fuselage. He looked around at the small clearing in the jungle, jammed with two warplanes.

"And bring me back a runway!" he hollered at the trees, scattering the monkeys and parrots that had been watching.

Ten minutes later Mike appeared. He handed Cody a flight suit and helmet, then produced two burgers, a pint of scotch and a flask with a Hello Kitty decoration on it.

Brennevin scowled at the flask, then shrugged his shoulders. "As long as it doesn't leak." He filled it with scotch. "Do you want to get the Beauty by yourself?"

Mike took a deep breath. "Yes."

"Well, step out of character and try to be charming." Cody raised his flask in a mock-toast.

Mike squinted at the afternoon sun and tried to think of another option. There was none. He bumped to Tina's front door and knocked.

At the Kaelite headquarters, Simone watched Syndor monitoring the news. She considered the situation. The SAW was probably gone, and the Gen II had no energy-shield. Only a scattering of soldiers were still alive. Mike was in the area and knew that she had turned traitor, and aligned with the Kaelites.

She walked to the bedroom and stood before the window, gently touching the healing wound where her finger had been. "We almost made it, Angel. We almost became the ruler of mankind." Her reflection stared back at her, pensive and determined. "What should we do, Angel? The world is against us." She continued to assess her circumstances.

Two nations had been attacked and their militaries were certainly closing in around them. The five other Gen II fighters were out of reach on DuoSol. She peered at the thick rainforest surrounding the compound and decided to look through the house and see what supplies she could put together, just in case. "We're not going down with this ship, Angel. If the world is against us, then we are against the world! We will do this on our own if we have to!"

"Any news from Commander Mora?" Syndor called to his assistant, who ran out to the Gen II where the radar was located.

"None, sir," he called through the door to the prince.

Syndor was quiet for a moment. "Very well. We will see if the energy-shield can be repaired. Then we will prepare to hunt down the other SAW, and Mike. I need him out of the way before I can continue our attack against Earth."

Simone took note and continued to gather extra clothes, a knife, matches, and one of the Kaelites' portable radios. Any useful items she could find were jammed into a daypack.

In Colorado, Tina and Jennifer were starting to prepare for dinner when they heard Mike knock at the door.

"Daddy!" Jennie hugged her father as he entered the apartment.

"Hi, Sweet Pea!" He temporarily forgot his troubles and squeezed his progeny.

Tina smiled from around the corner and Mike smiled back. But their eyes betrayed their concern.

"Tired of jungle food?" she tried to joke, then became serious. "Are you up to date with the news?"

"No, I'm not."

"Dinner can wait." Tina was urgent. "You must see this." She activated her computer.

Mike, Tina, and Jennifer crowded at the monitor. There were images of the smoldering Pentagon. They switched stations and checked on Los Angeles. Billows of black smoke loomed above different sections of the expansive city.

"We have to stop this." Tina looked desperately at the riots breaking out in the City of Angels. "This can't go on, so many people are dying, and hurting each other."

Mike looked at the monitor. The death toll was immense. Corpses were beginning to rot where they fell in the streets. He watched the footage of a man who had been mugged and robbed. His assailants hit him on the head with a brick. *I could heal his injuries in an instant if I was there,* Mike thought. Frustration and anger rose in his body.

"First we need to stop any more attacks. Then we can go and help these people," he said abruptly. "Cody and I have two fighters now. The SAW from DuoSol and another fighter from the U.S. Air Force."

"Do you think that's enough to stop that alien ship? It keeps shooting planes out of the sky all over the country." Tina was unconvinced.

"It's enough," Mike said confidently. "Major Brennevin has an F-4 Phantom, with two missiles, and I've got the SAW. But there's one problem."

Tina remembered what Mike had described about the SAW being powered by a cerebral connecting the engines to Continuum. "You need a pilot."

"No, I need someone else who can connect to Continuum."

"No, you need a pilot. You connect it to Continuum and handle the guns, I'll fly it," Tina said with finality.

Mike tried to think this new perspective through.

Tina explained. "I am an experienced pilot, not a gunner. You have done both, but aren't really experienced at either. Although I'm sure that you've been learning quickly," she added.

Mike remembered the dogfight that he and Brennevin had that morning. Cody had piloted the SAW and Mike had shot Mora into the ocean. "OK, I'll be the gunner and cerebral."

Jennie folded her arms. "What do I do?"

"Stay here!" Mike and Tina commanded in unison.

"But I'm learning so much about Continuum! Probably more than you think. Just being with Tina for two days has taught me a lot," Jennie complained.

"I couldn't stand to have you hurt again, or worse." Mike hugged her. "I couldn't bear it."

"What about me?" Jennie argued. "I don't want to lose you either. I could help."

"OK," Mike offered. "You stay here as our backup and be ready to join us if we need help. One of us will come back for you."

Jennie placed her hands on her hips and scowled doubtfully at her father. She knew that he was just trying to get her to compromise. "All right," she relented.

It became late and Jennie prepared for bed. Tina and Mike sat together on the couch.

"So we'll have two planes against one," Mike began. "Our SAW is loaded with missiles and can turn just as sharply as the Gen II. Their ship has energy cannon that can demolish just about anything, and an energy-shield. Plus it's faster than the SAW. But with two ships, hopefully we can drive it into an ambush, or pin it between us."

"And you or I can bump our ship," Tina added.

"Yes, so essentially we can move faster than the Gen II, if we can anticipate where it's going."

"And are we going to try to rescue Simone?" Tina questioned.

Mike leaned back and sighed. "You were right. She was just using me when it was to her benefit. She shot us when we tried to pick her up this morning. Apparently she has aligned with Prince Syndor and the Kaelites." He turned towards Tina. "She always mentioned conquering another nation, perhaps she has higher aspirations now."

"I'm sorry that you have been betrayed." She placed her hand on his.

They heard Jennie close her door and flick off the

light. Tina rose to prepare for bed. "We need to get an early start tomorrow." She headed for the back of the apartment.

Mike thought of Brennevin, with his two burgers and flask. He would be OK for the night. They would attack in the pre-dawn.

Mike followed her until he got to the closet. He opened it and reached for his blanket and pillow. Tina gently pushed his hands away and closed the closet door.

"Don't you think you'll get a better rest on a bed?" She smiled.

Mike looked into her chocolate-brown eyes and visually traced the outline of her lips. Her auburn hair softly settled onto her shoulders. He could feel the wisdom and compassion that she had gained by living for more than eight thousand years. He lowered his eyes and watched her chest rise and fall with each breath.

"I don't know how much rest we'll get, but a bed sounds wonderful. As long as you're there next to me." He leaned to her and they kissed. His hands reached around her back and pulled her against his body. They fit together perfectly.

She turned and took his hand. "Come with me, Michael." She quietly opened the door to her suite, and closed it behind them.

With Jennifer sleeping across the hall they whispered and quietly fumbled with the buttons on each other's shirts. Mike pulled Tina's blouse open and admired her firm breasts, curving out of her lacy bra. Tina threaded her fingers into the hair on Mike's strong pectoral muscles. They reached for their belts and kicked their pants off. Mike lifted Tina onto her queen-sized bed and stood before her. She rubbed his swelling penis through his underwear, then stretched them down over his erection.

"Nice." Mike moaned.

"Shhh," Tina admonished him and reached behind her back to unhook her bra. She tossed it on the floor and looked up at Mike.

He gazed at her lovely face in the partial light. Then he leaned over and cupped her round breasts while he kissed her again. Tina reached to her bedside table and produced a condom, which she placed on the head of his penis and carefully rolled down its length. She leaned back and carefully clutched his balls, pulling him onto her. He gripped the elastic waistband of her panties and peeled them over her hips and down her curvy legs. Tina rocked back and forth to help him undress her.

"I've wanted you ever since that first day we met," she cooed.

Mike settled his body on hers and explored her lips and neck with his mouth, kissing her down to her cleavage. She caressed his back and buttocks, then slowly wrapped her legs around his hips and pulled him closer. Mike wiggled around until the tip of his erection was at the opening of her pussy. Then he slowly pushed.

"Uuuuuuoooooo," they quietly moaned. The lovers locked their mouths together and rocked in unison, savoring the sliding sensation. Mike lifted his head up so they could see each other. The expression of ecstasy grew on their faces as they tried to keep silent. They reached the limit of what they could endure and released themselves onto the waves of rapture. Wrapping their arms tightly around each other they felt the pulses of pleasure surge through their bodies. Mike rested his head next to Tina's and breathed heavily into her warm neck. They let the climax pass and relaxed together, then fell asleep, their last moments of peace together.

Mike woke early and reached for Tina in the darkness. He was alone. Opening his eyes he searched the room. Nope. He sat up and looked around for his clothes and pulled them on. As he opened the door he smelled coffee and heard female voices. Jennie looked up from her cereal. "Hi, Daddy."

"Good morning, Sweet Pea." He gratefully accepted a mug of coffee from Tina and quickly glanced at her eyes. They shone with affection. Mike sat down and felt himself waking up. Then the frightening reality of the coming day entered his mind.

"We should be off after we eat," Tina was firm. "The Kaelites might regroup and attack another city at any time." She looked unhappy, but determined.

"All right," Mike agreed and rubbed Jennie's shoulders.

"I'll watch you from here, through Continuum," she said to comfort her father.

"I know you will." He smiled.

They finished breakfast and Mike kissed Jennie one last time. Then he bumped himself and Tina to the dark clearing in the Panamanian rainforest where the two fighters were sitting. Cody was finishing pissing into a bush at the edge of the forest. He spotted the couple by the Phantom.

"You didn't happen to bring a toothbrush, did you?" He slid his tongue over his teeth. Scotch and two burgers did not leave a pleasant aftertaste.

"Nope, sorry," Mike informed him.

"You always were worthless." Brennevin zipped up and stepped towards the planes. "Mornin'," he addressed Tina.

"Good morning," she returned the greeting. "Do you have any thoughts about how we should proceed?"

"Why, yes I do. I want you and Mike to blast over their encampment and strafe the place with machine-gun fire, hopefully damaging that Gen II fighter of theirs and killing more of those ugly fish-goons." Cody plugged one of his nostrils with his thumb and emptied the other one into the grass. "I'm pretty sure they'll get airborne and chase after you. I know they'll see me on their radar, but if they focus on you, I might be able to cut into them sideways and unload my missiles into their flank. My ship only has two missiles, plus machine guns." Brennevin straightened up. "What do you think?"

"You're the expert," Tina replied doubtfully. "Mike needs to show me the basics of this SAW fighter. Then we'll be ready to go."

Cody shook his head and muttered his way to the F-4. He pulled on his flight suit while Mike and Tina entered the SAW and went over the controls and capabilities of the alien fighter. She caught on quickly and familiarized herself with the placement of the handles and levers. Then she checked the radar. "The sky is empty, so far. It looks like we'll be the first in the air."

Mike joined Brennevin in the Phantom and sat in the copilot's seat. He bumped the fighter to Aeropuerto Senegal, twenty-eight miles away, which had a long, empty runway. "Good luck. We'll meet you in the air." He bumped back to the SAW.

Mike checked the sensors around the cerebral's seat, adjusted them so they faced him at the gunner's chair, and mentally bumped to the boundary of Continuum. The atomic engines surged to life. He activated the protective energy-envelope.

"I wondered what that would feel like," Tina commented as her hands and arms vanished.

"It's pretty strange," Mike acknowledged.

"You never looked so good," she teased, gazing at Mike's empty clothing sitting at the gunner's controls.

"Ready?"

"Let's end this."

CHAPTER 23

BRENNEVIN'S END

"Here we go," Tina confirmed as she fumbled with the handling of the warship, but the SAW rose into the air and faced Syndor's compound.

They heard approaching thunder as Brennevin cut through the air behind them and roared to the south, towards the ocean.

"He looks like he means business," Tina commented and directed the SAW forward. She accelerated, then accelerated some more. "Holy smokes! This thing is a rocket!"

"Try a few turns, and then reverse direction," Mike suggested.

Within minutes Tina had a feel for the capabilities of the plane. She checked her radar. Brennevin was far to the south over the Pacific, and starting to curve back towards the mainland.

"Prince Syndor!" A soldier had run into the house. "Two planes appeared on our radar. One flew away, over the ocean, but the other is headed directly towards us."

Simone stood nervously behind Syndor, who was following the early morning news on the internet. As

Syndor raced for the door, she headed for the back of the house and grabbed her pack of survival gear. It was still dark outside, but the dawn was peeking through the trees.

"Grab the cerebral and get her in the fighter!" he ordered. "Cut a digit off her brother's hand and clamp the device on his other paw!"

Quint sat up when the lock to her cell was opened. As she was rushed to the Gen II she looked at the small, concrete building that held Drake. She considered bumping into it right then but was still unsure of Kresta's fate. She decided to wait before making her escape. She was pushed into the cerebral's chair in the fighter and the monitor was turned on in front of her. She could see her brother struggling against two Kaelite soldiers who clamped the cutters on one of his fingers and closed the jaws.

He screamed pitifully as vermillion fluid poured from the wound and through the fingers of his clutching paw. But the soldiers continued to wrestle him down and clamped the jaws on another digit.

"Hang on, Drake," Quint sobbed under her breath. "Kresta and I will rescue you soon."

"Some encouragement for you to stay focused on our mission," Syndor snarled at Quint as he moved towards her on the flight deck. "Engage the engines and activate the protective medium!"

Quint obeyed the order, and steeled her mind in preparation of her next move.

"What is the status of the energy-shield?" Syndor bellowed at the mechanic as he shoved him out of the rear hatch.

"I have taken the eight major cables that were partially singed and combined them into three functioning sections of the energy drive …" the mechanic began.

Syndor clutched the engineer's neck. "Answer the question."

"You're at one-third capability," he croaked before he was tossed to the ground.

The rear hatch was slammed shut and the Gen II was airborne within seconds. Syndor flipped the switch, activating the crippled energy-shield.

"Where the hell is my pistol?" He reached into his empty holster. "Forget it! Let's move!" Syndor grabbed the controls and rapidly rose above the compound as Tina and Mike roared overhead, hammering the Gen II and the surrounding hacienda with a flood of machine-gun fire and air-to-ground missiles.

Windows shattered as the buildings were sprayed with bullets. Several of Syndor's soldiers writhed on the ground with burns and gunshot wounds.

"Damn! Their energy-shield is deflecting our fire," Mike hollered above the sound of the guns.

"Let's get out of here!" Tina pressed the accelerator and the SAW rocketed over the trees to the west.

"Simone!" Syndor bellowed into the radio. "Get those wounded off the ground and organize our ground troops!"

Simone ignored the cackling radio in her hand, grabbed some last-minute items from the house, including her translating headpiece, and fled into the jungle. The remaining Kaelites gathered their wounded in the courtyard.

"Planes aloft!" the radar technician for the small American squadron in Costa Rica reported to the commanding officer. "They have left the aliens' stronghold."

"It's time to move in," the C.O. replied. "Notify the

Panamanian military to advance their ground forces into the area. We'll go through first and pummel the place with machine-gun fire."

"Simone! Where the hell is she?" Syndor was enraged.

He circled the hacienda one time with the Gen II, searching for his princess, then raced after the SAW, which was fleeing towards Panama City. The gap between the powerful warships closed as they approached the location of the 40 mm anti-aircraft guns that had fired on Mike and Mora the previous day.

Mike watched the trees thin out and knew that they were close to the cannons. He bumped the SAW fifteen miles straight ahead.

Syndor prepared to fire on the SAW just as it disappeared. "Find it!" he commanded his copilot, who was scanning the radar. Suddenly shells burst all around him as the Panamanian military opened fire, defending their territory. Two of the explosives struck the ship. The energy-shield held up, but was deteriorating. Syndor pulled up hard and the Gen II immediately soared out of range of the ground-fire, straight up. He leveled off at 35,000 feet and searched for the SAW.

"There, sir, over the ocean, to the north."

Tina directed their fighter north over the Atlantic in order to draw Syndor in that direction. Meanwhile, Brennevin had turned his Phantom northeast and flew low over the mountains, hoping to hide from Syndor's radar. Tina continued north at her top speed until the Gen II closed the distance between them, then she sharply turned southeast and headed for Columbia to, hopefully, cross paths with Cody.

"This isn't working! That thing's too fast!" Tina was panicking. Syndor had easily matched her evasive turn.

"I'll bump us behind it and take a shot at it." Mike readied his missiles and bumped their SAW two miles behind their current location. They appeared a quarter mile behind the Gen II and fired. The missiles soared towards Syndor's fighter but he caught them on radar and instantly plunged to a lower altitude and cut his velocity so that the missiles, and Mike's SAW, roared harmlessly above him.

"Damn! He's just too fast!" Mike was getting concerned. "Keep heading southeast. We need to intersect with Cody." They crossed into Columbian airspace.

Within seconds, Syndor had regained altitude and was closing in on the SAW from behind. "Extend the front cannon, Harmonic-mode. Fire when you have them." His gunners fingered the triggers.

"Get us out of here!" Tina screamed. All of her attention was focused on flying the warship.

Mike bumped them down to eight hundred feet above the trees. Syndor found them on his radar and dropped behind the panicking couple.

"Flash around all that you want to, Mike. I'll get you." Syndor's confidence rose as he relentlessly hunted the other ship.

Brennevin watched all of this develop on his radar as he sped over the landscape. Suddenly Mike's SAW streaked across his field of vision. He knew the Gen II was right behind them. Cody fired his two missiles as he roared over the forest towards the two fighters.

BLAM! One missile passed in front of the supersonic plane, but the second one struck Syndor's fighter behind the starboard wings. The immense release of energy from the missile's warhead knocked the Gen II sideways. The hull withstood the blow, but the energy-shield collapsed.

"That is one tough airplane." Cody shook his head as he wheeled around to stay in the fight.

"The shield is gone," Syndor's copilot confirmed.

"Get back on Mike's tail, we can go back and take

that Earth ship down whenever we want to." Syndor focused his rage on Mike, and the SAW.

The three ships passed into Venezuelan airspace.

"It looks like Brennevin hit the Gen II!" Tina called back to Mike. "Syndor suddenly shifted to the left on the radar, it must have been from the impact of an explosion."

"I wonder if the energy-shield is being worn out?" Mike questioned.

"I don't know, but we can take another shot at it." Tina was still in the game.

"I'll bump us closer again." Mike readied his guns.

Syndor smiled with anticipation. "Extend the rear cannon, Harmonic mode. He's going to try to duck behind us again," the prince said, predicting Mike's next move. "Gunner! As soon as I give the order, fire the aft cannon."

"Yes, sir."

Brennevin tried to keep up with the Kaelite fighters. His Phantom II raced across Venezuelan airspace at 1400 miles per hour, but Mike and Syndor were outpacing him.

Tina watched Syndor catching up to them on her radar. "They're closing in."

Syndor watched the gray-blue ship in front of him get closer. "Ready gunners!"

Tina began winding left and right to avoid taking a direct hit.

Syndor drew a breath to give the order to fire. The SAW vanished.

"Fire!"

The rear cannon of Syndor's fighter blasted their pulses just as the SAW reappeared, directly above the Gen II.

Tina felt the atmosphere shudder as the intense shockwaves shuddered the surrounding air. She looked ahead. "What is that?" Thirty miles away the Earth seemed to vanish at a mysterious edge.

A huge rift in the Earth's crust would soon be passing below them. The cliffs were over three thousand feet high and were home to the tallest waterfall on the planet, Angel Falls.

Syndor didn't bother checking his radar, he looked up through the canopy at the bottom of the SAW.

"Turn the machine guns facing up and blow that thing apart."

"His energy-cannon all fire horizontally around the sides of the ship, he can't shoot us up here," Mike explained. "Now we'll bum …"

Machine-gun fire burst through the floor of the SAW. Tina slumped forward against her console, dead. The cerebral's sensors exploded and a large chunk flew across the flight deck, striking Mike in his right temple. He twisted out of his chair and flopped onto the floor, unconscious, arterial bleeding spraying the flight deck.

The energy-engines in the SAW shut off when Mike blacked out and the emergency rockets engaged to lower their ship to the ground. The crewless fighter spun dizzily as it slowly descended to the Earth.

The Gen II sped on for several miles as Syndor checked his radar. "I did it!" he exulted, watching the SAW slow to a standstill on his radar. He relaxed and looped the scarlet warship, heading back to the site of the fallen fighter. "Set the front cannon for a combination beam, Harmonic and Biological. I'm going to blast that ship, and Mike, to atoms!"

The Gen II flew low over the jungle and lined up on the SAW, which had landed perfectly between the trees. Syndor guided his fighter to point-blank range. "Fire!"

The Gen II heaved as the impulses from the cannon struck the disabled SAW. The plane and the surrounding jungle exploded into a ball of flame. A gaping crater in the jungle floor was all that remained.

Mike opened one eye, then both eyes. He didn't understand.

"Daddy?"

He looked up at Jennie's face. They were on the carpet of Tina's apartment.

"Jennie!" he cried. "Tina!"

"I didn't bring her back. She was dead."Tears streamed out of Jennifer's eyes and she heaved with sobs.

Mike sat up and held his daughter. "I guess you weren't kidding when you said that you had learned a lot about Continuum." He tried to comfort her. "Cody!"

Prince Syndor turned the Gen II up in a gentle curve as he celebrated the burning hole that indicated where the SAW had been.

His radio came to life. "Base to Prince Syndor."

"Go ahead."

"We have new information on the whereabouts of Commander Mora and the SAW."

"About time! I could have used him a while ago. Where is he?"

"The news confirms that authorities have found the wreckage of his ship on the ocean floor, fifteen miles out to sea."

"Damn! And where the hell is Simone? She was supposed to be organizing our troops."

"I don't see her, my Lord."

"That's strange." Syndor solemnly looked out of the canopy at the approaching rift. "That is unfortunate about Commander Mora. He will be buried with hon … Ahhhh!"

The prince quickly pulled the receiver away from his head as ear-splitting machine-gun fire blasted over the radio. Kaelite soldiers could be heard hollering in the background as six F-15 Eagles roared above the hacienda, showering it with bullets. The radio went dead.

Quint, sitting in the cerebral's chair, overheard the news about Mora's SAW, and realized that Kresta had died. "I'm done waiting." She looked at the video feed of her brother in his cell. "If Kresta is dead, it's time to get us out of here."

In the meantime, Brennevin seared through the Venezuelan sky, catching up to the Gen II.

"Incoming!" Syndor's crew sprang back to life as Cody caught up to the Kaelite ship and hammered it with gunfire, then turned and headed towards the gigantic cliffs.

"Ha!" Cody watched the bullets puncture the Gen II. "Your shield is gone, peckerhead."

The bullets tore into the Gen II, but did little damage.

"After him!" Syndor accelerated the powerful fighter and chased the Phantom towards the rift, just five miles away.

Brennevin tried to think. He was out of missiles, Mike had vanished from his radar, and he had just passed over a smoldering crater in the forest. Now the fastest warship in the universe was trying to kill him.

At the same time in the hacienda, after the strafing by the fighter planes, the Panamanian troops stormed across the grounds, searching for any survivors. They threw open every door and looked in every hiding place. Any alien that the troops discovered was immediately shot in the forehead. Drake huddled in his cell, alone, holding his bleeding injury. His guards had fled after the fighter planes shot the compound to pieces. He listened as the human troops systematically searched every corner of the compound, searching for Kaelites. Scattered gunshots could be heard, marking the execution of another alien. Drake unclamped the cutters that were on his paw. Heavy footsteps approached the small building that he was contained in. The lock was shot off and the handle turned on the door to his cell.

Brennevin cleared the cliff edge and gasped as the surface of the Earth fell away below him. His thoughts coalesced into an idea and he smiled a peaceful smile. He turned the F-4 upside down and looked through the top of his canopy at the rainforest speeding past, three thousand feet below him. He pulled the stick and arced downwards towards the Earth, three fifths of a mile away. He continued his backwards circle and leveled off so that he was facing back towards the immense, gray cliff of the rift. He accelerated and rushed directly at the colossal rock wall.

Above him, in the Gen II, Quint went into action. She bumped out of the fighter and appeared in Drake's cell beside him. The energy engines in the Gen II stopped immediately and the emergency rockets automatically ignited to lower it to the ground. The ship coasted over the lip of the cliff.

"What the hell is going on!" Syndor screamed at the crew, who were now visible.

Brennevin pulled the nose of his plane up when the solid rock wall was just six hundred yards away and lit his afterburners. The Phantom jet rocketed straight up, skyward, along the cliff face. His timing was perfect.

As the Gen II cleared the edge of the massive rift, the Phantom flew straight through its belly at over four hundred miles an hour. The fuel on both planes erupted into a blinding fireball and the ships exploded into shrapnel.

Both crews were instantly killed. The flaming pieces of the planes and their crews spun towards the jungle floor, far below.

Drake cried out with shock when Quint suddenly appeared next to him. The door to his cell opened and the human soldiers raised their rifles. Quint quickly touched Drake and the two of them vanished, appearing on the rocky topped mountain. They were six miles away from where Simone was making her escape.

CHAPTER 24
STRAINED ALLIANCE

Simone ran through the jungle until she felt her lungs ache. The gunfire behind her confirmed that the hacienda had been overrun by the military, and was back in the hands of the human race. She sank to the ground and leaned against a tree, catching her breath. Closing her eyes she scanned Continuum. She could detect that Mike was back in Colorado, with someone else ... Tina?

"No." Simone panted. "You're not Tina. I'd know her signature anywhere."

She examined Continuum, searching for Tina. "You're gone." Simone smiled with satisfaction. "So long, Tinker Bell, see you in Neverland."

Her brow furrowed. "But who is that new person with access?"

She continued searching Continuum and detected two more signatures in her area, deeper into the mountains.

"It must be those two cerebrals."

Her breathing returned to normal and she looked up at some colorful parrots, preening in the branches above her. Her breasts ached, which reminded her that she was pregnant. She turned on the portable radio and searched different frequencies until she found the Panamanian military.

"… has confirmed the destruction of two planes over the Venezuelan rift, an F-4 fighter plane from the United States and a red, alien ship. The destruction was complete. There were no survivors. In the interior of the …" Click. Simone turned off the radio.

"Damn you, Michael! First you abandoned me to the Kaelites and took up with that waif, Tina. Then when I regroup and form a new allegiance, you kill my partner." Simone held her hand out in front of her and examined the royal ring.

She stood up and turned towards the rocky topped mountain. "I'm not finished yet, you asshole! I'm the rightful ruler of Kael when the queen dies." A murderous strategy developed in her mind. "Those cerebrals are going to bump me back to DuoSol and I'm going to return to Earth with the Gen IIs."

She charged through the jungle with renewed vigor. "I told you before, Michael, I will never be dominated again." She scowled and focused into Continuum, gathering her hatred for Mike into a tight field of rancor and revenge. Then she directed it through the Sea of Energy, into his mind.

"Oh no!" A wave of terror surged through Mike as he sat on the floor in Tina's apartment. "She's still out there somewhere. She's going to kill me, and as many other people as she can."

"Who?" Jennie was still crying over Tina's death.

"Simone, the woman who started all this. She's still crazed with delusions of conquest."

"How do you know?"

"I'm not sure. Suddenly my mind went black. I couldn't see anything, but I could feel the hatred. She will not stop until she has wreaked her revenge on mankind, or dies." Sweat beaded on Mike's brow. He examined the blood that covered his shirt.

Jennie was quiet, scanning Continuum. "You're right. Simone is still in Panama. And so are two other beings with access to Continuum."

"Cerebrals," Mike realized. "Somehow they survived." He raised himself to his feet. "I must help Brennevin, but how?"

As the afternoon light darkened the jungle, Simone continued to struggle through the thick undergrowth. "This is too hard." She panted. "I need to find a place to hide for the night."

Eight miles away, a scaled, horned creature crawled out of the Pacific Ocean. Commander Mora, utterly exhausted, had clung to the buoyant cushion of his pilot's seat after he ejected, and swam to the coast. When his feet finally touched the sandy bottom he collapsed and let the waves wash over him. With his last strands of strength he struggled across the beach and into the woods, where he sank to the ground.

"I'm coming, my Prince." And he passed out.

From the peak of the rocky topped mountain, Quint and Drake worked their way downhill.

"Where are we going?" Drake asked his younger sister.

"We must find water, and a place to sleep." Quint maneuvered through the darkening woods, wondering what sort of predators lurked in the trees.

"We need to go back and get Kresta."

"She died, Drake. The plane with Commander Mora was destroyed, everyone was killed." She choked back the urge to cry. "But we're going to survive. How's your finger?"

"Gone. And it hurts like crazy." He plodded a few more steps. "You mean Mora is dead?"

"Yes, thank goodness for that." She saw an outcropping of boulders. "We'll sleep up among those rocks. Tomorrow we can decide what to do."

Night rolled over the Western Hemisphere. The fires raged in Los Angeles, but the jungle of Panama grew still. Only the wind blowing through the trees, and the occasional hoot of an owl broke the huge silence of the woods.

Simone climbed a massive tree and nestled herself between three branches. Visions of snakes and jaguars haunted her weary mind until she could not hold her eyes open any longer. She pulled the handgun and a jacket from her pack, then drifted to sleep.

Mike turned on the lights in Tina's apartment. The emptiness was overwhelming without her presence.

"Is she gone forever?" Jennie asked quietly.

"I don't know. She said that she has died and returned to life many times. Perhaps she can do it again." Mike thought about the serenity that Major Brennevin had described in the afterlife. "But who knows? Maybe she won't want to return."

"What about the aliens, and the attack? We have to

stop them." Jennifer was determined.

"I'm not sure. We shot their SAW into the ocean, but the Gen II shot us down. So Cody and Syndor must still be out there."

"Dad. Simone won't quit, I can feel it. She will never stop unless she is dead." Jennie crossed her arms across her lanky figure.

Mike realized that she was right. Simone had never swayed from her ambition to dominate mankind.

"You have to go kill her."

Mike gasped to hear the violence in his young daughter's voice. "Kill her?"

"Yes, she is the key to everything. When she is dead, the invasion will stop."

"How can you talk like this? You're a child!"

"My powers are growing, and my experience in Continuum has taught me a unique perspective that you can't understand." She paused. "I'll go kill her myself."

"All right, that's enough. You're not killing anyone." Mike was amazed at the ferocity that his fourteen-year-old daughter was capable of.

"You have to do it, before she organizes something else."

"All right, I see your point." *How did I become a killer?* Mike reflected on the growing number of humans and aliens that he had murdered. *I brought this havoc to Earth, I need to end it.* His eyes narrowed to determined beads. "I've got to do this. Can you guide me to Simone's location?"

Jennifer silently reached up and touched the sides of her father's head. They both focused on their inner minds, and Continuum. The sensation of Simone's location grew in Mike's brain.

"OK, I can feel where she is now."

Jennie looked sternly at her father and nodded in

affirmation.

Mike took a deep breath. "Here I go." And he went.

The jungle was almost completely dark, Mike instinctively crouched as low as possible. His eyes slowly adjusted and he began to distinguish the shapes of the thick tree trunks. There was no sign of life. He took a few tentative steps, softly crunching the plants beneath his feet, and began wondering if he was in the wrong location.

"Are you here to kill me?" A disembodied voice spoke to him from above.

Mike stepped away from the base of the tree and searched the sprawling branches overhead. A dark figure began climbing down.

Simone jumped the last few feet to the ground and stood facing her assassin.

"I've been keeping track of you, and your little friend." She moved from the dark shadows into an open space where Mike could see her in the moonlight. "Well, are you?"

"You shot me!" Mike didn't know where to begin.

"You left me with those creatures! They cut off my finger *again* and threw me in a cell," Simone seethed. "You abandoned me. But I don't need you, I can make my own way."

"Your way is killing millions of people. Why are you doing this?" Mike noticed that her right hand was held behind her back.

"I told you before, I will never be dominated again. You're just like all the rest. A pig! A raping, molesting animal. All you ever wanted from me was sex!"

"How can you say that?" Mike was incredulous. "What the hell else did you offer besides sex? You used me to pursue this obsession of yours to wreak revenge on mankind."

Simone's head tipped down and she adjusted her footing. "Yes, I did. And your usefulness is over. One final thing, Michael."

Mike prepared to vanish her.

"I'm carrying our baby."

"Wha…?"

"Are you surprised?"

"You're lying!"

"I'm not. Our child is developing right in front of you, inside my womb."

Mike scrutinized Simone. There were no outward indications to verify what she was saying.

"Don't be stupid, Michael. I'm less than two weeks along. It will be a special child, with both of our powers combined."

"You're even more dangerous now."

"Perhaps. But can you kill your own child? As I recall, you have already done that once before." Simone sent the stinging accusation straight to Mike's heart.

The truth of her words crushed him and he hesitated. *I've got to do this! Focus!*

Simone whipped her handgun around. Mike reacted instantly and accessed Continuum. He disappeared from the woods. Simone laughed victoriously. "You could never hurt me, Michael," she scoffed, then spoke tenderly to the empty woods, "You still love me."

Jennifer glared at her father as soon as he reappeared in Tina's living room. "She's still there. What happened?"

Mike sat down and groaned miserably. "I couldn't do it, she says that she is pregnant with our child."

"You have *got* to be kidding! That witch is going to have my half brother or sister?"

"I don't know what to believe." Mike gathered his thoughts. "But either way, she must be neutralized, somehow."

Simone shouldered her pack and scanned Continuum for the location of the cerebrals. They were a mile and a half away. Energized by adrenaline from her brush with death she marched through the darkness.

"Kresta died in Mora's SAW." Simone reviewed the facts as she hurried through the woods. "That means that Quint must have figured out how to bump with someone else, so that she and her brother could escape."

The trees thinned out and Simone could see outcroppings of rocks on the hillside to the north.

"That's all I need, someone to bump us back to DuoSol, where I can get those planes. If one Gen II can destroy Los Angeles, the remaining five of them can conquer Earth." She made a fist around her ring, the ring that verified her status as princess of Kael, and followed the signature of the young Kaelites to their hiding place.

Drake heard the sound of small rocks being loosened and tumbling against each other. He shook Quint awake and the siblings peered out of their alcove.

Simone put on her translating headpiece.

"Quint! Is that you?"

Quint and Drake were startled to hear a human voice. They tried to press themselves deeper into the crevices.

"Quint, it's me, Simone. Are you all right?" Simone listened, but heard nothing. She searched around until she caught a glimpse of Drake's clothing between two dark boulders. She carefully approached the young Kaelites.

Quint recognized her and came out of hiding.

"Simone! We wondered what happened to you after we were separated."

"I was taken by Syndor, he used me to translate for him." Simone noticed Drake's severed finger. "Maybe I have something to help that." She dug through her pack and examined the medicines that she had quickly grabbed. There was antiseptic and pain killer. She helped wash the wound and wrapped it in a clean sock.

Quint and Drake both noticed the royal crest on her ring as she secured the bandage.

"You are one of them!" Drake accused, pulling back his injured paw. "You are Syndor's mate!"

"Yes, I am, just listen to me! I was trying to do anything to get us out of there. I pretended to be on his side and help him. That was how I got out of the cell and was able to get these supplies." Simone sounded sincere. "Who knows? If we can get back to DuoSol it might be helpful. I am the princess of Kael, and have the power to protect all of us."

"How can we get back to DuoSol?" Quint asked excitedly.

"The same way that you escaped from captivity. Since you are able to transport yourself out of a cell, you can learn how to bump us across outer space, back to Kael. Drake can learn too."

The young siblings looked at each other. They had never dreamed that they could return home. They took Simone back into their trust and shared some of the food that she had brought.

"Is everyone else dead?" Drake asked.

"I think so. The SAW and the Gen II were destroyed, and the basecamp was overrun by soldiers."

"Soldiers almost shot us." Drake remembered his narrow escape with Quint.

Simone was quiet. "OK then. When we get back to DuoSol, I'll become the new queen, and you two will be my wards. But for now we need to find some shelter. A place where we can be safe." Simone stood up. "You both need to learn how to bump through space, and take some large objects with you."

"Large objects?" Quint and Drake looked confused,

but said nothing more. They were happy and comforted that Simone would be taking care of them, and that they would be going home soon.

The sky was beginning to show signs of daylight. The trio gathered their few belongings and began walking downhill, towards water, but away from the hacienda. After another three hours, Drake noticed a shiny, sharp stone and picked it up.

"This is glass," Simone observed. "People have been here before."

They continued searching and discovered what appeared to be an abandoned field lab. Some scientists had built a sturdy structure out of wood and corrugated metal while they were studying the fauna of the rainforest, and then abandoned it when their work was finished. Two of the windows were cracked, but it looked weatherproof and secure. A rusting jeep sat on flat tires next to the shed.

"This is a blessing." Simone was tired of walking, and pleased to enter the building and find a place to sit. There were several chairs, a table, and bunks.

Drake and Quint walked in and looked around. It suited them fine. As soon as they expanded their powers to bump with other objects, they would be going back to Kael.

The morning sunshine peeked through the branches and shone on Commander Mora's face, waking him up. The sound of the breaking waves, just fifty feet behind him, reminded Mora of his recent ordeal. He stood up and cautiously examined his surroundings. He was at the end of a long beach, a tourist beach. At this hour, not a soul was in sight.

"What have we here?" Mora crept towards a garbage

container. He plied through the rubbish and salvaged half a cheeseburger and a chicken dinner, which he greedily devoured. Turning inland he contemplated the rolling hills of the jungle before him.

"This might take a while, but I'll get back to head-quarters. Then we'll track down Mike with our Gen II and destroy that bastard." He mentally found his bearings and entered the jungle, striding in a determined path towards the destroyed hacienda.

Mike kissed Jennie on the forehead and went to Tina's computer. "Let's see if we can get an update on what is going on over there."

The news was full of stories. The Panamanian government was reporting the complete destruction of the alien stronghold in the rainforest. Every creature had been killed.

A backcountry outfitter in Venezuela had witnessed the collision of two planes near Angel Falls. One was bright red, with double wings, and the other had emblems from the United States on it. The planes were demolished and there were no survivors.

"That's them!" Mike was elated to learn that the Gen II had been destroyed. *Way to go, Old Man.* He felt sad that Cody had died, again. But then remembered that Brennevin had expressed how peaceful he had felt in Continuum. *At least you died in your plane, saving the Earth. And I'm sure that your flask was tucked into your flight suit. Rest in Peace, old friend.*

In other news, the National Guard was desperately working to bring supplies to the greater Los Angeles metropolitan area, but it was a losing battle. The light from the flames on the computer screen flickered on

Mike's face. "Look at that! It's a war-zone! A war-zone! We have to stop this, somehow."

Hours later, Commander Mora crossed a stream in the jungle, and heard indiscernible voices. He decided to circumvent the outpost and turned away from the noise, trotting between the trees. He kept the small group just beyond his range of vision.

"Yaa!" Drake hollered as he rounded a large tree and walked directly into Mora's chest.

"You!" Commander Mora grabbed the youth by the shoulders, capturing him. "What the hell are you doing out here? You deserted our camp!"

"Simone!!"

Simone rushed from the cabin towards the cry for help, abruptly running face to face with the commander. His large, blank eyes and horned head made her gasp. "Mora!"

"Princess Simone!" He released Drake and stood, dumbfounded. "What is happening?"

She regained her composure. "The Earth military advanced into our compound. Everyone has been killed."

"What about Prince Syndor, and the Gen II?"

"I am sorry to report that our great prince has died. The Gen II that he was piloting was destroyed." She urged Drake to run ahead to the shack. "We fled into the jungle when the soldiers attacked our base. We are all that's left."

Rage burned in Mora. "This is impossible! If it weren't for Mike and his control of our SAW this would never have happened." He tried to assimilate this new information, and to evaluate their present situation. "We must hunt him down and destroy him, then we can proceed with our conquest of this planet, and avenge Prince Syndor's murder."

"That is our plan, Commander." Simone spoke quietly. "One of these young cerebrals is capable of transporting herself through space. As soon as she can reliably bump us all back to Kael, we will assemble a larger force of troops and bring the five Gen II warships back to Earth."

Mora nodded as they slowly walked to their temporary shelter. "With five Gen II fighters we will be invincible."

"I am putting you in command of the entire operation, Commander Mora," Simone declared, assuming her role as the new princess.

Mora paused, displeased that Simone was now giving him orders. "I shall not fail. Our beloved prince shall be avenged, and the Kaelite nation will conquer and colonize this planet."

They entered the open area around the cabin where Drake had joined Quint.

"Simone! Watch." Quint grabbed Drake's paw and touched the decrepit jeep. Everything vanished and reappeared fifty feet away.

"We only have these two cerebrals." Mora eyed the young siblings. "We cannot power five warships with just two cerebrals."

"These two will not be serving as cerebrals anymore. They are now my personal assistants."

The commander looked disdainfully at the young Kaelites. "They are part of our machinery, nothing more."

"No longer," the princess corrected him. "They will serve as my aides. I will power the Gen II ships another way."

"As you wish, highness." Mora tried to hide the doubt in his voice.

Simone turned to Drake and Quint, who was clearly

pleased with her ability to bump the heavy jeep. "Nice job!"

"Are we ready to go home now?" Quint eyed the commander standing next to Simone and shied away.

"Yes, we will return to DuoSol." Simone breathed with satisfaction, remembering the beautiful castle that would soon be hers. "And you're going to take us there."

The four beings held hands in the clearing before the little shack.

Commander Mora swelled with anticipation for his revenge. "Soon we will return to this place, and we will be victorious."

CHAPTER 25

F-33

"They're gone!" Jennie startled Mike as he scanned the news on the computer.

"What are you talking about?" He left the horrors on the screen and turned to his daughter.

"Simone and the cerebrals are no longer in Panama. Their signatures in Continuum have disappeared from that area."

"Can you tell if they are on DuoSol?"

"Let's see." Jennifer searched the immense expanse of Continuum, and was drawn to the distant planet, where she detected the three beings who had access to the Sea of Energy. "Yes, they are out in space, on another planet."

"No! This means that at least one of the young Kaelites can bump her through Continuum. Maybe they are capable of bringing the Gen II fleet back to Earth!"

Mike's cell chimed. "Hello, this is Mike." He rubbed his forehead.

"Mr. Kruger, this is Special Agent Bristol."

Mike sat upright and pressed the phone against his ear. "Yes, sir."

"We would like for you to meet with our science expert, here in Washington, at your earliest convenience."

"Yes sir, as soon as possible would be a good idea."

Bristol was silent for a moment. "Well then, are you available this morning?"

"Yes. I can bump over there at any time." Mike wasn't certain where he should go, but he remembered visiting the National Mall as a schoolboy. "Can we meet at the Lincoln Memorial in twenty minutes?"

"I'll be there."

Mike and Jennie freshened up as best as they could and bumped together to the nation's capital.

"Welcome, Mr. Kruger. It's a pleasure to see you and your daughter again. I'm sure that you are aware of the recent military actions in Central America, and the severe situation in Los Angeles. Let us take you to my office." Bristol's greeting was terse.

Minutes later the four of them arrived at a temporary office. The furnishings were plain and functional and the walls were devoid of any decorations. Lieutenant Forbes was already seated.

Bristol waved Mike and Jennie into chairs. "My office in the Pentagon was destroyed. We are set up here for the time being."

"We'll get right down to business, Mr. Kruger. Do you have any knowledge of the alien forces and aircraft that have been attacking various targets in the Americas?" Forbes asked.

"I do," Mike replied. "I've been to their planet and I met the prince of their nation, who was also the commander of their military."

"Was?" Bristol leaned forward.

"Yes, sir, his plane was destroyed over Venezuela, near the rift at Angel Falls."

"We are aware of the destruction of those planes, and one more over the Pacific Ocean, fifteen miles offshore from Panama City. Their base camp in the jungle has also been completely overtaken by Panamanian troops and all alien lifeforms have been killed," Forbes said, with a slight show of pride.

"Do you have any more information?" Bristol pressed.

"I was a part of that air battle. We had stolen one of the alien planes and an F-4 Phantom II. Together we attacked their base and engaged their two fighters."

"You have flown one of those alien planes?" Forbes was astonished.

"Yes."

"Do you know how they can move so fast, and how the cannon and force-field operate?" Bristol couldn't hide his excitement.

"Basically. They're powered by Continuum: the universal matrix of energy that's all around us, everywhere. It's an endless source of atomic power." Mike thought about the Gen II's structure. "I would suggest that you recover the wreckage of the plane off the coast of Panama City. One of the keys to accessing this power is the sensors located on the flight deck."

"The remains of that ship have already been recovered and are being analyzed as we speak," Bristol revealed.

"You said 'one of the keys to accessing the power,' what is the other?" Forbes wondered if they could recreate this technology on Earth.

"You need a person, or being, who can access Continuum, like I can. The ship's drive is connected to the power of Continuum through that person's mind. The Kaelites called this person a cerebral. That's why you need the wreckage of that plane, to get the sensors out of the bridge."

"So, if we can replicate the sensors from the alien ship, you could be that cerebral and access this power?"

"Yes."

Forbes turned to Jennifer. "And you as well?"

Jennie squirmed in her chair. Her powers already exceeded those of her father, and she could sense his anxious thoughts. "No, sir, I'm just a kid."

Forbes' phone beeped and he spoke into it. "Excellent, send her in." He looked up and turned to Bristol. "The new eighth generation fighter, the F-33 Conquistador, should be able to accommodate this new technology. There are five nearing completion. We must confer with the engineers and designers to see if those planes can be made compatible with this new system."

Mike interrupted. "Sirs, I am also aware that the Kaelites are completing five more of these planes, the Gen IIs, on their home planet. If they can find enough cerebrals to power them, they will be impossible to repel unless you can match their fleet." Mike paused before he clarified the bad news. "The problem is, no matter how many planes you have, there is only myself who can take the position of being the cerebral, and powering one of those fighters." He glanced at Jennie and subtly shook his head.

"That's right," Jennie added.

"So essentially you have just one plane," Mike concluded.

"Hmmmm." Forbes pondered this limitation. "Do you think it's poss …"

The door opened and a professional-looking woman entered the room. Forbes looked up.

"Ah, Doctor Rydall, thank you for joining us. We have a very promising situation here and we need your expertise." Forbes stood up and motioned Dr. Rydall into a chair at the table. "Mike and Jennifer, this is Dr. Liza Rydall, our science consultant. Physics and the structure of outer space are her specialty."

Agent Bristol brought Dr. Rydall up to date, while Mike and Jennifer sat quietly, listening to the unbelievable information that was being relayed to the eminent physicist. She absorbed everything and nodded slightly, then turned to Mike.

"Do you use your brain to make this connection with Continuum?" she asked for clarification.

"Yes, I began by meditating very deeply, but now I can easily channel and focus my mind to access Continuum," Mike summarized.

Rydall scrutinized Mike. "Would you say that you *think* about this process, or is it a more intuitive experience?"

"I don't think. It is more of a feeling, deep within my brain."

Dr. Rydall considered this for a few moments and then addressed Forbes and Bristol. "I believe that this is not a process that occurs in the cerebellum. It isn't high-order thinking. Rather it's a basic, primitive connection that occurs in the brain stem. This ability has not developed over time, it's been there since the beginning. As humans evolved over countless generations, it has been covered up and overlaid by higher functioning sections of the brain. It's been buried, but now Mike has delved deep enough to access it."

Forbes and Bristol waited, hoping that Rydall would clarify what she was getting at.

"My point is, we don't need entire people to make the connection between the engines of the planes and Continuum, we only need brain stems. And we can grow those."

Jennie's eyes widened with horror at the thought of a brain sitting in a jar in the cerebral's chair. Mike sat back, sickened, and murmured, "A cerebral is nothing more than a life-support system for a brain stem."

Bristol smiled, his eyes clearly showing that he was developing a plan. "You're familiar with the operation of these planes, and their cannon and energy-shields?" He looked at Mike.

"Yes. I'm not an expert, but I am familiar with their operation."

"Perhaps we can use you as a consultant while we analyze the salvaged sensors and incorporate them into our five new fighters?"

Mike imagined the terrible air battle that Bristol seemed to be planning. "Yes, I can. Are you considering an attack on DuoSol?"

"No, Mr. Kruger. We are determined to develop the ability to defend ourselves against further attacks from this species." Forbes tried to assimilate all of the information that he had garnered in the last half hour. "Are you available now to assist in the modifications of the F-33s?"

"Yes sir, I'll do the best that I can." Mike was relieved to know that future invasions might be repelled, if the retrofit of the sensors, and the brainstems, worked.

"Excellent, I'll give you the location of the facility in Missouri where the Conquistadores are receiving their final adjustments before being battle ready. We will see if they can be modified to draw their power from Continuum."

The meeting was adjourned and they all stood up. Mike and Jennie acknowledged the three other people in the room, and bumped back to Tina's apartment to gather their things. Then they bumped to the immense buildings where the new F-33 Conquistadores would be retrofitted, hopefully before Simone returned to Earth with the Gen IIs.

CHAPTER 26
THE QUEEN

Simone, Mora, and the cerebrals appeared in the lush woods surrounding the nation-city of Kael. Both suns were up and it was baking hot. Quint and Drake smiled wide smiles and ran through the trees with their arms outstretched.

"Home again!"Commander Mora scowled at the childish behavior.

Simone looked across the wide valley and saw the buildings and castle of Kael, nestled against the cliffs of the Shillus Mountains. She examined her hands. One was missing a finger, and on the other hand she wore the royal ring. Her previous experience in Kael had been horrible, but she was prepared to reverse the situation and become the monarch of this beautiful nation.

"That was unbelievable." Commander Mora marveled at Quint and Drake's ability to bump them across the galaxy. "These cerebrals have developed fantastic abilities."

"I suggest that we bump into the queen's main conference room and meet with her." Simone was ready to get started.

"I agree." Mora looked over the valley and smiled a crooked smile when he saw the red-roofed hangar that housed the Gen II warships. Then his face grew concerned. "She will be distressed to hear of Prince Syndor's death."

Simone gazed back at the castle. Its beautiful architecture had few rivals on Earth. The delicate arches and towering spires were breathtaking. Colorful pennants fluttered in the wind. "Quint! Drake! We need to keep moving."The siblings ran to her side.

"We need to get into the castle and have an audience with the queen."

"If you show us where you want to go, I can take us there." Quint was excited to infiltrate the headquarters of the royal family. She was no longer a slave, she was the princess's personal aide.

Simone stood up and tried to straighten her hair with her fingers. "We all look like hell."

Mora looked down at his uniform. It had a crust of salt from the ocean and was torn in several places. "We have been in battle, Queen Cassilius will understand."

Simone looked at the royal ring on her thumb and beckoned her charges to come close and hold hands again "OK, let's go see what we can do." She checked that her translating headpiece was secure.

The four of them appeared in the queen's formal council chamber.

The expansive room was empty. A long table with chairs stood silent in the center. *I'm going to need some custom-built furniture for myself,* Simone noted as she observed the small size of everything. *Thank goodness the ceilings are high enough.* They walked across the parquet floor and opened the door to the hall. A guard immediately spotted them and rushed over.

"Do not move!" He pointed the barrel of his weapon at Simone's face.

"Put that down!" Simone demanded. "I am here to see my mother-in-law, Queen Cassilius. Go inform her that I request a meeting with her." She raised her hand and showed the guard her ring, and the royal crest that was embossed on it.

Commander Mora exited the room behind Simone and glowered at the guard. "We have returned from our invasion on the alien planet Earth. Go inform the queen of our presence at once!"

"Yes, Commander … and your Majesty." He bowed and hurried around the corner of the hallway, where he immediately reported the situation to his superior.

Simone heard a multitude of boot steps running towards them from all directions. She grabbed Drake's paw. "Be ready to bump us back to the woods." The guards appeared and surrounded the newcomers.

"Commander Mora! You have returned, and you have recovered these escaped prisoners."

"You will address me as your princess." Simone extended her fist and displayed her ring. "Prince Syndor and I became life partners. I have returned from the battle on Earth to confer with the queen. Delay me no more!"

In another section of the castle, Lord Territhade listened intently to his phone. He hung up and addressed Queen Cassilius. "My Queen, the guards report that Commander Mora has returned from the battle on Earth with the female alien and two young Kaelite youth. They appeared near your counsel chamber and are requesting an audience with you. The Earthling female is wearing a ring with the royal crest and claims to be Prince Syndor's partner!"

Cassilius opened her mouth, but was speechless. Her advanced age was obvious as she gingerly rose from her chair. She pulled a colorful scarf completely over her head to ward off the chill of the stone castle and began carefully walking towards the door. Territhade followed close behind as they slowly made their way through the halls until they encountered the group of guards.

Simone, Mora, and the young siblings emerged from the crowd and bowed generously as the queen approached. Cassilius carefully examined the ring.

"We have returned from the battlefront to bring you information about the war on Earth, your highness." Simone coyly placed her hand on her pregnant tummy and looked directly at the queen. Cassilius noticed the gesture.

"Welcome, Commander Mora, and Simone." The queen ignored the youth.

Lord Territhade dismissed the guards and opened the door to the council chamber. Simone, Mora, and the cerebrals reentered the room, followed by the queen and Territhade.

"This is quite a surprise." Cassilius cautiously eyed Simone. "What news do you have?" She burst into a fit of coughing and produced a handkerchief to cover her mouth.

"Your son the prince and Commander Mora have destroyed the power supply to one of the major cities on Earth. The population of Earthlings living there is starving to death and killing each other as they compete for fresh water and food."

Cassilius and Territhade turned to Commander Mora, as if seeking verification.

"Princess Simone and Prince Syndor became life partners. She has assisted him while he investigated the alien planet, and translated for him when he destroyed the headquarters of their primary military force." Mora strained to hide his disapproval.

Territhade noticed the missing digit on Drake's paw. "Are these the cerebrals that power the three ships that Prince Syndor has at his disposal?"

Simone clarified, "Yes, they have also developed the ability to transport us through space, as Michael did. However, they will no longer serve as cerebrals, they are my personal assistants."

Quint lowered her head at the memory of Kresta. Drake reached over and held her paw.

"And how is it that you and my son are life partners, and you are now in possession of one of the royal rings?" Cassilius leaned forward and stared at the golden band on Simone's thumb.

Commander Mora sat rigidly still. His blank eyes glared directly at Simone.

"As you know," Simone began, "Michael and I came to Kael in order to form an alliance with the rulers of DuoSol. He has become a traitor to us and is now fighting for the Earthlings, but I remained true to my purpose and aided Prince Syndor as he began to conquer Earth. We quickly developed a relationship and vowed to support each other as man and wife. Together we were dominating the military on Earth. And yes, I am now the princess of Kael." Simone raised her chin slightly and smiled at the queen.

Cassilius coughed. Her frail frame shook with spasms. Territhade poured her a cup of water, which she carefully sipped. Then she drew her scarf closer around her head.

Simone and Mora sat in silence.

"What news does my son send his mother?"

"My Queen," Mora began. "Our great and revered Prince Syndor has been killed in battle." He lowered his head.

"How did this happen, Commander?" Cassilius scowled from under her head wrap.

"He engaged two fighter planes with the Gen II." Simone filled in the details. "The prince successfully destroyed one of the ships, but died when he collided with the second fighter."

"We must avenge his death! And continue our conquest of this dangerous planet." The queen brought her kerchief up to her mouth and made gagging noises.

"With your permission, my Queen, and Princess, I would like to immediately transfer to the hangars and prepare the Gen II fighters for our return to Earth." Commander Mora felt charged with energy and revenge. "We have inflicted severe damage to their civilization and we must return before they are allowed to recover."

Cassilius nodded and waved him to be dismissed as she fought to regain her breath.

"Yes, Commander. I will join you soon to discuss the replacements of the cerebrals." Simone also dismissed the commander.

Mora turned his emotionless eyes at Quint and Drake and scowled. Then he bowed slightly and left the room. The guards in the hall quickly parted as their commander marched straight through them.

"Well, my child." The queen returned Simone's gaze after she had regained her ability to speak. "I must welcome you to our family. We shall arrange a formal presentation to the council for the next brightness."

"Thank you, your Majesty." Simone lowered her head and touched her hand to her heart. "It is my honor to serve at your side."

The queen returned a slight nod and discreetly peered at Simone's tummy. She coughed again and began to rise from her chair. Territhade assisted her until she was on her feet. "You may use Syndor's bed chamber. It seems only reasonable, since you are his widow." She looked at Quint and Drake. "These two may stay in one of our guest quarters."

"With your permission, my Queen. These young Kaelites are serving as my personal squires. May they stay in my chamber?"

The queen studied the two youth. "As you wish," she replied coolly. "We will have extra sleeping pads brought to your room. And we will bring some proper clothing for you, after you bathe." Territhade opened the chamber door and aided Cassilius as she exited the room.

Moments later an assistant entered and led Simone and her acolytes to Syndor's bedroom. "Dinner will be after the first sun sets." Then he left them alone.

"They're going to make us operate the planes again!" wailed Quint. "Commander Mora was looking right at me!"

"Nonsense. Soon I will be in charge here, and I will never allow that to happen."

Simone and her companions relished the opportunity to soak in hot water and put on fresh clothes. She admired herself in her royal robes. They were colorful and airy as she turned to consider her reflection in the mirror. "Look at me, Angel, I'm a real princess! Hmmm, I hope they have a crown for me." She pouted at her image.

The following morning, two of Cassilius's aides came to Simone's quarters and led the three newcomers back to the formal council chamber. The room was almost full this time with the queen's councilors sitting around the large table. Simone was directed to the chair at the queen's right side. Quint and Drake stood respectfully near the back of the room. Commander Mora, in a crisp new uniform, sat next to Lord Territhade.

"My councilors, I have grave news to share with you." Cassilius paused for breath.

"Our beloved Prince Syndor has died in battle during our attack of the planet Earth."

The counselors rumbled with shock and sorrow. Territhade raised his hands to quiet the room.

Cassilius continued. "Our warplanes and troops have

inflicted great damage on this alien civilization; however, they need reinforcements. Commander Mora has returned to Kael to lead the Gen II fighter fleet back to this planet and complete our conquest."

The room erupted in cheers of approval, but the counselors could not refrain from staring at Simone, who towered over all of them.

"As you can see," the queen continued, "we have a new member to our parliament. In fact, she is a new member to the royal family. This is Simone, Prince Syndor's widow." Cassilius directed her hand towards Simone and presented her to the counsel. "They were joined as life partners on the battlefront. As I have lost my beloved son, I now welcome my new daughter."

"Welcome, Princess Simone." Territhade, the head counselor, confirmed acceptance of his new leader.

Simone bowed her head.

"As a native of Earth, Princess Simone will be a powerful force in our government as we subdue and colonize this planet." Cassilius sat down, weary from the exertion of speaking.

Lord Territhade stood up and dismissed the counselors, then comforted the queen. Commander Mora quickly returned to the airbase, where he was working with the engineers to strengthen the protective energy field around the Gen IIs.

"May I have a private audience with you, my Queen?" Simone whispered and placed her hand on her abdomen.

Cassilius was fascinated by Simone's developing secret and quietly replied, "Yes, I think that would be most beneficial. Come to my private meeting room this evening, after dinner."

When dinner was over, Simone gathered her co-conspirators in their bedroom. "I will be speaking with the queen now. Wait here, in our room, until I return. By midnight I will be the new ruler of Kael." Quint and Drake nodded with excitement. Simone took a deep breath and prepared to put her plan into action. As she left her room and walked through the castle she made a point of greeting every guard along the way. Then she knocked on the door to the queen's meeting room and entered.

"Greetings, my Queen." Simone bowed slightly.

"Enter." The queen was already seated. The room was decorated elaborately, with tapestries and embroidered cushions on the fine furniture. Colorful fish swam in a beautiful tank near the window.

Simone selected a comfortable chair, adjusted the pillow, and sat down.

"You are bearing a child. Is it Prince Syndor's?"

Simone feigned indignation. "Queen Cassilius. Your son and I shared a special bond. We did not think that it would be possible for our two species to conceive a child, yet we have been blessed with an heir to the throne of Kael."

"Indeed." The queen was clearly skeptical. She coughed and reached for her glass and the pitcher of water.

"Allow me, your Majesty." Simone quickly rose and walked behind the queen. She reached over and grabbed a large cushion, pulling it into Cassilius's face. Simone coiled her arms around the queen's head and constricted her grasp with all of her youthful strength. The fragile, older woman scrambled against the attack but was as helpless as a bird in the jaws of a tiger. She went limp and hung like a doll. Simone maintained her death grip and counted to five hundred before releasing the warm corpse onto the sofa. She checked the room to make sure that nothing had been disturbed and opened the door to the hall.

"Thank you," she addressed the guard. She locked the

door and closed it behind her. As Simone retraced her path to her own bed chamber she politely acknowledged every sentry. Once in her room she closed the door and ran to the young Kaelites.

"We must move quickly! Quint, bump us all into the queen's parlor."

Drake and Quint jumped up and the three of them vanished, appearing back at the scene of the murder.

"Oh my goodness!" Quint held her paw to her mouth and pointed at the dead figure.

Simone quickly wrestled the queen's clothes off of the body and set them on the chaise.

"OK, now bump us, and the body, into the queen's bedroom."

"I don't want to touch her!" Quint squealed.

"Hush! We only have one chance at this." Simone grabbed the dead body and joined hands with the cerebrals. They vanished from the parlor and appeared in Cassilius's bedroom chamber.

"Drake, help me to drag her into the bathroom."

Once the limp form of the queen had been pulled onto the cold tiles of the bathroom floor Simone held the cerebrals' hands once again.

"Now take us back to the parlor."

Quint bumped the trio into the queen's parlor.

Simone picked up the queen's clothes and handed them to Quint. "Here, put these on."

"They're still warm!" Quint complained as she held the robes.

"Hurry up and stay focused." She helped to pull the fine material around the young Kaelite. "I knew you would fit into her clothes. Now pull the scarf over your head and cover your face. Just leave enough open so you can see out."

"This is perfect." Drake watched the transformation.

"You look just like her."

Simone and Drake stood back and scrutinized their work.

"Not bad at all." Simone smiled with confidence. "Walk across the room and let us take a look at you."

Quint hunched over and tried to mimic the queen's rheumatic gait.

"Something's wrong." Drake watched, confused.

"That is definitely not convincing," Simone agreed. "You're too damned healthy and young." *Maybe I should break her toes.* Simone considered the problem.

"I have an idea." Drake went to the fish tank and reached onto the bottom, pulling out a pawful of decorative gravel. "Put this in her shoes."

"Brilliant." Simone moved quickly.

They sprinkled some of the coarse pebbles into Quint's shoes and had her walk again. She creaked painfully across the floor.

"Perfect!" Simone whispered. "Do you know the way to the queen's bedroom? Where we just came from."

"Yes." Quint peered out from under the scarf.

"Good girl. Keep the shawl around your face when you walk over there. If anyone speaks to you, just shake your head and cough. Got it?"

"Yes."

"OK, first you're going to bump me and Drake back to the queen's bed chamber and come back here. Then go out this door and walk directly to meet us."

Simone checked that she had Quint's clothes. They held hands and bumped back into the bedroom suite, where the queen lay dead in the bathroom. Then Quint returned, alone, to the parlor and faced the door.

"Auurrf auurrf." She tested a few coughs. They sounded more like mouse farts.

The young Kaelite carefully unlocked and opened

the large door, entering the hall. Two guards bowed and stood aside.

Quint advanced painfully in her gravel-filled shoes. She tightened the scarf around her head and proceeded through the long corridor, passing more guards who stood at stiff attention. There was only one turn, then Quint made her way towards the bedroom. Her shuffling footsteps echoed in the spacious castle as she neared her destination. She heard small chips of rock fall out of her shoes and onto the smooth, polished floor.

There were two more guards posted on either side of the entrance. They each brandished a large rifle.

"Shall I turn your bed down this evening, Majesty?" one of them queried.

Quint shook her head and grumbled an incoherent reply in as low a voice as she could muster.

"As you wish, my Queen." He opened the door for her and stepped back to let her pass.

Quint slid her feet across the threshold, trying to stop the chips of colorful gravel that she was leaving behind her. She entered the room and pushed the door closed. Simone was standing right there and quickly locked it.

"Nice job." Simone hugged Quint and whispered excitedly. Quint beamed with pride as she removed the scarf and took off the queen's clothing. Then she re-dressed in her own outfit.

Simone carried the royal robes to the bathroom and pulled them back onto the lifeless queen. She filled a cup with water. Then, grabbing the dead woman by the hair, she opened Cassilius's mouth and poured water down her throat. Simone arranged the queen on the tile floor and set the spilled cup next to her outstretched paw.

"That looks good enough to me." Simone approved of her handiwork. She pulled and rumpled the covers on the bed. "OK, we all need to bump back to our sleeping chamber." They held hands and bumped to their own quarters.

"Nicely done," she complimented her assistants. "I am now the rightful queen of Kael. Tomorrow you must simply be quiet and act surprised." Simone glowed with accomplishment as she stood before the mirror. "I did it, Angel, I am the queen of Kael. Soon I will be the supreme ruler of two planets! Then I will personally have Michael brought before me so that I can execute him myself. And nothing can stop me."

CHAPTER 27
FUELING THE WAR MACHINES

Mike and Jennifer were met by an officer of the Burling Space and Defense facility in Missouri. "Lieutenant Forbes phoned ahead and requested that I meet you. I am Dr. Klocke, VP in charge of Electronics." The mature woman was both professional and cordial. "I understand that we are about to install some remarkable modifications to our fleet of Conquistadores."

"Yes, ma'am. I am Mike Kruger and this is my daughter, Jennifer."

"Welcome. I'll give you a brief tour on our way to your sleeping quarters. Forbes, Bristol and Rydall will join us in the morning. The salvaged sensors are on that platform over there. We will return and have a look at them after you settle in."

"Thank you." Mike looked at the familiar sensors that had been recovered from the SAW that he and Brennevin had shot into the Pacific Ocean.

"Wow." Jennie gave a hushed exclamation of approval. The colossal structure housed over twenty-four acres under the roof. The five F-33 Conquistadores could be seen at various locations in the building. Every inch of the plant was spotless, from the hard, concrete floor to the endless rows of lights hanging fifty feet overhead.

The black profiles of the warplanes were as sharp as a razor. Lethal.

If anything can take on the Gen IIs, those machines can. Mike and Jennie felt exhilarated to join this team. They followed Dr. Klocke to their on-site apartment.

The following morning, on DuoSol, Simone was awake before dawn. Today was her big day. She tried to be patient until it was time to gather her squires and head to the dining hall for breakfast.

When they arrived, the servants were standing idle, waiting for the queen to enter the room. Lord Territhade sat at the table with a pensive look on his face. He stood up when Simone entered the room.

"Good morning, Princess."

"Good morning, Lord Territhade." Simone scanned the room, as if looking for the queen. She sat calmly at her place at the table.

Cassilius's personal aide rushed in and hurried directly to Territhade. "Sir, the queen does not answer when I knock at her door."

Concern spread over his face and he quickly left the room. Simone followed him through the castle until they arrived at the door to the queen's bed chamber. Territhade was knocking loudly as she arrived.

"My Queen! Are you all right?" He tried the door and found it locked. Territhade produced his own set of keys and opened the door. He entered and pulled the door closed behind him. Simone braced herself and prepared for the acting performance of her life.

"Yaaah!" An anguished scream could be heard from inside the room. Simone opened the door to find Lord Territhade on the phone. "Send the royal surgeon immediately!" He was desperately calling into the receiver.

"What's going on?" Simone sounded alarmed.

"Our queen … she is dead."

Simone's mouth dropped open and she looked anxiously around the room. "Where is she?"

Territhade ran back into the bathroom and Simone followed.

"Oh no! I just spoke with her last night!" Simone seemed horrified as she crouched down and felt for Cassilius's pulse on her cold, stiff wrist.

"Oh, my dear queen, to die alone, after all these years." Territhade was crushed.

The castle was a flurry of activity. Territhade consulted with the captain of the guard and found nothing irregular. The queen had retired to her chamber alone, and no one else had entered or left all night.

The doctor confirmed that the queen had suffocated, apparently from choking on her water. Funeral and cremation arrangements were organized for that same evening.

Simone paced around, holding her head and asking Lord Territhade how she could help and what the proper procedures were.

Commander Mora appeared. His military boots pounded the freshly swept hallway as he briskly marched to Cassilius's suite. "What has happened, Lord Territhade?"

"Our beloved queen had died. First Prince Syndor, and now this."

"Yes, quite a coincidence," Mora practically growled. He looked directly at Simone. "How was the queen when you had an audience with her last evening?"

"We spoke for several minutes. She coughed and needed to catch her breath, but nothing suggested that she could not take care of herself."

"And the guards witnessed Queen Cassilius as she entered her room?"

"Yes, Commander," one of the queen's personal sentries confirmed.

Mora pondered this information and tried to reconstruct what might have occurred. "Then I suppose there is no need for an investigation." He looked again at Simone and his jaw ground to the side. "Long live the new queen." He bowed his head slightly.

"Thank you, Commander." Simone felt cautious relief as she returned a small bow.

"My Queen, we have many arrangements to make." Territhade beckoned Simone to follow him.

With one last glance at Mora, Simone hurried off to prepare for the funeral, and her coronation.

Commander Mora watched the queen's small procession recede down the corridor. He stepped back and felt a slight crunch under his boot heel. Looking down he saw a patch of freshly ground maroon dust. The color was unnatural.

"Something is amiss here," he snarled to himself. "As the chief commander of our military, I am the next in line to succeed the throne. Perhaps one murder should be followed by another?" He slowly returned to his transport, which took him to the hangars to complete the preparations on the Gen IIs. The citizens of Kael were informed of their queen's passing, and that King Syndor's widow was now the queen of Kael.

"Long live the queen!" was repeated wherever Simone went.

The funeral proceedings were dignified and simple. Cassilius rested on a large pyre while Lord Territhade delivered a eulogy praising her long reign as queen. The fire was lit. Towering flames licked the sky, and gray smoke billowed upwards. The citizens of Kael listened, spellbound, as Territhade introduced Simone, their new ruler.

The crowd was astonished to see the alien woman, dressed in the royal robes, with the light of the great fire illuminating her face. Her thick black hair rolled onto her shoulders and her green eyes glowed. The ring, with the royal crest, sparkled on her hand. There was no debating it, she was Syndor's bride, and therefore their new queen.

The coronation immediately followed the funeral.

Nice! Simone smiled broadly as a highly jeweled crown was placed on her head.

She stood straight and faced the multitude that was gathered before her, her new subjects.

"I will serve you and the great nation of Kael in the same tradition as Queen Cassilius. In honor of our fallen Prince Syndor, and to continue Queen Cassilius's aggressive plans to protect our planet, DuoSol, from alien invaders, we will return to Earth to conquer and colonize that hostile planet for ourselves."

The crowd cheered enthusiastically and seemed pleased. Simone beckoned Quint and Drake to follow her. She turned with a flourish of her robes and left the stage. "Now we will begin our revenge against mankind."

The following morning in Missouri, Mike was reconnected with Dr. Rydall, Lieutenant Forbes, and Special Agent Bristol. The four of them, and Jennie, met in a small conference room and sat around a table.

"You mentioned before that you believe that access to Continuum might have a genetic component," Forbes was asking Mike.

"Yes, sir, that seems to be the case."

Dr. Rydall leaned forward. "In order to modify stem cells that have this genetic coding, we are going to have to ask you to donate a sample of your own DNA."

"You mean that you need to take a piece of my brain?!"

"No, Mr. Kruger," Dr. Rydall explained. "We can harvest this from your hair follicles."

"So you're going to pull out some of my hair." Mike was relieved.

"Basically, and it might hurt a bit. We will incorporate your DNA into the stem cell. After we grow a mass of this tissue, we will see if we can induce it to become a conduit between Continuum and the sensors for the plane's engines."

"Let's get started." Mike nodded.

"If we can accelerate the growth of the stem cells after they are merged with your DNA sample, we should be ready to install the brain stems in front of the sensors within one week," Dr. Rydall explained.

"How long will it take to install and connect the sensors in the Conquistadores?" Bristol asked Forbes.

"The crew chiefs report that the salvaged sensors can be reused, after they are cut into smaller sections. The assembly and installation will only take five days, if there are no setbacks."

"That's amazing!" Mike couldn't help but be impressed.

"These are the best in the world," Bristol replied with obvious pride.

The meeting broke up and Dr. Rydall led Mike to the Burling medical offices, where they carefully pulled out some of his hair by the roots.

"That's sort of funny," Jennie pointed out. "A handful of your hair is the key to protecting Earth."

"Let's hope it works."

"Take me to the Gen II planes that are under construction," Simone instructed Lord Territhade.

"Yes, my Queen."

Simone and her young Kaelite aides were driven to the immense bunker where the five warships were lined up. They looked like a covey of angry red dragons, raising their wings.

"They're fantastic!" She swelled with pride. Everything in the kingdom of Kael was under her authority, including these new fighters.

"Yes, your Majesty, the Gen IIs are complete." Territhade brought the queen up to date. "The main challenge at this point is the availability of cerebrals that are needed to drive the engines." Lord Territhade paused, and eyed the young Kaelites by Simone's side.

Quint and Drake recoiled with fear at the thought of being tortured and forced to serve as cerebrals again.

"My squires will not be used for this purpose," Simone stated sternly. "Take me to speak to our scientists who are working on this project."

"This way, your Majesty." Territhade led Simone and her aides across the gigantic hangar to a series of offices and laboratories. There he introduced her to the head scientist.

"Queen Simone, this is Master Karyyel, chief scientist in charge of the Gen II project. Master Karyyel, may I introduce our new queen, Queen Simone."

Karyyel bowed respectfully. "It is my honor, Queen Simone, to serve you in the capacity of Chief Scientist."

"Thank you. I would like to discuss the cerebrals that are needed to connect to Continuum."

"Yes, my Queen, this is a challenge. We have begun searching for family members of the former cerebrals, or anyone who has developed the gift of access." He noticed Drake's missing digit.

"We will not be using cerebrals as we have done before," Simone directed.

Territhade and Karyyel looked up, mystified.

"The cerebrals access Continuum with their minds. Therefore, all we need are minds that can access Continuum. We don't need the bodies."

"Yes, my Queen," Karyyel agreed, but was unclear how this was going to be accomplished.

"I have the ability to infuse a brain with the gift of access. We only need five brain stems, not five cerebrals." She addressed Lord Territhade. "Instruct the army to capture five Pacabrians. They are disposable. Bring them to Master Karyyel."

"Yes, my Queen."

Karyyel tried to understand. "Are you saying that you want us to decapitate these prisoners, surgically harvest their medulla oblongata, pons, and midbrain, and then sustain them with artificial life-support?"

"If that's how you say 'Kill them, chop off their heads, scoop out their brain stems, and put them in jars of formaldehyde,' then yes." Simone looked at the fleet of blood red fighters. The fastest and deadliest warships in the known universe. "I will do the rest."

"Yes, my Queen." Lord Territhade pulled out his radio to organize a hunting party.

"I will return tomorrow to complete this process," Simone said to set the timeframe.

"Yes, my Queen."

My Queen ... I like that.

Simone, Drake and Quint were driven back to the castle. Cassilius's suite was now Simone's. Quint and Drake left their new queen and walked to Syndor's former chamber.

As Simone began rearranging the furnishings to suit her preferences, someone knocked at the massive, carved door to her private bedroom.

She pulled the door open a few inches. Commander Mora was uncomfortably close to the opening. Her guards were not at their usual post flanking the entrance.

"Yes, Commander?"

"I have need of your counsel, my Queen." His fly-like eyes betrayed nothing.

"It is not appropriate for you to visit my personal chamber. I will join you in the conference room in fifteen minutes." She pushed on the heavy door, but Mora blocked it with his heavy boot. His powerful arm shot out and he clamped his four thick digits around Simone's neck. "I will see you now."

CHAPTER 28
BACK TO LIFE

"Initiate primary test of the Continuum engines." Lieutenant Forbes spoke into his radio. The five F-33 Conquistadores were now retrofitted with the brain-stems, and the sensors were connected with the turbines. One of the sleek warships had been towed from the hangar to the airfield, and was ready to test its new capabilities.

Mike, Jennifer, and Special Agent Bristol joined Lieutenant Forbes in the control tower.

"Engaging the energy drive," the test pilot replied.

The angular, black plane sat at the head of a ten thousand foot runway.

Forbes stroked his chin and studied the most sophisticated fighter jet on Earth. It sat still.

"This is going to happen quickly." Mike stepped closer to the windows and smiled at Jennie. He had seen the power of the energy-engines in action. The whole room would be stunned when it ripped down the runway.

It sat still.

"Lieutenant Forbes, I have attempted to connect the cerebral unit to the engines several times, but nothing happens. The gauges indicate that the connection is good, but there is no power," the pilot radioed to the tower.

"Shit!" Forbes pounded the table with his fist, making everyone in the room jump. "We might come under attack at any time!" He turned to Mike and tried to calm his voice. "Any ideas what is wrong?"

Mike was dumbfounded. "I don't know. I guess my DNA didn't grow into the stem cell."

"Well, that's a fine pile of crap. Now we've got five fighters, with their fuel systems disconnected, and a hunk of worthless brain stinking up the cockpit."

Forbes leaned into his mic. "Tow it back into the hangar." He picked up his private phone. "Is Dr. Rydall down there? … good … I want to meet with her in three minutes." He turned to Mike. "Take the rest of the day off," he ordered venomously.

Mike grabbed Jennie's hand and they walked through the facility to the commissary. He grabbed a coffee and the two of them walked out onto the patio.

"What the hell!" he agonized. "This whole thing is falling apart!"

"We'll figure it out," Jennie tried to console him.

Mike groaned and slumped back in his chair. He sipped his latte, extra shot.

Jennie's attention was drawn to a lovely woman walking through the doors and entering the patio.

"That's so pretty," she said quietly as she admired the woman's colorful, silk sari.

The Hindu woman peered around the array of benches and tables, then approached Jennie and Mike. Her light brown skin glowed in the afternoon sun. A bright red bindi decorated the center of her forehead. "May I join you?"

"Sure," Jennie said shyly.

Mike was engrossed in his disappointment and barely acknowledged the visitor.

The woman sat and peered at the drink in her hands as if she were deep in thought. Her thumb stroked the lip of her cup of tea, and she brushed the blowing strands of hair from her forehead.

"I've been searching for you, Michael." She abruptly looked up. "I traveled a great distance to find you."

Mike's eyes popped open. He peered at the woman. Her eyes were chocolate brown with small flecks of orange in them. "Traveled a long distance? You mean like, from the other side of death?" He smiled.

Jennie sat up. She quickly checked the woman's signature in Continuum. "Tina!"

"Yes. I have returned."

They both rushed to embrace their resurrected friend. Jennie's eyes filled with tears. "Oh my gosh. Tina!"

Mike held his arms around her shoulders and buried his face in her hair. Tina wrapped her arms around Mike and Jennie. "It's so good to see you again."

They separated and sat down, pulling their chairs close together.

"It's good to see you again, even though you look completely different!" Jennie examined Tina's new appearance.

"I wondered if you would come back." Mike's smile was as wide as his face.

"I wasn't going to," Tina admitted. "It is so tranquil in the realm of Continuum, and humankind is so disappointing to me. I have tried for so long to bring peace to Earth, but I keep failing," she said sadly.

Mike gently stroked her hand.

Tina reminisced about her days in Continuum. "Brennevin is there, and Prince Syndor ..."

"They were together?" Mike interrupted.

"Yes," Tina said gently. "Just as you say, they were together. It is not like our physical world. All beings are everywhere, and nowhere, there is no separation. The energy flows together and we are all one unity." She looked at Jennie.

"I remember." She nodded quietly.

"And you came back." Mike's voice was hushed.

"Yes, I came back for you. I still have hope for mankind and I will help to end this conflict with the Kaelites. That is why I have returned many times from Continuum: to try to bring peace to the human race."

"Thank you."

"However, things seem different this time. Continuum is becoming active, undulating, as if something is about to change."

"I have felt it too," Jennie confirmed. "What is happening?"

"I don't know. It's impossible to understand. We will just have to see what develops."

Mike's thoughts returned to the day's failure with the F-33 Conquistador. "We have tried to modify some of the Air Force's fighter planes and power them with Continuum. But it isn't working."

Tina listened attentively as Mike explained the situation.

"Instead of cerebrals, we have taken brain stem cells and tried to infuse my DNA into them. These tissue samples have been installed in front of the sensors. But when we tried to power the engines, the system failed."

"Perhaps that is what is disturbing Continuum. More and more beings are using the infinite fabric of time-space for destructive purposes," Tina mused. "I believe that your configuration would function fine, if it had more time to develop. I will see if I can instantly align these brain stems with Continuum, and complete the process."

"We need to do this as quick as we can," Mike urged.

They left their unfinished drinks and Mike led them back into the gigantic hangar and over to Lieutenant

Forbes, who was engaged in a heated conversation with Dr. Rydall.

"I told you to take the day off." Forbes's irritation seethed through his words.

"I could do that, or we could fix this problem," Mike snapped back.

The lieutenant glared at Mike's disrespectful attitude, but Dr. Rydall interjected before he could speak.

"What are you thinking, Mike?"

"This is Tina. She is a good friend, and has very strong access to Continuum. She might be able to connect with the brain stems and conjoin them with the energy source."

"So far this voodoo is failing miserably." Forbes looked as the Conquistador that was being towed back towards the giant building.

"Please come with me." Dr. Rydall ignored Forbes and gestured the trio towards the returning warship. "Clearly this power is available, we simply need to figure out how to complete the connection."

They walked outside and met the towing vehicle before it passed through the massive door.

"Hold up!" She halted the truck and walked towards the F-33. "Bring a ladder over here!" The flight crews jumped into action and rolled a ladder against the sleek plane.

Rydall and Tina ascended to the cockpit, where the pilot obligingly opened the canopy. Tina looked at the new system, jammed into the rear of the confined space.

"Just give me a minute." She spoke quietly, and focused on the gob of living tissue. It was primal, the most elemental portion of the human brain. Tina could detect Mike's DNA in the glistening, gray matter. But it was underdeveloped. She accessed the infinite realm of Continuum and felt the brain stem respond. Using her ability to couple with other minds, Tina directed the small mass to the Sea of Energy. She felt the living tissue integrate with Continuum, like two magnets clicking together. "This plane is now connected to Continuum." Tina returned to her normal state of consciousness.

"Amazing." Dr. Rydall watched with wonder, then addressed the driver. "Tow it back out to the runway."

The cockpit was closed and the Conquistador was maneuvered away from the building, and onto the open tarmac.

"Let's give it another try," Rydall encouraged Forbes, who picked up his radio.

"Initiate primary test of the Continuum engines," the lieutenant repeated to the test pilot.

"Engaging energy drive," crackled back over the radio.

The ground rumbled. All eyes turned to the black plane on the runway. The turbines roared to life.

"I can't see my hands!" the test pilot reported.

"That's normal, the energy envelope is working," Mike explained excitedly.

"That's normal, all systems are functioning properly," Forbes directed the pilot. "Proceed with the test flight."

The Conquistador lurched briefly as the pilot tentatively tested his throttle. The ailerons flexed slightly. Then the thunder of the engines rose to a higher pitch and the warship virtually vanished as it instantly accelerated down the runway.

The F-33 was in the air within seconds and piercing the cloudless sky above the Burling facility as dozens of workers watched the test flight in amazement.

"Now the terror is on our side!" Forbes was exultant.

"Let's connect the other four planes." Rydall motioned Tina to follow her into the hangar.

"Good job, Kruger," Lieutenant Forbes acknowledged. "We are ready to attack DuoSol."

"Attack?" Mike was stunned. "I understood that this entire project was to defend Earth in the event that the Kael tried another invasion!"

"That was our original plan. However, the high command has decided that if an intergalactic battle is imminent, we would rather have it happen on their planet than risk destruction to our own cities and citizens."

Mike silently moaned with frustration.

"We still need to test all five planes and arm them. But they are ready." Forbes scanned the fleet with pride. "Be prepared to transport, or bump, our squadron to this alien planet tomorrow morning."

"Yes, sir," Mike muttered. *I need to think about this.*

CHAPTER 29
DEATH SENTENCE

Simone kicked frantically at Mora's crotch, but she was already stumbling backwards onto the marble floor. Commander Mora jammed his knee into her breastbone and pressed his weight onto her ribcage. His grip choked her carotid arteries.

"Get off me, you raping bastard! What the hell are you doing?" Simone gagged. The tips of Mora's claws punctured her skin and blood oozed down her neck.

"Following your example, Highness. You murdered Cassilius to become queen. Now I will kill you and become the king!"

Simone's vision was turning black. "You need me, you stupid toad."

"Nobody needs you. You may have seduced Prince Syndor, but on this planet you are hideous and repulsive. You have no power over anyone here!"

"I'm the only one who can connect the Gen IIs to Continuum." Her voice gurgled and her frantic eyes pleaded with her assassin.

Commander Mora hesitated. "We will use those two cerebrals of yours."

"That's only two, and you will never capture them

now that they can bump through space." Mora's grip loosened slightly and Simone desperately sucked in lungfuls of air. Her blue face returned to its normal golden tone. "You need us to connect all five ships to Continuum and then bump them to Earth. Otherwise you are stuck here with a fleet of warships that you can't even get out of the hangar!"

Mora pushed one of the claws on his other paw against Simone's left eye and brought his horned face within inches of hers. "That is exactly what you will do. If you fail, I will kill you."

"Not if I kill you first." Simone tried to push against the commander's bulk. It was futile, she was completely overpowered.

"From this point on, I will have my special forces sharpshooters watching you. Their orders will be to shoot you in your grotesque head if you deviate the slightest bit from your purpose. You will connect those fighters to Continuum, and then transport them to Earth." He pushed his claw against her eye. And squeezed her neck.

"Yaaaa!" Simone urinated.

Commander Mora released his grip and stood over her, placing his thick boot on Simone's chest as he rose. "I hereby sentence you to death. Your execution will only be postponed for as long as you follow my orders." He turned and yanked the thick door open, then carefully closed it behind him.

Simone sat up on the hard floor. Her elegant robes were soaked with piss. Blood seeped down her chest and back. "You should have killed me, asshole. Nobody dominates me."

* * *

After Tina connected the remaining four F-33s to

Continuum she joined Mike and Jennie as they walked out of the assembly plant.

"Now we are capable of defending against an attack by the Kaelites," Tina concluded. "Shall we bump back to my apartment in Colorado and see if there is anything in the refrigerator?"

Mike was silent.

"That is not a happy face." Tina placed her hand along Mike's cheek. The three of them bumped to Tina's apartment and poured themselves three waters.

Mike sat down on the couch next to Jennie. "The planes are complete. The F-33s will be flight tested today. From what I can see, they are as fast and maneuverable as the Gen IIs. They don't have energy cannon, but our air-to-air missiles are powerful enough to eventually disintegrate the Gen IIs' shields."

"And we are invisible to the Gen II's radar. So we are prepared if the Kaelites initiate an attack," Tina concluded.

"That's what I was hoping, that we were preparing to defend ourselves. What I prayed for was that we would not be the aggressors. If Kael takes a defensive position against us, and we take a defensive stance as well, and neither one of us attacks, then there will be no more fighting."

"That sounds like a common hope for most of the people on Earth."

"But Lieutenant Forbes just informed me that the U.S. wants to take the Conquistadores up to DuoSol and attack. They don't want to risk waiting to see if Kael makes a move first."

"We could refuse to transport them up to DuoSol," Tina suggested as she set drinks on the coffee table.

"I thought of that, but what if Forbes is right? If there is an attack on Earth it would be catastrophic." Mike slumped into the couch.

"Maybe we can help to negotiate a truce?" Jennie suggested.

"That's an excellent idea," Tina complimented Jennie. "How about we just destroy the planes?"

"Then we would be defenseless!" Mike complained.

"Not *our* planes, I mean how about I go up to Kael and destroy the fleet of

Gen IIs? All I have to do is touch each one and vanish it. Then the U.S. won't have anything to fear from them and will have no need to attack." She smiled at Jennie. "This is a great idea."

Mike was silent and slowly sipped his water. "I should go. I have the power to vanish objects too. Plus, I have been there before so I might be able to find where the planes are being constructed more easily than you can."

"I can scan Continuum and locate Simone. You can't do that. In general my abilities are much stronger than yours. You and Jennifer remain here. She can monitor where I am."

"I don't like this. One of your best gifts is the ability to spread peace. I have already been in combat. I've killed people. I can cope with the stress of this mission better than you can."

"Now you're really reaching for an excuse," Tina scolded him. "I was in the SAW right next to you over Panama. If you don't think that I have managed stress in my eight thousand years of existence then you don't know your history."

Jennie nodded in agreement.

"I don't know. Let's think about this and come to a rational decision."

"I'm done thinking." Tina stood up. "I'm sick to death of that woman! All Simone does is bring chaos and death anywhere she goes. I'm going to go up there and destroy that fleet, and maybe slap that psychotic bitch across the face while I'm at it."

"Whoa, calm down." Mike set his drink down. "You're getting all worked up. That's no way to enter a situation like this. You need to have a clear head and make good decisions. Charging up there in an emotional state is a good way to get killed."

"I've never seen you like this." Jennie was clearly concerned.

"This is a good way to be," countered Tina. "I'm pissed. And I'm ready to put a stop to all of this violence!" She vanished.

"Oh shit!" Mike stood up. "I'm going after her."

"No, Dad! She can handle it!"

Mike held his fist to his mouth and forced himself to remain in the room. "Who knows what she's going to find up there?"

The following morning Simone gathered Drake and Quint and headed to the hangar where the five new warships sat, ready to attack. There was only one more detail that needed to be completed.

"Have you acquired the brain stems?" she asked Dr. Karyyel.

"Yes, my Queen. They have been placed in preservatives and attached in front of the sensors."

"Take me to them." Simone peered around nervously. *I wonder if my head is in somebody's crosshairs right now.*

Simone entered the first fighter and examined the fresh tissue that had been sealed into a clear container. She focused into Continuum and connected with the dissected portion of brain.

Other people's minds are what I'm good at. She smiled as she sensed the coupling of the slab of tissue and the

Sea of Energy. Then she frowned. Something was different about Continuum.

She exited the first plane and worked her way through the hangar, linking each fighter with the infinite power of Continuum.

"You may inform Commander Mora that my fleet of Gen IIs is ready for battle," she ordered Karyyel.

"Thank you, my Queen. Commander Mora has been observing us the entire time."

Simone looked across the expansive building. Mora stood like a statue, in full uniform.

"We're bumping back to my chamber," she told her young Kaelites. And they were gone.

"Are you OK?" Quint asked Simone once they were back in the castle.

"I think so."

"You fixed those planes so easily," Drake complimented.

"I'm not sure." Simone's thoughts seemed far away. "It was like Continuum was resisting me. I've never felt that before."

"What happens now?" Quint could detect that her guardian was deeply troubled.

"As soon as Commander Mora is organized, you two are going to bump those planes to Earth. Then the attack begins."

Twelve miles away, Tina waited in the woods surrounding the nation-state of Kael. "Ok, let's put an end to this." She noticed the two suns, in different parts of the sky, and the unusual plant-life. The great city baked in the sunlight against the cliffs of the mountains. "This place is really pretty. I'll be saving two civilizations as soon as I vanish those war machines." She scanned Continuum to locate Simone. "That figures, you're in the castle. But that doesn't help me to locate the Gen IIs."

Waves of invisible energy twisted and congealed around DuoSol.

Tina shook her head. *Something feels strange.*

Simone felt it too. "Will you two stand guard outside the door for a while? I feel like I'm getting a migraine, or something."

Drake and Quint looked at each other with concern and left the room.

Immediately, Lord Territhade approached the door to Simone's bedroom.

"Master Drake, I must relay an urgent message to the queen."

Simone rubbed her temples and then jumped at the sound of loud knocking at her door.

"Simone!" Drake called through the door. "Something strange has happened in the hangar where the ships are being armed."

"What is it?"

"Master Karyyel is trying to figure it out. They request your presence, it's urgent."

"I will be there shortly."

She met Drake and Quint in the hall and they bumped to the hangar. Simone looked nervously around for Commander Mora, but spotted Lord Territhade.

The mighty planes were complete. Crews were loading armaments onto the dual wings. Simone glowed with power as she appraised her fleet of warships. Soon she would ravage the planet that she longed to dominate.

"My Queen, a most strange phenomenon has occurred in one of the planes." Lord Territhade bowed a greeting.

"Yes?" Simone looked at the row of fighters. Everything seemed to be in order.

"Inside this second plane, a light has appeared."

"Show me."

Territhade led Simone past the first Gen II and directed her into the rear hatch of the next fighter. Drake followed her inside the ship. Master Karyyel was already inside, staring at the strange apparition.

A light, the size of a small marble, was floating in the middle of the flight deck. It glowed like a candle.

"What is this object, Master Karyyel?" Simone was cramped inside the plane.

"I believe that it is a hole, my Queen." Karyyel turned to face her. Lines of concern and wonder were etched on his face.

"A hole? How did it get here?" Simone became intrigued with the odd object hovering before them.

"It appeared when we activated the power drive."

"Can't you turn off the drive and make it go away? If you created it, you can get rid of it." Simone waved her hand impatiently.

"Thank you, my Queen. We tried that. It doesn't seem as though we created it. It is more like we attracted it, and it appears to be here to stay."

"Why did you call it a hole?"

Karyyel pulled a long pen from his pocket and carefully reached towards the glimmering sphere. He dangled it directly above the small light. Then released the pen and let it drop towards the luminous ball.

It fell into the small object and vanished.

Simone was startled and pondered the foreign specter.

"Can you push it out of the plane?"

Karyyel carefully backed away from the light. "No, my Queen, anything that touches it is absorbed and lost forever. It is consuming its surroundings and taking them into another realm."

"What kind of realm?"

"Out of the universe. This is the Oculus. The eye. The

opening to the original experience that existed before our universe was formed. It is not part of our cosmos."

"How can it not be part of the universe? It's *in* our universe."

"Yes, my Queen. Imagine a bowl of pudding, and you insert a straw into it. If you blow into the straw you will create a bubble within the substance. That bubble is inside the gel, but it is not part of the actual pudding. We have a pocket here that is not part of the universe. It is the non-universe."

"Does Continuum extend into it?"

"What is on the other side is as deep a mystery as what is on the other side of death."

Simone stared at the light. It was now the size of a ping pong ball. "It's growing!"

"It is feeding on our universe, devouring it." Karyyel looked at the Oculus with reverence. "The universe formed at the moment of the great expansion. I believe that this is the reverse process. All of the elemental modules of the universe are being absorbed through this opening. Matter and anti-matter are being forced together, becoming pure energy. It is recreating the original unity. What we see is the event horizon. What is inside this surface of light is beyond our comprehension."

"At this rate it will take a helluva long time to suck up the entire universe."

"Yes, my Queen. However, the Oculus seems to be doubling in size at regular time intervals. This is exponential growth, and it will soon expand at an astonishing rate." Karyyel reached towards the flickering surface of the light, as if to caress it, then quickly withdrew his paw.

"Hmmmm." Simone was feeling cramped in the plane. The apparition was distorting Continuum, and she was getting a new impression from the surrounding forest. She crawled out of the rear hatch. "Place an armed guard at each ship," she directed Lord Territhade. "I want them to have strict orders to shoot and kill any alien, besides myself, who enters this hangar. I have a feeling that something is about to happen."

"As you wish, my Queen." Territhade turned to carry out her orders.

"What do think of that Oculus thing?" Simone consulted Drake, who was walking by her side.

"It is very strange. It seems dangerous, yet I felt calm when I looked at it."

"If we can't get it out of that ship, we will only have four Gen II planes." Simone turned back and studied the second warship. "I wonder if that thing can be useful? A bubble that is not part of Continuum might be quite handy."

The armed guards took up their positions at each plane. Simone was deep in thought. "We must be prepared to initiate our attack against Earth at any moment. If the Oculus keeps growing it might consume that whole plane, and then move on to the others. Damn!"

She held Drake by the shoulders. "You and Quint are the only Kaelites that can bump those planes to Earth. Stay close. We might need to move quickly."

"I understand." Drake nodded. "I'll go tell Quint."

Simone walked to a secluded corner of the spacious building and tried to focus into Continuum. "Who are you?" she murmured as she examined the new signature to Continuum that was lurking at the periphery of Kael. "Your signature is familiar, yet different."

"Ah ha!" Tina exclaimed from her hiding place in the forest. Simone's signature had moved from the castle, along with the two Kaelite siblings. "I wonder if you are with the Gen IIs?"

"My Queen!" Territhade startled Simone out of her thoughts. "The Oculus continues to grow. It has practically filled the flight deck on the second Gen II. Soon it will envelop the entire plane."

Simone looked across the hangar at the second warship. From the outside there was no indication of the expanding sphere within, the gentle glow of light was barely visible through the transparent canopy.

"Alert the pilots and air command. We may need to initiate our attack, very soon."

"Yes, your Highness." Territhade hurried to his radio. "I will alert Commander Mora."

Simone looked at the five planes. The armed guards were alert at each ship.

She cocked her head, sensing a strong presence affecting Continuum nearby. "That's strange," she murmured. She peered around the expanse of the hangar and turned directly into Tina's angry glare.

"Who the hell are you?" Simone was shocked to see another female of her species.

Tina looked at Simone's royal robes, the crown, and the opulent ring. "Don't tell me, you're the ruler of this city?"

"I asked you a question, dot-head, 'Who are you?' and yes, I am the queen of Kael." Simone checked the guards with her peripheral vision. They had not noticed the new Earth-woman.

"We have met before. I'm the most powerful being in the universe." Tina practically spit her answer at Simone's face. "Your trail of selfish terror and murder is over."

"Ah." Simone scowled with recognition. "Tina vanished from Continuum, and you appeared, didn't you?" She critically eyed Tina's new body. "Are you and Michael together now? What a letdown for him."

Tina frowned. "I'd kill you, but I'm here to stop this violence before it begins, not add to it."

"Oh, you're such a goodie-goodie," Simone laughed,

taunting the smaller woman. She surreptitiously cast her eye around the room. The guard of the first ship noticed Tina and tentatively moved closer with his weapon.

Simone slid one hand behind her back and made a motion like pulling a trigger with her finger and pointed towards the other Earthling. The guard stared, uncomprehending. Simone, exasperated, turned and glared at him with her piercing green eyes. He raised his rifle.

Tina noticed the movement and instantly bumped into the nearest plane to avoid being shot, and to vanish the warship. It was the second Gen II in the line. The plane instantly disappeared. So did Tina.

"Oh my God!" Simone looked at the glowing sphere, floating where the second Gen II had been sitting. "No way! It can't be that easy." She laughed. "What a fool! The most powerful being in the cosmos just bumped right out of the universe!"

CHAPTER 30
THE OCULUS

"**D**addy!" Jennifer rushed from the kitchen.

"What's up, Sweet Pea?"

"Tina's gone!" Her eyes were filled with tears.

"She's gone? What does that mean? Can you find her?"

"No, this is different. She's really gone, there's no trace of her anywhere."

"How can that be?"

"I don't know." Jennie was crying now.

"I'm going to find out," Mike panicked.

"No, Dad! Stay here," she wailed. "Something bad is going on up there. Continuum has a blind spot in it. I can feel it."

"Wha—?" Mike held his hands out, uncomprehending.

"She's gone. Really gone." Jennie collapsed onto the couch and sobbed.

Mike sat next to her and tried to comfort his daughter. He looked around the apartment at Tina's's belongings. *How can she be gone, that's impossible!*

"Screw this! We're going to take those planes up to DuoSol and find her!" Mike rose and picked up his phone to call Lieutenant Forbes. "This will be dangerous, I want you to stay here."

Jennie wiped her eyes and gave her dad a stern, *not happenin'* look. "We're going to do this together. Continuum is distorted and I can't find Tina. Whatever is going on up there, it will take both of us to fight it and rescue her."

Lieutenant Forbes answered his private line and confirmed that the squadron was ready to go, and they needed him. Mike and Jennie bumped back to the Burling Space and Defense facility in Missouri. They would begin transporting the F-33 Conquistadores up to Duo-Sol as soon as the pilots were in the planes.

Simone continued to celebrate Tina's annihilation, but her laughter was cut short as she watched the Oculus grow. It was now over ten feet high, and extending into the floor. The gentle yellowish light seemed peaceful, but the expanding sphere was relentlessly absorbing everything in its path.

"What the hell is that?!" Commander Mora demanded.

Simone looked over her shoulder at her nemesis.

"What are you doing?" he continued with a menacing tone. "Did you create that thing?"

"No, but I can control it and we can use it to our advantage." Simone's eyes glowed, an evil smile spread across her face.

"What happened to the Gen II that was sitting there?" Mora accused, as he peered around the periphery of the hangar, looking for his sharpshooter. At that moment Simone's skull was in the crosshairs of a high powered rifle.

"That light absorbed the Gen II," Simone began. "It was a terrible loss, but I can use this sphere against the fighters on Earth. Come and see."

"I asked you before, what the hell is that thing?" Commander Mora stared at the surface of the Oculus. The glowing globe was like a phantom: it was visible, but its surface was indistinct.

"It is an Oculus. It absorbed our fighter, and we can take it to Earth and use it to absorb their entire fleet! Let me show you."

Mora looked skeptically at Simone, then smiled as he noticed the bruise by her eye and the puncture wounds on her neck.

A slight heat emanated from the sphere as they approached it.

"Watch." Simone pulled a coin from her pocket and gently tossed it at the luminescent surface. It passed through the glowing shell and disappeared.

"Where did it go?" Mora hadn't heard it strike the floor.

"It is gone, forever. This is how we will conquer Earth. You try." She handed the commander another coin. Mora tried to focus on the phosphorescent globe as he prepared to throw it.

"I can't see where it begins." He squinted.

"You can actually see inside the surface, if you try."

Mora leaned closer to the radiating orb, careful not to touch it.

"Uuuufff!" Simone drove her shoulder into the commander's back as if her life depended on it. Mora instantly extended his hands to break his fall, but they passed through the undulating surface of the globe, and he stumbled into the Oculus.

"Repulsive and grotesque, am I? I told you that you should have killed me. Now I got you first," Simone crowed with triumph.

"Get the pilots and crews into these planes!" she hollered, and grabbed a portable radio from a nearby table.

Everyone in the room turned.

"Now!" she shrieked.

Simone marched over to Drake and Quint. "Lower your weapon!" she yelled at the hidden sharpshooter.

The Special Forces assassin lowered his scope from Simone's head, confused. His orders had been to shoot her if she deviated from Mora's intention to take the planes to Earth. However, she was clearly following through with that plan.

"It's even bigger!" Quint watched as the Oculus reached the ceiling of the assembly plant.

The pilots scrambled into the fighters.

Simone looked at the huge sphere, and gloated. "That thing cost us a plane, but it killed two of the creatures that were standing in my way." She pushed the young Kaelites towards the planes. "We are bumping these to Earth, right now."

"OK." They ran under the glistening warships.

"Drake, take that one, Quint, you take that one. I'll guide us. Ready?!"

They nodded and focused.

"Let's go!"

The brilliant fighters disappeared from the hangar and appeared on Earth, in the serene fields of central France.

"Perfect!" Simone looked around at the surrounding miles of wilderness. "Now go get two more. I'll wait here."

Quint and Drake vanished. Simone looked at her two warships.

"Are you ready?" she called up to the pilots over the radio.

"Yes, Queen Simone."

Two more planes appeared.

"Good job." The fleet of four planes crouched in the grass, ready to annihilate another city.

Quint was wide-eyed with terror. "The ball of light is huge now!" she reported.

On DuoSol, the Oculus was now consuming the entire city of Kael. Its surface expanded at a fantastic rate, absorbing everything. Major Cody Brennevin's grave vanished. Three minutes later, DuoSol was gone.

In Missouri, the pilots ran to the F-33s.

"How will this work?" Forbes asked Mike.

"Jennie and I will each touch the outside of a plane and bump it up to DuoSol. Then we'll return and get two more, then one more trip to get the fifth one. As soon as we set the first two on the runway they should take off, so the next two can line up."

The lieutenant looked at the tremendous warplanes. "Are you sure that you can transport all of this mass across the galaxy?"

"Yes, we're ready." Mike hurried towards one of the jets.

Jennie was not so sure. "Where are we going, Dad? I know where DuoSol is, but where are we going to set the planes? I need to copy the location of the runways from your mind, into my mind, so I know where I'm bumping."

Mike knew the position of the airfield well. He had traveled to DuoSol, and back, twice before. He focused, but became confused. "I should know this," he muttered to himself and rubbed his palm against his forehead. "What's going on?"

"Dad?" Jennie, Forbes, and the ground crews could see that Mike was having difficulty.

"We're depending on you, Kruger. What are you waiting for?" Forbes was growing impatient. His planes and crews were ready to go. The alien invasion was imminent.

"Something is wrong. It's not just that the planet doesn't exist anymore, the space-time coordinates don't even exist. That section of the universe is gone!"

Jennie tried to help by accessing Continuum and locating Simone.

"Oh no! Dad!"

"What?"

"Simone is on Earth, with the two Kaelites. Somewhere across the ocean."

Mike and Forbes looked at each other.

"She bumped here first!" Forbes realized. "We've got to get our fighters over there!"

"OK, Jennie, can you direct us to her location?"

"Yes."

"All right, you go make physical contact with a plane and I'll get another. Guide us at least three miles in the air above Simone." He looked at Lieutenant Forbes. "Have them fire up the engines."

"We're in the damned hangar!"

"We won't be for long. We need to bump them into the air, ready to fly. I don't know where a runway is over there. As soon as we bump the planes, they need to accelerate like hellfire so they don't fall to Earth. The energy engines should be powerful enough to do it." He touched the side wheel of the nearest plane and looked at Jennie. She touched a front wheel under her jet as the engine howled to life. They disappeared.

The two Conquistadores appeared sixteen thousand feet in the air over the French countryside, turbines blazing, and quickly flew under their own power. Jennie and Mike fell towards Earth for an instant before they bumped back to the hangar.

"That was crazy!" Jennie exclaimed, wide-eyed. Her hair was whipped around her head like cotton candy.

"Get another one." Mike ran for the next F-33 and ducked beneath the trembling jet. They bumped to the atmosphere above France for the second time and returned for the fifth Conquistador.

Simone looked up at the four F-33s as they aligned into attack formation above her. "We're bumping out of here!"

Drake and Quint ran to touch two planes. Simone guided them and they all bumped to the hills outside of Paris, leaving two planes sitting in central France.

The pilots in the F-33s reported to base. "Lieutenant Forbes, we have located two of the red, alien warships. They're sitting on the ground."

"Blow them to bits!" Forbes couldn't believe that they had wasted the time to call him.

Simone looked at their new situation. She had two of her warplanes and Paris was in sight.

"Go get the other two!"

The Kaelites vanished and returned in seconds. Just as the F-33s were lining up to fire their missiles at the grounded Gen IIs, Simone stood in the middle of her four fighters, overlooking Paris, the European capital of fashion, art, and intellectuals.

"Lieutenant Forbes, the planes have vanished."

"Damn it! How can we keep up with them?" The lieutenant looked desperately at Mike.

"She's bumping them to different locations!" Mike was panicked.

He looked helplessly at Jennie. "We can't bump into the cockpits of the Conquistadores, there's no room."

"Well, we sure can't hang on to the outside of them while they're flying," Jennie added.

Simone barked into her radio. "Destroy that city and return here. Use the combination cannon, both Harmonic and Biological beams. Kill everything and demolish every structure."

The four scarlet warplanes rose straight up into the air and turned towards the ancient city.

Forbes pulled headphones over his ears and listened intently. He went pale and looked up. "NATO reports that four alien planes are destroying Paris. Our squadron is five hundred miles away."

"That's about twenty minutes," Mike realized helplessly. There was no way that he could bump them into battle. "Get those planes to Paris!" Forbes ordered into his mic.

The four Conquistadores turned and accelerated towards Paris.

Mike, Jennie, and Forbes looked at the fifth F-33, idling in the hangar.

"I know the location of Paris," Mike realized. He looked at Jennie, his precious child that was returned to him from the dead. "We're going to bump that last F-33 to the skies over Paris. I have an idea."

CHAPTER 30
APOCALYPSE

While night covered the western United States, the National Optical Astronomy Observatory monitored their telescopes. "Sir, I don't even know how to describe it, but something new has appeared along the Orion arm." Several scientists crowded around the screen and stared at the foreign object. It hadn't been there the previous night.

"It's huge! Bigger than several galaxies," one woman observed. "It might even be visible to the naked eye."

"And it's getting bigger, fast."

Several people left their stations and walked out into the Arizona night. Looking skyward they could easily detect the light, bigger than a star, glowing in the interstellar medium.

"A supernova!" the group excitedly agreed. They rushed inside to share their observation with their colleagues.

"It's not a supernova," one woman concluded, looking at the information coming in from their radio telescopes. "It is not emitting nearly enough energy to be a supernova."

"Then what is it?" The crowd stared in bewilderment at the mysterious ball. "Whatever it is, it's expanding towards us."

News of the strange light spread rapidly and families on the dark side of the Earth gathered in their back yards to stare and wonder at the shimmering specter, which swelled at an observable rate.

Mike and Jennie were unaware of the growing Oculus. Everyone inside the hangar was entirely focused on the invasion from Kael.

They both touched the fifth F-33, piloted by Major Tam McGinnis, and bumped into the airspace over Paris, then immediately bumped to the ground, a safe distance from the attack. McGinnis fired his afterburners and identified the alien ships on his radar.

Paris was in ruins beneath him.

The four Gen IIs had flown side by side, straight through the heart of Paris over the Seine River, hammering the Earth with their energy cannon. Every living creature was vanished, and the buildings were shattered by the Harmonic beam.

The Eiffel Tower, Louvre, and the great cathedral of Notre Dame crumbled into rubble. Flames erupted, filling the air above Paris with gray smoke.

After their first pass, the Gen IIs split into pairs and circled around to cut another swath of destruction. McGinnis pursued the two red warplanes turning south. He was invisible to their radar and closed in as close as he could before he was spotted visually.

"Enemy plane!" Simone's radio came to life.

"Just one?" she responded. "Shoot him out of the sky! The rest of you continue your bombardment of the city."

Simone, Drake and Quint searched the firmament above the burning city, trying to catch a glimpse of the action.

"What's that?" Quint noticed the pale, orange circle

on the edge of the horizon.

"That's the …" Simone stared, it wasn't the moon. "What the hell?"

The sound of her fighters circling above drew her attention away from the mysterious sphere. "Take one more pass and then return and land," she commanded into her radio, then looked at the menacing globe. "That's the Oculus!"

McGinnis readied his ordnance and accelerated towards the two Gen IIs. They split up. "I've hit you before, I'll hit you again." He pushed the new energy-engines to full power and selected one of the fleeing fighters. This time he could keep up with the alien plane.

The Gen II turned sharply skyward, trying to shake the major, but McGinnis stuck with him, hammering the air with his turbines.

"Get this guy off my back!" Simone heard over her radio. But it was too late.

The F-33 Conquistador fired two air-to-air missiles, one after the other. The Gen II turned sharply to avoid the first one, but the second sidewinder exploded between the dual wings. The energy-shield deflected the explosion.

Tam didn't let up. Another missile left its trapeze and bore into the alien plane.

The immense impact of the second warhead overpowered the Gen II's defenses. The surrounding air crackled like lightening as the energy-shield was annihilated.

"Damn! What do I have to do to blow that thing up!" McGinnis fired again. His final missile chased down the Gen II, ramming it behind the wings. The explosion blew the plane in two. The main hull exploded into a fireball and hurled to the ground.

Simone's head turned towards the flash of light in the sky. "That doesn't look good."

The three remaining Gen IIs, following her orders, approached and landed on the hillside. The heat emanating from the idling warplanes felt like a furnace.

She checked the glowing ball on the horizon. It had grown. The entire sky was tinted orange. "That thing isn't going to stop." She raised her radio to her mouth. "I need this plane vacated." She pointed at the windscreen of the closest Gen II. The pilot saluted and the crew crawled out of the rear hatch.

"Get in there." She shoved Drake and Quint.

One and a half miles away, Mike and Jennie watched the obliteration of Paris. Through the smoke they could discern the complete destruction of the holocaust. They heard the sonic booms, thundering engines, and explosion of the Gen II. The F-33 roared over them as the flaming wreckage of the alien ship hurtled to Earth.

"Where's Simone?" Mike looked intently at Jennie. "I want to bump to her, and kill her."

Jennie held her father's hand and they appeared in the grass, between the remaining three Gen IIs.

The crew that was standing outside the planes reached for their guns. Jennie and Mike vanished them instantly. Mike looked at the three scarlet war machines surrounding him. Drake was climbing into the rear hatch on one and Simone was impatiently waiting for her turn.

"I'm ending this!" Mike focused into Continuum.

Simone heard him. "You can't hurt me, Michael! I know that you love me!" She stepped one leg into the opening.

"I never loved you!" Mike screamed.

"I'll kill her myself!" Jennie was done talking.

"Are you a baby-killer too?" Simone accused, mockingly, as she slipped into the red warplane and quickly locked the hatch behind her.

Mike and Jennie stood, stunned. It took them too

long to recover from the searing insult.

"To hell with the engines! Pick a location in space, in the opposite direction of that Oculus, and bump us there now!" she screamed at Drake.

Drake immediately complied and the Gen II vanished from Earth, reforming in deep space.

The sky over France rumbled as the original four Conquistadores arrived and joined Major McGinnis. They bore down on the three scarlet planes sitting helplessly in the grass.

Mike grabbed Jennie and bumped them both to the next hillside, where they watched the F-33s hammer the Gen IIs.

Nine air-to-ground missiles exploded within the small area, blowing craters in the ground and destroying all three alien ships.

Mike watched the flaming remains of the Gen IIs burn while the victorious Conquistadores soared into the orange-hued clouds.

Jennie looked up at the sphere in the sky. She could begin to see details in its surface. Yellow, orange, and brownish veins of light swirled across its face. It was active, seemingly alive, and filled the sky above them.

"That's the hole," Jennie said quietly. "The hole in the universe, that I felt."

The Oculus consumed Jupiter and approached the outer atmosphere of Earth, its gentle heat warming the planet.

Mike looked sadly at the carnage. The burning ruin of Paris, the smoldering wreckage of the Gen IIs. All around him were the miserable consequences of hatred. He sadly wrapped his arms around Jennie. "It all seems so pointless." They were absorbed into the Oculus with the rest of Earth.

Looking back through the canopy of her Gen II, Simone could see the glowing sphere in the far distance.

She scanned Continuum. "They're gone," she could hardly believe it. "DuoSol is gone, and now Earth is gone. We're the only ones left." She looked back at the Oculus. It was now expanding at a rate that enveloped galaxies. "Bump us farther away!" she ordered Drake.

He looked through the glass and picked a distant point of light to aim for. The Gen II leapfrogged ahead of the pursuing globe. They looked back. A tiny speck appeared, and swelled until it filled one of the windows. Now the Oculus was absorbing clusters of galaxies.

"Outrun that damned thing!" Simone grabbed Drake's shoulder and shook it.

Drake selected another distant point of light and bumped the plane, their lifeboat, as far as he could manage. The three passengers anxiously looked back. Nothing but stars. Simone nervously peered at the heavens behind them.

"It's there!" Quint spotted it. The Oculus began to fill the space behind them like a pupil of an eye, expanding in reaction to its darkening surroundings.

"It's coming!" Quint began to cry.

"Go!" Simone pounded Drake's chair.

He looked out of the canopy. There were barely any spots of light left in front of him. The entire universe was to their rear. "There isn't much to bump to anymore." He was awed by the strange sight, the end of space, as dark as obsidian.

"Go go go!" Simone screamed above the noise of Quint's sobbing.

Drake selected a solitary smear of light and bumped to it. He looked behind the plane. The entire view was a golden yellow. The event horizon of the Oculus rushed at them at a speed that was unknown to physics.

"Keep going!" Simone urged. She looked at the blank, black space in front of them.

"There's nowhere to go!" Drake panicked. "We are surfing on the edge of the expanding universe. Continuum and all of the energy in the cosmos are behind us! There is nothing in front of us!"

Simone grabbed the back of Drake's neck and pushed his face towards the glass of the canopy. "We're going out there! Now bump us forward!"

Drake tried the impossible, to travel where there was nothing. He transformed the crew and ship into pure energy and bumped away from the leading edge of the Oculus. In doing so he confirmed that the universe was a torus and entered the back side of the absorbing light.

The first experiment of life was over.

Thank you for sharing this adventure.
I hope you enjoyed it.

Please review the book on Amazon, it really helps!

BOOKS BY STUART CHURCH

Conquest by Seduction
Science Fiction Fantasy

Europa's Gate
Science Fiction Adventure

Metahuman on Trappist-1e
Science Fiction Adventure (Due May 2018)

To join our mailing list or post a review please check out our webpage at stuchurch.com and receive a note when my next sci-fi adventure hits Amazon. Your email address will not be shared with anyone else or used for any other purpose. You can unsubscribe at any time.

To send me a note please go to stuartchurch@gmail.com
I would love to share ideas with you.

See you next time!
Stuart